BURDEN OF PROOF

A RAIN CITY LEGAL THRILLER

STEPHEN PENNER

INKUBATOR
BOOKS

Published by Inkubator Books
www.inkubatorbooks.com

ISBN (eBook): 978-1-83756-134-6
ISBN (Paperback): 978-1-83756-135-3
ISBN (Hardback): 978-1-83756-136-0

1

"All rise for the jury!"

Attorney Daniel Raine was already standing before the bailiff bellowed the exhortation. Everyone in the courtroom knew the jury was about to come in. That was the reason they had assembled there in the first place: to receive the jury's verdict after a weeks-long trial. Raine turned to his client, the one who would take the brunt of that verdict if it wasn't favorable. He placed a hand on his shoulder. "You ready, Patrick?"

Patrick shrugged the hand off his shoulder. "Don't touch me, man." He was a young man, tall and lean, dressed in a tight suit he got on sale at the mall. "And I told you, it's Pat, not Patrick. The jury made their decision, so you can stop calling me 'Patrick' all the time to make them like me or whatever."

Raine didn't suppose that tactic had worked anyway. He didn't like Patrick much himself.

Raine put on a tight smile and turned his attention back to the proceedings unfolding in the courtroom. He hated taking verdicts. The result was so important for everyone involved, yet the procedure of telling those same people that result was so drawn out. Even after seventeen-plus years as an attorney, he still felt a queasy twinge in his stomach whenever it was time to read the verdict. And the décor in the courtroom didn't help any. Someone had decided to combine black and white checkerboard marble flooring with carved mahogany for the jury box, judge's bench, and counsel tables.

"Please be seated," the judge instructed everyone once the jurors had completed the process of filing out of the jury room and into the jury box. Raine and his client complied, as did everyone else in the courtroom.

Judge Elaine Hightower was perched above everyone on the mahogany bench, her bailiff and court reporter tucked into built-in cubicles immediately beneath her flowing robes and harsh countenance. She had short white hair, smooth brown skin, and a pair of clear-framed reading glasses perched on her nose. Hightower had been a judge longer than Raine had been a lawyer, and was starting to show it. She definitely acted it. She hadn't rotated out of that courtroom in a decade and treated those who entered like props in her own personal legal drama. Except for the jurors. The jurors were her audience, and she treated them as the honored guests Raine supposed they sort of were.

"Will the presiding juror please stand?" Hightower addressed the jury box.

Juror number 7 stood up. He was a middle-aged man with a protruding stomach and receding hairline. Raine hadn't liked him very much during jury selection, but there had been worse potential jurors to eliminate with his limited number of strikes. That he had been elected foreperson was not a good sign for Patrick.

"Has the jury reached a verdict?" the judge asked. Again, formality over function. Of course they had reached a verdict. That was what they had told the bailiff an hour earlier. That was what the bailiff had told Raine and the county prosecutor when he called and instructed them to reassemble in the courtroom. That verdict was the entire reason everyone in the courtroom was there, nauseated by both the disorienting décor and the unbearable drawing out of the result of the trial. Yes, they had a verdict.

"Yes, Your Honor," juror number 7 answered.

"Please hand the verdict forms to the bailiff," Judge Hightower instructed.

The bailiff climbed out of his box and marched to the jury box, chin raised in accordance with the solemnity of the proceeding. He accepted the forms from the juror, then returned to his corral and handed them up to the judge.

"Those bastards better have found me not guilty," Patrick whispered. It seemed like it was more to himself than to Raine, so Raine didn't bother replying. Their relationship was about to end anyway.

"The defendant will stand for the reading of the verdicts," Judge Hightower instructed.

Patrick stood up sharply and raised his face defiantly to the judge. Raine pushed himself to his feet and glanced over at the jury. They were all looking away from the defense table. That wasn't a good sign either.

Hightower adjusted her reading glasses and held the verdict forms at arm's length to read them aloud. "In the King County Superior Court, Seattle Division," she began, prolonging the nausea by reading every last word on the document before the one word—or, as Raine hoped, two words—everyone cared about. "The *State of Washington versus Patrick Emmanuel McCollum*. Case number CR-1-04598-3. Verdict Form, Count One."

Raine took a deep breath and exhaled it out again. He really hated this part of his job.

"We, the jury," Judge Hightower continued, "find the defendant, Patrick Emmanuel McCollum…"

She paused. Of course she paused.

"… *not guilty* of the crime of Assault in the Second Degree."

The nausea washed away. Most of it anyway. The floor still looked atrocious with that wood. Raine patted Patrick on the shoulder triumphantly. Patrick shrugged it off again. "I told you, don't fucking touch me."

Raine forced another saccharine smile and turned his attention back to the judge. They weren't quite done yet. He stole a quick glance at the assistant DA at the next table. He was a young guy, in a suit only slightly nicer than Patrick's. He was obviously disappointed in the first verdict, but his eyes were glued hopefully on Judge Hightower as she turned the page and read the other verdict form.

"Verdict Form, Count Two. We, the jury, find the defendant, Patrick Emmanuel McCollum… *guilty* of the crime of Attempting to Elude a Pursuing Police Vehicle."

Raine pursed his lips, but nodded. It was a fair verdict.

"The fuck does that mean?" Patrick turned and demanded of him.

"It means they think you didn't pull over for the cop," Raine explained, "but they don't think you tried to run him over with the car like he claimed."

"So I'm guilty?"

"You're half guilty," Raine qualified. "But it's a good result. With your history, you would have gone to prison on the Assault Two. Eluding is just a Level One offense. Maximum sentence is ninety days, and you'll be eligible for work release."

"I don't even have a job," Patrick hissed.

"Yeah, about that." Raine opened a hand toward him. "You still have a small unpaid balance on your retainer…"

"I'm not paying you shit," Patrick barked. "You just got me convicted."

"I just got you acquitted of the more serious charge," Raine countered, "and kept you out of prison."

"You're fired," Patrick responded.

This was all unfolding in front of the judge and jury. It wasn't going to help him at the next hearing.

"You still have sentencing," Raine reminded him. "You might want a lawyer at your sentencing."

"Man, I might not even show up for that," Patrick scoffed.

Raine nodded. "That's exactly why they convicted you of trying to elude the cop."

And it was exactly why Raine hated doing criminal cases. Guilty clients who could barely afford to pay and were ungrateful for anything less than a full acquittal of the crime they had definitely committed. The sentencing hearing was scheduled for thirty days out. Raine left the courthouse hoping Patrick really would fire him, but cognizant that an attorney could only be let out of a criminal case by order of the judge. Hightower wasn't going to let him out of the case, and Patrick wasn't going to pay him another dime. And he really could have used that dime.

Raine's office was only a few blocks from the courthouse. Up the hill to Fifth Avenue, then south a few blocks to Washington Street, where downtown Seattle started to turn into the International District, but not quite as desirable as that. The office was in a one-story commercial building that had a large glass window in the front that used to have painted on it:

Hawkins & Raine, Attorneys at Law

Except Hawkins just got himself elected judge, and when Raine walked up, a worker was scraping the last of the *s* in

"Hawkins" off the glass. His former partner was more eager to cut ties with him than Raine had realized.

"You want me to scrape it all off, right?" the worker asked, seeing Raine approaching. Raine was tall—six feet three—in his mid-forties, with short black hair starting to gray at the temples, wearing a suit, and carrying a briefcase. He looked like a lawyer.

Raine frowned at the man's handiwork. And what it meant. "Nah, you can leave the rest of it," he answered. "I'm not going anywhere."

The worker tipped his hat back and gazed at the window. He was an older man, wearing white coveralls and already sweating at the neck from the exertion of his task. "'And Raine'?" he questioned. "That's a sentence fragment."

Raine didn't appreciate the grammar lesson. "Maybe I like sentence fragments. Just clean it up and leave the rest for now."

For now. It had been "Hawkins & Raine" for almost a decade. Mike Hawkins was a great guy and a great lawyer. They had struck up a friendship at the courthouse when they were up-and-coming attorneys in their early thirties, and let it blossom into a mutually beneficial professional partnership, handling everything from divorce to personal injury, bankruptcy to wills, and even criminal cases at first. Criminal could keep the doors open, but Raine had worked hard to establish a practice that wasn't dependent on unreliable and ungrateful clients like Patrick McCollum. Everything was great until it wasn't. Hawkins had decided he should be a judge, the voters agreed, and Raine was left facing an uncertain future.

He opened the door to the office and walked inside, to be faced with a more certain aspect of his future. Although not one he was any happier about.

"Dan. Finally." It was his wife, Natalie, and their younger

son, Jordan. More precisely, it was his soon-to-be ex-wife, Natalie, and his soon-to-be-estranged teenager Jordan. They were sitting in the waiting area just inside the door. Natalie stood up as soon as he walked in. Jordan didn't look up from his phone.

"We've been waiting for almost twenty minutes," Natalie complained.

"I had to take a verdict," Raine explained. "I didn't even know you were stopping by. Why—?" But then he saw the papers in her hand.

Natalie held them up for him. "These are the final orders for the dissolution. My lawyer just needs your signature, and we can file them."

"Dissolution", lawyer-talk for divorce. Another years-long partnership that hadn't worked out. Sixteen years, four months, and twelve days to be exact.

Raine took the papers and started to thumb through them. He knew they were the ones he had already agreed to in principle. It hadn't been a contentious divorce. Just two people who had grown apart, each making enough money not to need child support, and agreeing to split custody fifty-fifty, the kids shuttling back and forth between the house Natalie was keeping and the apartment Raine would be renting while he looked for a more permanent residence.

"Where's Jace?" Raine asked about their older child.

Natalie frowned. "He's in the car. He didn't want to come in."

"He didn't want to see his old man." Raine knew only too well.

"It's been harder on him than Jordan," Natalie defended. "Can you please just sign the papers so I can get back out there to him?"

Raine sighed, but he could hardly argue. Or rather, he could have argued, but to what end? They were getting divorced, his oldest son didn't want to see him, and his younger one still hadn't looked up from his phone. He pulled a pen out of his suit-coat pocket and signed the last page of his divorce decree. He handed the papers back to her.

"You look nice today," he remarked. She did. Thick brown hair, stylish shirt and pants combination, new boots.

But she put up a hand. "Don't, Dan. Just don't. Not in front of Jordan. This is hard enough as it is."

Raine shrugged. "Well, thanks for coming by, I guess." He reached out and tousled his son's hair. "Nice talking to you, pal."

Jordan just frowned at him and smoothed his hair back into place. Thirteen going on Jace. "Can we go now, Mom?"

"Yes, honey." Natalie put her arm around him. Then she offered Raine a lopsided smile. "Thanks for signing these, Dan. I know it's not what either of us planned."

Raine didn't know what to say. With Natalie, he never did. That was probably part of why it didn't work out. "Good to see you, Nat. Have your lawyer send me copies after they're filed."

And then she was gone, with their boys.

Raine took a moment to assess his surroundings. He was alone, finally. Their one employee, a receptionist, was on her lunch break. He put his fists on his hips and took a deep breath, ready to have important thoughts about life and change and things that end up as quotes on motivational memes. But then he heard an unfamiliar voice coming out of the hallway that led to the individual offices in the back.

"I'm telling you, Hunter, I can lease this place in a week. Faster if your guy finishes scraping those names off the window today."

Raine turned to see a woman about his age walk out into the lobby, dressed to kill on a random weekday afternoon, with long perfect platinum hair, even more perfect makeup, and a phone call obviously going on via her earbuds.

"No, no, I didn't bother him," the woman continued, still oblivious to Raine. "I used the keys to come in the back entrance. I just need to—"

She stopped in her tracks when she saw Raine. "Oh crap, the tenant is here," she told "Hunter". "I'll call you back in three."

She waited a moment for the call to disconnect, then extended a heavily ringed hand to Raine. "You must be David Raine. So nice to meet you."

"Daniel," he corrected. "Daniel Raine." There were two nameplates on the reception desk. Hawkins hadn't taken his down yet. Raine pointed to his own.

Sommers squinted at the brass plaque. "J. Daniel Raine," she read aloud. "Oh, okay. Yes. Daniel, not David. My bad." Then she asked, "What does the *J* stand for?"

Raine sighed. He liked how using his first initial made his name more lawyerly, but the name behind the initial less so. "Jack," he admitted.

"Ooh, Jack Raine." Sommers tried the name on for size. "I like that. Sounds like a private eye. I always thought I'd make a great private eye. What do you think?"

"I have no idea," Raine answered. "I don't even know who you are, or why you're in my office. What are you doing here?"

"Oh my God, right." Sommers waved a bangled arm at him. "I'm Rebecca Sommers."

Raine waited for more. There wasn't any. "Okay. And?"

"Rebecca Sommers?" she repeated. "*The* Rebecca Sommers?"

Raine shook his head. "Sorry. Should I know you?"

Sommers cocked her head at him. "Yes, as a matter of fact, you should. I am the number one commercial real estate agent in Seattle—downtown core and First Hill—for three quarters running."

Raine narrowed his eyes at her. "Real estate agent? But I'm not moving—"

"Not yet, Jack." Sommers laughed. "But you will be. You just haven't figured it out yet. Your partner has left your business, and you guys were late on the rent twice last year as it was. You think you can keep this place afloat by yourself? This is a prime location, or it will be soon. I didn't become the number one commercial real estate agent in Seattle—"

"Downtown core and First Hill," Raine interrupted.

Sommers smiled, but not as warmly as her previous grins. "Yes, that. I didn't get there by sitting back and waiting for listings to come to me. I do my homework. This place is prime to flip, and I'm the one to do it."

Raine closed his eyes and shook his head. "Okay, let's just slow down a minute. First of all, it's Dan, not Jack. Please don't call me Jack. That was my dad's name, and he was the sort of guy who thought naming his kid 'Jack Daniel' was funny. So don't call me that. Second, I'm not moving. I've been in this office for ten years—"

"Nine," Sommers corrected. She tapped her temple. "Homework."

"Nine and a half," Raine allowed. "I understand that my partner is leaving, but I have a long-term lease and—"

"The law firm of Hawkins and Raine, LLC, had a long-term lease," Sommers interjected, "but that entity no longer exists. As such, your lease has converted to month-to-month. And no one thinks you're going to make the next month, especially not your landlord, who is my client, by the way."

"Well, I think I'll make rent," Raine protested. "I have a plan to keep this practice successful enough to more than cover—"

"Your last client," Sommers interrupted again. "Did he pay you? Like, in full?"

Raine exhaled through his nose. "I'm not sure what that has to do with—"

"Hold on." Sommers raised a finger at him and tapped her earbud. "Hey, Hunter. Yes. Sorry. No, I guess I'm going to need like one more minute with this guy. Yeah. Yeah, I know, right? I'll call you back. Don't worry, we got this."

She returned her attention to Raine. "Hunter is my broker. He runs the office, and he can be very demanding. What were you saying again? Some lie about being able to keep this place open on less than half the receipts you brought in last year?"

Raine was about to argue that he had been responsible for bringing in slightly more than half of their receipts the previous year but was interrupted by the woman who exploded through the front door. She appeared to be in her early forties, but fighting it, dressed in a fashion-forward pink suit with a wide-brimmed pink hat and a rhinestone-encrusted purse.

"I'm Abigail Willoughby!" she declared. "I need attorney Daniel Raine!"

2

R aine took a moment before answering, "I'm attorney Daniel Raine."

There were any number of reasons a person might be looking for him. Some were good, but a lot were bad. The woman who had suddenly appeared in his office might be a relative of the guy who just got convicted of Eluding, unhappy about the result. She might be a creditor on one of his bankruptcy cases, upset at receiving pennies on the dollar. She might be an angry victim on one of those criminal cases he tried to, but couldn't quite completely, avoid. Or, and this was the reason he'd decided to go ahead and identify himself despite all of the other negative possibilities, she might be a prospective new client. If he hadn't been willing to take that risk normally, the vulturelike presence of Rebecca Sommers focused his mind.

"You are Mr. Raine?" the woman almost challenged. She had a pleasant face, with a bit more makeup than women in Seattle usually wore. Her hair was blonde and straight, cut harshly just above the shoulder. She held herself with confidence.

"I am," Raine confirmed. "How can I help you?"

Abigail Willoughby stepped forward to inspect the man she had come to see. Raine reflexively took a half step back as the woman sidled into his personal space. She scanned his face and attire up close, squinting thickly mascaraed eyes and pursing fire-red lips. She even sniffed at his neck, which only caused him to become suddenly aware of her own scent. Her perfume was pleasant enough, in a flowery sort of way. Or maybe fruity. Possibly both. He wasn't quite sure. But he was sure he didn't like her so close to him.

"Yes, you'll do," Abigail announced just as Raine was about to back away from her. Instead, she took a step back and nodded at him. "You'll do nicely."

"Do for what?" Raine was not enjoying the interaction so far.

"I have need of an attorney," Abigail answered.

"I gathered as much," Raine replied. "For what? And why me?"

Abigail's head swiveled as her eyes darted around the room; she clutched her purse tighter. "Is there somewhere we can talk alone?" she whispered. "I wish to speak in private."

Raine frowned. He was relieved that Abigail Willoughby was new business and not someone seeking revenge, but her appearance and affect were setting off alarm bells in his mind. Privacy was certainly important when speaking with a lawyer. Discretion was a pillar of the profession, and attorney-client privilege extended to conversations with prospective clients even if the person never ultimately hired the attorney. On the other hand, it wasn't advisable to meet alone with a woman whom he'd just met, who was acting strangely, and whose stated reasons for bursting through his door had yet to be confirmed. For all Raine knew, Abigail Willoughby —if that was even her real name—could have been one of those disgruntled people after all and had sought him out in order to set him up with a false accusation of impropriety behind closed doors.

That was one of the reasons why Raine and Hawkins usually did their initial consultations together—so they always had a witness. People who needed lawyers were often not the most reputable people. But Raine had lost Hawkins, and his receptionist, Laura, wouldn't be back for another forty-five minutes—longer if Laura stopped for a coffee on her way back. He could ask Abigail to wait for nearly an hour, but she didn't seem like a woman who was used to being told to wait. She might just walk right out the door again, and Raine could resume his conversation with Rebecca Sommers about how he was going to lose his office.

Or he could get creative.

"Of course," Raine answered. "We have a conference room around the corner. Let's the three of us head back there, and you can tell us what's brought you here today."

"Three of us?" Abigail and Sommers asked in unison.

"Why, yes," Raine answered with a cool smile. He gestured to Sommers. "This is Rebecca Sommers, my investigator."

He smiled at the stunned real estate agent and hoped she'd meant what she'd said earlier about wanting to be a "private eye".

"Anything you say in front of me," he continued, "you can say in front of her."

Raine waited a beat to see how his gambit would go over. Sommers was still processing, but Abigail seemed satisfied with that suggestion.

"Excellent," Abigail declared, and she marched between them toward the conference room.

But Sommers blocked Raine's way. She crossed her arms and raised a bemused eyebrow at Raine. "Your investigator?"

"I need another person in the room," Raine confided. "I'm

not meeting with a woman I've never met before without a witness."

"So tell her that," Sommers suggested.

Raine frowned. "I'm afraid she won't wait while I line up a real investigator for the case. Besides, it's fifty-fifty she even has a case worth taking. But I don't want to just let her walk out the door without finding out."

"Are you that desperate not to lose new business?" Sommers asked before adding, "Although, I suppose maybe you should be."

Raine shrugged. "You said you always wanted to be a private investigator, right?"

"I said I would be a good one." Sommers laughed. "And I would. But I'm quite happy in my chosen career, Jack. Besides, I wouldn't know the first thing about being a private eye."

"Okay, first of all, it's Dan, not Jack," Raine replied. "Second, no one says 'private eye'. It's just 'investigator'. Third, I just need another person in the room in case it turns out she's crazy and accuses me of something inappropriate."

"What are the odds of that?" Sommers raised her other eyebrow.

"Her accusing me, or me doing something?" Raine asked.

"Well, either one, I suppose," Sommers answered. "I should probably know that if I'm going to be your 'investigator'."

"The chance of me doing anything inappropriate is zero," he assured her, "but I have no idea what the chances are that she might accuse me of something. I just know it's not zero."

Sommers frowned, but hadn't said no yet.

"I just need someone to sit there with me while she tells me what she wants a lawyer for," Raine assured her. "Just take notes or something. That's all a real investigator would do anyway."

Sommers took a moment, then checked the time on her phone. She nodded. "Okay, you know what? Why not? I have thirty minutes before my next appointment. This might be fun. And you're going to pay me."

That last part wasn't a question.

"Pay you?" Raine balked. "I didn't say anything about paying you."

"You said you wanted me to do a job for you," Sommers recounted, "and I don't do jobs for free. My time is money, honey."

Raine rubbed the back of his neck. If he paid Sommers but Abigail didn't hire him, he would literally lose money on the consultation. Maybe Abigail would be willing to wait for his receptionist to come back after all.

"Are the two of you coming or not?" Abigail shouted from inside the conference room. "I don't have all day."

Sommers crossed her arms and smirked at Raine. "Do we have a deal, Mr. Raine? Or am I going outside to tell that guy to scrape your name off the window too?"

Raine sighed hard through his nose, then nodded his head. "Okay, fine. Thirty minutes, standard investigator rate."

"Thirty minutes, standard rate for the number one commercial real estate agent in Seattle—downtown core and First Hill—three quarters running," Sommers countered.

Raine shook his head at her. "Do real estate agents even have hourly rates?"

"No," Sommers allowed with a laugh, "but I'll think of something. Now let's see what Ms. Abigail Willoughby has to say. This should be fun."

Raine sighed again. He wasn't so sure.

It was a small conference room. The table could seat eight, but it took up most of the space; the chairs bumped the wall when they were pulled out. The three of them squeezed into position, Abigail Willoughby on one side, hat and purse placed on the table in front of her, and Daniel Raine on the other, his new "investigator" at his side.

"What can I do for you, Ms. Willoughby?" Raine began.

"It's my husband, Mr. Raine," Abigail declared with a toss of her hair. "I fear what he may do."

Raine frowned. She wanted a domestic violence protection order. He hated DV protection order cases, maybe even more than criminal cases. At least with criminal cases, he had a shot at winning on the merits, and there was enough work to do to justify a healthy retainer—even if the client didn't always pay all of it. But protection order hearings were short and sweet, and whether the order was granted or not was a crapshoot that depended more on which commissioner was assigned to hear the case than any of the facts alleged in the pleadings. The retainer wouldn't cover even one month's rent, and there was an even chance his client would be upset with the result.

"What might he do?" Raine asked.

"And why?" Sommers put in.

Raine glared at her. *Just take notes*, he thought, but he couldn't say it out loud.

"Lord knows what he'll do," Abigail answers, "but he'll do something when he finds out I'm filing for divorce."

Oh, a divorce case. Raine's spirits lifted. A messy divorce case could be quite lucrative. Even more so if the other side was easily upset. Raine's own divorce had been amicable enough to avoid outside lawyers, and it had still been time-consuming. A nice contentious divorce with multiple hearings and fights over everything from the beach house to the spice rack could generate enough billable hours to keep his office door open for a long while. And Abigail Willoughby looked like the kind of woman who had a beach house. Probably a few of them.

"Well, I think I can help you—" Raine began before Sommers interrupted him.

"Willoughby," Sommers said the name aloud, as if swirling it in her mouth like a sip of wine. "Your husband is Jeremy Willoughby." It wasn't really a question.

Abigail smiled slyly, exposing bleached teeth behind the cherry lips. "The one and only," she confirmed.

"I'm sorry." Raine looked between his not actually investigator and his not yet client. "Who is Jeremy Willoughby?"

"Only one of the richest tech moguls in Seattle," Sommers answered. "He took his money and went into real estate. Smart move. He owns half the office space downtown now. I would know."

Abigail tilted her head slightly. "Forty percent," she corrected. "And why would you know that?"

Raine's heart sank, but Sommers didn't miss a beat. She lowered her voice and delivered a line straight from a 1940s film noir. "It's my job to know, Ms. Willoughby. I'm a private eye."

Raine pushed back in his chair. The game was up. *Oh, well.* Maybe he could find a cheap office space under where the freeways met.

But Abigail pointed at Sommers and grinned. "What did you say your name was again, darling?"

"Sommers," she answered. "Rebecca Sommers, private eye."

"Wow. Okay." Raine leaned forward again and tried to regain control of the consultation. "So you need a lawyer because you want to file for divorce from one of the richest men in Seattle?"

"Exactly that." Abigail nodded.

Raine liked the sound of that. Rich clients paid their bills, and paid bills kept the doors open.

"You've come to the right place, Ms. Willoughby," Raine said. "We handle all sorts of cases here at Hawki—here at Raine Law Offices, but divorces are sort of our specialty."

"Do you have experience in high-asset divorces?" Abigail asked.

"Oh, of course," Raine assured her, trying not to sound like a used-car salesman. In truth, most of the divorces he had handled were the typical middle-class divorces he'd gone through himself, where the only major asset was the family home. Sell the house, split the proceeds, then argue over the children's residential schedule. But he wasn't about to cop to that. "I assume that's why you sought me out," he tried.

Abigail's mouth dropped into a half-pout. "In truth, I reached out to Michael. We knew each other when we were children. This is a delicate matter, and I wanted someone I could trust. But apparently Michael is going to be a judge or some such, so he said I should speak with you. He wasn't wrong, was he?"

"Michael? Wrong?" Raine waved the suggestion away with a laugh he hoped wasn't as nervous as he felt. "Michael is never wrong. That's why he's going to be a great judge. And I'm going to be a great lawyer for your divorce."

Abigail Willoughby didn't seem convinced.

"Let's start with the basics," Raine pushed on. "Are there any children from your marriage?"

"No," Abigail answered. "Jeremy has a son from his first marriage, but he's an adult now, and Jeremy cut him off years ago when he refused to go into the family business."

"Real estate?" Raine thought he recalled.

But Abigail frowned at him.

"Tech," Sommers corrected. "Real estate investment is a fruit of the business, not the business itself."

"Correct," Abigail confirmed. She took a moment to size

up Daniel Raine one more time. She raised a hand to her chin, her rings fighting to sparkle in the fluorescent light of the conference room. "You know, I'm not so sure—"

"Your assets," Sommers interrupted before Abigail could decide to take her business elsewhere, "are they in a SLAT?"

Raine cocked his head at Sommers. "SLAT?"

"Spousal Lifetime Asset Trust," Sommers translated.

"I know what it is," Raine defended. "I'm just surprised you know about them."

"I know a lot of things," Sommers informed him.

"But that's more of an estate planning tool," Raine said. "That is, wills and trusts, things like that."

"I also know what estate planning is." Sommers frowned. "And I know that a SLAT can be used during a marriage to avoid taxes while providing funds to a spouse. Those funds can be substantial, even enough to purchase real estate."

"Ah." Raine finally understood how Sommers knew about them.

"Do you two work together often?" Abigail questioned, watching their uneven dynamic.

"Mr. Raine isn't my only client," Sommers explained before Raine could reply. "Sometimes he forgets the breadth of my experience."

Raine was beginning to suspect that was true.

"So, is there a spousal trust?" He decided to pursue Sommers's line of questioning. "We'll need to know all of the financial arrangements, especially if they're complex."

"Oh, they're complex," Abigail confirmed. "The SLAT was set up at the same time we executed the prenuptial agreement."

Raine winced. Of course there was a prenuptial agreement.

"I wasn't about to sign everything away," Abigail continued, "without getting something in return. A well-funded irrevocable trust seemed like a good start."

"A good start," Raine conceded, "but maybe a bad ending. That prenup is going to be a problem. We have to get past that prenup before we can reach any of the assets. Getting something in exchange for signing it will make it hard to claim you didn't understand what you were doing."

"Well, that's why I've come to you, Mr. Raine," Abigail reminded him. "If I wanted to accept the terms of the prenuptial agreement, I wouldn't need a lawyer, now would I? I could just file whatever it is you file to divorce someone and walk away with whatever pittance I agreed to when we were married. But that was ten years ago. A lot has happened since then. I've grown and our business has too. I deserve more than a severance package."

"Of course you do," Sommers agreed.

Raine was agnostic on the question. He had no idea whether Abigail Willoughby did or did not "deserve" more than she bargained for when she'd married a very rich man who then became even richer. But it didn't matter. He was a lawyer; he did what he was hired to do. A case wasn't a moral question to be answered. It was a puzzle to be solved.

"Who deserves the assets won't mean anything if we can't reach them because of that prenup," Raine repeated.

"Well, that kind of feels like your job," Sommers pointed out.

"Yes, Mr. Raine," Abigail agreed, "how will you invalidate the prenuptial agreement?"

She was challenging him. He didn't mind a challenge.

"I need to see it before I can know for sure," Raine was sure to caution, "but there are a few general lines of attack we can expect to take. The first will be to attack its legality at the time of execution. We claim that it was signed under duress or that its terms are so unfair as to make it unconscionable on its face. If that fails, we can argue that there's been a change of circumstances sufficient to render its original purposes unattainable, maybe even contrary to public policy. Finally, we may be able to point to a series of actions over the last ten years that indicate an intent by you and your husband to abandon the agreement."

"I assure you," Abigail said darkly, "Jeremy has never intended to abandon it."

"I said we look for actions that allow us to argue that," Raine clarified.

"Oh," Abigail responded. "I like that. Very lawyerly."

"So that's step one," Raine continued. "Step two will be division of the assets."

"The real estate holdings, Abigail"—Sommers leaned forward and tucked a lock of her platinum hair behind an ear —"how are those held? Personally? Trusts? LLCs?"

"A mixture," Abigail answered.

"Are any of the real estate assets in your name, by any chance?" Sommers asked.

Abigail laughed. "Oh, no. Jeremy would never do that. He's too much of a control freak. Nothing is in my name."

"But you do want some of that real estate, right?" Sommers asked.

"Do I want some?" Abigail laughed. "What's that old saying about real estate? 'Invest in land, they aren't making any more of it.' Yes, I want my share of the real estate. I want my share of everything."

"We'll need a plan, then," Sommers declared. "Some of the properties are probably overvalued, and others are probably undervalued. Some probably need to be transferred into different forms of ownership, especially if the marriage is dissolving and won't exist anymore as a possible owner. That means transactions, and that means taxes."

"And commissions," Raine realized.

"Nothing wrong with commissions." Sommers flashed a grin at him, then turned back to Abigail. "That's just the cost of doing business. But there needs to be a plan in place that not only divides the properties, but does so to our maximum benefit."

"You mean Ms. Willoughby's maximum benefit," Raine suggested.

Sommers didn't look at him. "I said what I said."

Abigail smiled. "I like you." She pointed at Sommers and looked to Raine. "I like her. She'll be on the case all the way until the end, right?"

Raine forced a tight smile. "If that's what you want, Ms. Willoughby."

"Don't worry, Ms. Willoughby," Sommers said. "At the end of this case, when that property transfers to you, I will absolutely be there to help you maximize its value."

"Wonderful," Abigail said. She stood up and extended a hand for Raine to shake. "You're hired, Mr. Raine. Where do I sign?"

———

ABIGAIL WILLOUGHBY SIGNED two documents before departing. One was the fee agreement; the other was a retainer check more than large enough to pay Raine's rent for the next six months.

"Congratulations." Sommers tapped the check Raine was still admiring in his hand. "I'll send you a bill for my portion of that."

Raine frowned at her. "Are you really going to do that? Aren't you going to make enough on your commissions when you become her Realtor at the end of it all?"

"That obvious, huh?" Sommers grinned.

"To me"—Raine shrugged—"but then again, I knew you were only pretending to be a 'private eye'. I'm pretty sure she thought you were actually interested in her best interests, not your own."

"Those can be aligned," Sommers returned. "And don't forget about your best interests. You just made rent for the next two quarters, which means I missed out on a nice commission for flipping this place—at least for now."

She stepped over and placed a hand on Raine's shoulder. "Listen, you seem like a nice enough guy, Jack, but I'm not about doing other people favors. I'm about doing favors for myself. You may never have heard of Jeremy Willoughby, but I have. I knew who Abigail Willoughby was as soon as she said her name. I just didn't know how I could turn things to my advantage, but then you invited me into the room! When she said she was going to divorce the man who owns half the office space in downtown Seattle—"

"Forty percent," Raine corrected.

"Fine, forty percent." Sommers surrendered a nod and removed her hand. "When Abigail Willoughby said she was going to divorce the man who owns forty percent of downtown Seattle, I knew I needed to be in the room when that happened. I'll get to see the deepest darkest details of their financials, I'll know exactly which one of them is going to own which assets before anyone else in the industry, and every asset that doesn't stay with Jeremy is going to need an expert like me to execute the transfer of title."

Raine wanted to be upset with her for twisting his client consultation to her own advantage, but he could only manage to be impressed.

"Plus," she continued, "I'll have the eternal gratitude of the woman who will likely end up owning twenty-five percent of the office space in Seattle."

"Twenty," Raine corrected. "Half of forty percent."

But Sommers smiled and patted his cheek. "Have faith in yourself. You can do better for her than a fifty-fifty split. And I'll be there to make sure you do. We're partners now, Dan."

3

"Partner" was too strong a word, Raine decided. Partners worked together toward a common goal, each helping each other and sharing the rewards. Rebecca Sommers's goal was her own, and Raine wouldn't share in her rewards. They would be traveling in the same train car for a while, but they had different destinations.

Raine frowned as he pulled on his coat. The weather had turned. A steady rain had been falling for the two days since Abigail Willoughby left his office. It was supposed to let up the next day or maybe the day after that. But the frown wasn't for the weather. It was for another partner, one who jumped off the train early. It would be good to see Hawkins again, but it wouldn't be the same. That was life though, Raine supposed. He grabbed his briefcase, pulled his hood over his head, and stepped out into the rain.

The Superior Court Clerk's office was on the second floor of the King County Courthouse. It was one of two places Raine would need to deliver the pleadings that would initiate Abigail's divorce from Jeremy Willoughby. Raine entered the clerk's office and made his way to the self-service filing counter. He extracted the original of each required pleading, stamped it with one of the several "FILED" stamps available to the public, and dropped the packet into the wire basket labeled "NEW FILINGS".

After the court clerk, the other person Raine needed to provide copies of the divorce papers to was the opposing party, Jeremy Willoughby. The clerk would be indifferent to Raine's filings. Just part of the job. Another case, another filing fee. But Jeremy Willoughby was likely to react adversely when served with divorce papers. Everyone did. Even if Jeremy didn't fly into a rage as Abigail feared, it was never a good feeling to be served with divorce papers. Raine knew that personally.

Whatever Jeremy's reaction, Raine wouldn't be witness to it. Lawyers didn't serve papers to opposing parties. Lawyers hired process servers to do that. For one thing, Raine would need proof the lawsuit was properly served, and he wasn't permitted to be his own witness. For another, he wasn't interested in participating in someone else's misery any more than professionally necessary. It was just a job for him too. Another case, another retainer.

He dropped the papers off at the process server's, then ducked back into the rain to trudge up Fourth Avenue and meet his lunch companion at what had become, over the years, their favorite lunch spot.

"All rise!" Raine called out as he stepped into the restaurant and spied his former partner waiting at the usual table. "The Honorable Michael T. Hawkins is in the house!"

Hawkins laughed. "You rise when the judge walks in, not when he's already here."

Hawkins stood up to shake the hand of the man he'd spent every workday with for almost a decade. He hadn't arrived much sooner than Raine; both of their hands were still wet around the edges from the rain they had traversed.

They grasped hands tightly, as if to defy the unavoidable truth that their closeness was doomed to fade no matter how many intermittent lunches they made time for.

Raine added a shoulder squeeze to his handshake and sat down opposite his friend. Hawkins had one of those faces that somehow looked ever younger even as the crow's feet grew next to the eyes and the gray hairs began appearing at the temples. He had thick brown curls cut short and perfectly straight teeth in a genuine smile. Raine already missed seeing it every day.

"How's the judge life?" Raine asked. "Put anybody in prison for the rest of their life yet? That sounds great. I can see why you wanted that sort of joy in your life."

Hawkins laughed. "It was time, Dan. I did the lawyer thing long enough. I wanted to do something more."

"I don't know, Mike," Raine replied with a shrug. "Some people might say taking off your helmet so you can pull on a referee's whistle is doing less, not more. You won't be in the fight anymore; you'll be watching it."

"Making sure it's a fair fight," Hawkins returned. "That's just as important as fighting the fight. Maybe more."

Raine was tempted to argue the point more—he didn't really agree—but he didn't want their short time together to be swallowed by an academic disagreement. "You're going to be the best referee on the field, Mike. The players are lucky to have you." He looked at the menu, but only for a moment before tossing it down again. "Our usuals?" he confirmed, starting to stand up so he could walk over to the counter to place their orders.

"Already taken care of." Hawkins gestured for him to sit down again. "I got you a green tea too."

Raine frowned. "That's not my usual," he protested.

"Maybe it should be." Hawkins flashed that strong smile of his. "We aren't getting any younger."

The reunion was already sliding off its foundation.

"How about you, Dan?" Hawkins asked. "How's the firm? Landed any new cases? How'd that assault trial go?"

Raine frowned. Where to begin. With the less interesting information, he decided. "It was a mixed verdict. Not guilty on the assault, but guilty on the eluding."

"That's a good result," Hawkins opined.

"Mr. McCollum didn't think so." Raine chuckled. "He wants to fire me and said he won't pay the balance of his retainer."

"Sounds typical for a criminal case." Hawkins nodded. "I'm not going to miss that part of private practice."

Which led to the more interesting information. "But I did just land a big divorce case. Thanks to you, I think. Do you know a woman named Abigail Willoughby?"

Hawkins grimaced. "Oh shit. Did she actually call you? Oh man, I'm sorry, Dan. I just told her I wasn't practicing anymore and you were my old partner. I didn't think she'd actually contact you."

"No, no, it's all good," Raine assured him. "Not only did she contact me, she hired me. Big fat divorce case with a bunch of complex assets. It'll take a whole lot of billable hours to divvy up that marital community. Should keep me in the black for a few months at least while I try to figure out how to survive without you."

But Hawkins shook his head. "Be careful, Dan. Abby and I knew each other when we were kids. Her family rented out the lake house next to ours one summer back when no one lived in Seattle and a cabin on a lake cost less than a new car. She was always a little off, you know. Super serious and had trouble making friends."

"Did you guys date?" Raine asked.

"We were ten, Dan." Hawkins frowned. "So, no. We hung out that one summer; then we kind of lost track of each other.

We lived in Seattle, but she lived way out in Issaquah back when the biggest business there was that feed store by the freeway."

Raine laughed. "Oh yeah, I remember that feed store. What was the name of it?"

"I think it was just 'The Feed Store'," Hawkins said. "Typical old Seattle, right?"

"Before they started calling it the Emerald City," Raine agreed.

"I liked Jet City," Hawkins said. "When everyone worked for Boeing instead of Amazon and Microsoft."

Raine nodded at the weather visible through the restaurant windows. "I always was partial to Rain City."

Hawkins laughed. "You would be, wouldn't you, Mr. Raine? Well, anyway, I knew Abby back when the Emerald City was still Rain City. Honestly, it took me a minute to remember who she was when she contacted me. She called me at my new judge's office number. She must have just googled me."

"Maybe she thought she could just hire the judge directly," Raine suggested. "Cut out the middleman, you know."

Hawkins chuckled but shook his head. "No, she may have been socially awkward, but she was smart. She just had trouble trusting people. And getting a divorce is so personal. It can be embarrassing. Like you failed at the biggest thing you'll ever do in life."

Raine just blinked at his friend, shoving his own feelings of embarrassment and failure back down into his stomach.

"Oh shit, Dan." Hawkins suddenly realized what he'd said —or rather, whom he'd said it to. "I forgot. I didn't mean it that way. I just—aw, shit."

"Don't worry about it, Mike." Raine absorbed Hawkins's gaffe. That's what friends do. "Besides, you're not wrong."

"How are you doing?" Hawkins asked. "I've been so

caught up in the transition to the bench, I haven't even checked in on you."

"I'm fine, Mike," Raine assured him. "I'm not a ten-year-old girl who can't make friends at the lake house."

"How are the kids?" Hawkins asked. "How's Natalie?"

Raine realized he really didn't want to talk about it. "Fine. They're all fine. It's all fine."

Hawkins wrung his hands in the ensuing silence, which he then felt compelled to break. Raine wished he hadn't.

"You seeing anybody?" Hawkins ventured. "Or too—"

"Yeah, too soon," Raine confirmed. "Natalie and I were together for a long time. You don't just move on from something like that."

"I suppose not," Hawkins answered. "At least Abby is going to help you move on from Hawkins and Raine. Honestly, I was a little worried about you, but I'm glad I don't need to be."

Raine put on his best smile. "Nope. No one needs to worry about me. I've got this."

⁂

THE SANDWICH WAS TOUGH, and the soup was cold. Raine didn't get past a first tentative sip of the green tea. And it was still raining. Only harder.

Nevertheless, he took the long way back to his office, hood up, bag on his back, and hands pushed into his pockets. He walked down Madison Street to the waterfront, past the public library and the old federal courthouse.

Madison Street ended in a T-intersection with Alaskan Way, the road that ran parallel to the shoreline. Raine crossed the four-lane boulevard to the boardwalk of the tourist-filled waterfront. The weather had thinned the usual crowd a bit, but there were still plenty of tourists who had spent good money to travel to Rain City and weren't about to let their plans be ruined because the city lived up to its old nickname. It was easy to spot the tourists; they had umbrellas. Locals like Raine had hooded coats and waterproof hats. You couldn't spend your life carrying an umbrella everywhere.

Raine peeked out from under his own drenched hood at the gray churning water of Elliot Bay visible between the piers housing attractions like the aquarium and the still relatively new Ferris wheel. On the edges of the boardwalk, T-shirt and jewelry vendors braved the elements under pop-up tents, offering inclement weather discounts: three T-shirts for $25, or buy one bracelet of threaded beads, get the second one free. None of the tourists were stopping to take advantage of the deals. Raine didn't either. He was there for the scenery, not the wares. The scenery and the tranquility he hoped it might offer.

Eventually, Raine passed the last of the tourist attractions, and the boardwalk gave way to a cement sidewalk, then to the railroad tracks and uneven asphalt of the city's working harbor. There was something cathartic about leaving new Seattle behind and stepping back into old Seattle, especially in the rain. He turned away from the water and crossed back over Alaskan Way, then took a left on Jackson and started up the hill toward his office.

He had expected to use the rain-drenched walk to ruminate on his failed marriage, his broken business, and the finiteness and futility of life generally. Instead, though, his mind emptied itself of any thought other than watching out for puddles and feeling the sting of the rain on his face. That must have been what he needed, Raine decided. Sometimes the best defense against being overwhelmed by big thoughts was to not think them. He could always return to them later; they weren't going anywhere, after all, no matter how much he might wish they would.

When he turned onto Washington Street, finally arriving at his office building, he felt strangely refreshed, ready to take on whatever challenges might be waiting for him. He just didn't expect the first challenge to be two men blocking his office door.

"Raine!" the smaller of the two men called out from under the umbrella the larger man was holding over him. Raine was a big man at six feet three, but the umbrella holder was even taller, with thick arms and a thicker neck, all wrapped in a black wool turtleneck and black overcoat. The man under the umbrella was several inches shorter than both of them, in a perfectly tailored suit but no overcoat. Raine also noticed his shoes. They looked very nice, with large gold buckles. He and his obviously very expensive outfit would have been drenched but for the services of his goon.

Raine stopped short. "Can I help you, gentlemen?" he inquired from a distance.

"I'm Jeremy Willoughby," the man under the umbrella announced, "and you just made a big mistake, my friend."

4

"I appreciate the sentiment, Mr. Willoughby," Raine replied, the rain dripping on his face from the edge of his hood, "but I hardly think we're friends yet. We just met."

"You think you're funny, Raine?" Jeremy took a step toward him, but tentatively, making sure the umbrella followed him.

"I think I'm a lawyer, Mr. Willoughby," Raine answered. "And I think this conversation would be a lot more comfortable inside my office. Can we go in, or are we really going to do this out here in the rain?"

Jeremy hesitated. On the one hand, it was all very dramatic to ambush someone outside his office. On the other hand, the rain was picking up, and his continued dryness depended on the skills of the man he'd brought most likely not for his talents with an umbrella.

"Fine," Jeremy finally relented. "Let's take this inside."

Not as inherently threatening as the phrase "Let's take this outside", but Jeremy did his best to make it sound menacing. Raine gestured invitingly toward his door, and

Jeremy and Umbrella Boy performed an awkward little dance as they tried to duck through the doorway without getting wet from the rain pouring off the collapsing umbrella. Raine watched with no little amusement, then followed his ambushers inside, pulling his hood back once he was fully out of the rain.

Raine was glad for the dry warmth of his office. In truth, he could have said whatever he needed to say to Jeremy out in the cold and rain, but Jeremy's companion suggested a desire to intimidate, and that could quickly escalate to assault. Outside, the only evidence that Jeremy himself had been involved in assaulting his estranged wife's lawyer would have been Raine's word. But inside, he could slick his hair back and introduce his guests to his receptionist, immediately converting her from staff to witness.

"Laura, this is Jeremy Willoughby," Raine called out. "He's the opposing party on our latest case. And the man with him I believe is his bodyguard or some other role designed to intimidate the riffraff like us. Is the conference room available?"

Jeremy looked flummoxed. He likely hadn't wanted to be identified, as Raine had suspected. In addition, Raine had called out the reason for bringing the goon in the turtleneck. It was all very transparent. The tech mogul's new clothes.

"Afternoon, Mr. Raine," Laura answered from her desk on the other side of the small lobby. She was fifty-seven, with gray hair that hung limply to her shoulders, large thick glasses, and no makeup whatsoever. Raine and Hawkins had hired her the first week of their partnership and she'd been with them ever since. She was a loyal employee, a good friend, a recent grandmother, and a smart cookie. "Nice to meet you, Mr.—Willoughby, was it? I'm afraid the conference room isn't available, Mr. Raine. The exterminators were just here, and they had to fumigate it. You'll need to use your office. I know it's too small for three people, so I'll put on a pot of coffee for Mr. Willoughby's companion. Maybe I can find something good on the TV. I'm sure you and Mr. Willoughby won't be long."

That was true. Raine was not a fan of speaking to opposing parties. It was always easier to deal with the other side through the other side's lawyer. Not that there weren't plenty of jerk lawyers in Seattle, but the caustic interactions with a jackass attorney were coated in at least a thin veneer of professionalism. They might call you an asshole, but they'd do it in writing, and in Latin.

"Thank you, Laura," Raine responded. It was a thank-you for lying and being astute enough to know to do it. The conference room had definitely not just been fumigated. Raine gestured toward his office. "Right this way, Mr. Willoughby."

Jeremy stood still for a moment. Not only had he been identified, but he was also being asked to shed his body-guard. One on one, Raine could probably take him. Definitely take him, Raine thought. He had several inches and more than a few pounds on Jeremy. More importantly, Jeremy had brought someone larger with him; that telegraphed feeling inadequate in his own ability to intimidate and/or win a fight. If they went back to Raine's office without his goon, it would be words, not fists. And when the weapons were words, lawyers usually won. Jeremy looked up at his companion.

"Do you take cream or sugar, Mr....?" Laura tried to coax another name into the official record. But Jeremy had his limits. Still, it distracted him enough to seal the one-on-one in Raine's office.

"You don't need to know his name," Jeremy snarled. "He'll take it black. This won't take long."

Raine led Jeremy down the hallway to his office, but was

just able to hear the Nameless Umbrella Holder tell Laura, "One cream and two sugars, please."

Raine smiled to himself and stopped at his office door, opening an arm toward the guest chairs. There were definitely two of them. "Here we are, Mr. Willoughby. Have a seat, and I'll be happy to answer any questions you might have about the upcoming process. Within the bounds of attorney-client privilege, of course."

Jeremy pushed past Raine, making an effort to lean a shoulder into him as he traversed the doorway. Raine decided to let it slide and followed his guest inside, taking a seat in his office chair across the desk from his client's husband. He could see why she didn't like him. He wondered why she ever had.

"I don't give a fuck about attorney-client privilege, Raine," Jeremy barked. "That's my wife you're talking about. You tell me whatever the fuck I want to know. You got that?"

Delightful, Raine thought.

"Mr. Willoughby," Raine replied evenly, "I would call you out on your tough-guy act, but I fear it would be counterproductive."

"It's not an act, Raine," Jeremy growled at him. "You don't know who you're dealing with."

Raine raised a calming palm at his opponent. "I can deduce from your presence at my office that you were served with the divorce papers today. You need to understand that the petition for dissolution has been filed with the court. This is happening. Menacing me won't change that. You need to focus on what is coming, not what has been."

Jeremy sprang to his feet and slammed the top of Raine's desk. "Now listen here, you little shit! You don't tell me what to do. I tell you what to do. And what you're going to do is march down to the fucking courthouse and withdraw that motion for divorce—"

"Petition for dissolution," Raine corrected, without standing up himself. "It's not called a 'divorce' in Washington. It's called a 'dissolution'. And it's a petition, not a motion. A petition initiates the dissolution; a motion comes between the initiation of a legal proceeding and its termination."

Another slam on the desk. "Goddamn it, Raine! You are going to listen to me, and you are going to do exactly what I fucking say."

Raine finally stood up. He did so slowly so that both men could be fully aware that he was the larger of them. "I do what my client says, Mr. Willoughby, and you are not my client. My client is your wife, and she is divorcing you."

Jeremy exhaled slowly through flared nostrils, fists still on the desk and looking up to stare Raine dead in the eye. After a moment, Jeremy broke off his gaze and stood up straight, his chest heaving in anger.

"Look, I understand this can be difficult." Raine tried to calm things down. "But the law provides for an orderly process in this type of situation, and it really is in everyone's best interest to allow the process to unfold."

Jeremy stepped away from the desk and toward the cabinet behind Raine's chair. He pointed to a framed photograph of Natalie and the kids that Raine probably should have put away by then. "That your wife and kids?"

Raine felt his heartbeat accelerate. His fists clenched reflexively. "Yes."

"How would you feel if you were about to lose her?" Jeremy asked.

"I already did," Raine admitted. Maybe it would create a bond. "And I survived. So will you."

Jeremy smirked, and Raine instantly regretted divulging even that small piece of personal information.

"Survived," Jeremy repeated. He picked up the frame. "Yeah, it'd be a shame if anything happened to them."

Raine squared his shoulders at Jeremy. "What did you just say?"

"You heard what I said." Jeremy laughed in Raine's face. He set the photograph down again. "And you know what I meant. I'm a powerful man, Mr. Raine. And you? You're not. Maybe you should think about what might happen to your family before you—"

Raine grabbed Jeremy by the lapels and slammed him against the cabinet, sending the picture of his family and half of the other things on the credenza crashing to the floor.

"Don't you fucking threaten my family, Willoughby," Raine growled, nose to nose, "or you'll be the one who doesn't survive."

Moments like that reminded Raine he was bigger than most men. A moment later he was reminded that he wasn't bigger than all of them. Umbrella Man stormed into the office and ripped Raine away from his boss. He picked Raine up by the shoulders and threw him across the room into the far wall. Raine's face slammed against the drywall, and he fell to the ground in a heap, head spinning. He started to force himself to his feet before the next blow, but Jeremy was magnanimous enough to save him from it.

"That's enough, my friend." Jeremy grabbed his body-guard's arm. "I believe Mr. Raine has gotten my point. I expect the petition for dissolution will be withdrawn by the end of the day."

Raine steadied himself against the wall as Jeremy and his goon exited. He reached up and touched his rapidly swelling cheek. It was bleeding. But he'd survive.

He stumbled to his office door and shouted after his retreating assailants, "I'll see you in court, Willoughby!"

5

Raine had several takeaways from his encounter with Jeremy. The first was that he was grateful Umbrella Man had pulled him away from Jeremy, facial laceration notwithstanding. The Bar Association would not have looked favorably on a lawyer assaulting an opposing party. He had already lost his wife and his business partner; he didn't need to add his license and livelihood to that list. The second takeaway was that he understood what the Willoughbys saw in each other. They both appeared to be entitled, petulant, and self-centered bordering on narcissistic. Neither of them gave a damn about him or probably anyone else. He was a tool in their fight. Not an atypical position for a lawyer to find himself in, but it led to the third takeaway. He wasn't going to meet with either of them alone ever again.

He definitely needed to meet with Abigail Willoughby again after being assaulted by her husband, or by his body-guard anyway. Which meant he needed a witness.

"Rebecca Sommers, executive Realtor," Sommers answered the phone when Raine called.

"'Executive Realtor'?" Raine questioned. "What does that even mean?"

"I'm sorry, who is this?" Sommers asked in a sugary tone that somehow also highlighted her irritation with the question.

"It's Daniel Raine," he identified himself. "Remember me?"

"Ja—er, Dan." Sommers caught herself. "Not Jack. Dan. Or maybe Danny. Can I call you Danny? What can I do for you, Danny?"

Raine sighed. "Danny" was better than "Jack". "I was wondering whether my," he went ahead and said it, "*partner* might be available for a follow-up interview with our client, Abigail Willoughby."

"Oh, Danny," Sommers practically gasped. "You really are including me? I thought maybe I'd have to fight you for access to my next big client."

"Speaking of fighting"—Raine decided he might as well ask, given how events were turning out—"you don't happen to know karate or tae kwon do or anything, do you?"

"Jujitsu," Sommers answered. "Brown belt."

"Really?" Raine was surprised. He'd meant it as a joke.

"Yes, really," Sommers confirmed. "Why?"

"Oh, no reason," Raine lied. "Just curious what an executive Realtor does in her spare time. Listen, we need to talk with Abigail again. I filed the divorce papers, and she was right about Jeremy not taking it well. I've decided I'm not going to be alone with either of them again if I can avoid it."

"Ah, hence the question about jiu jitsu," Sommers deduced. "You think Abigail might beat you up or something?"

"Are you available or not?" Raine ignored the jab.

"I'll make myself available," Sommers assured him.

"Thanks. I appreciate that."

"Oh, it's not for you, Danny," Sommers said. "It's for Abigail."

"It's for Rebecca." Raine knew.

"Well, yes," Sommers agreed with a chuckle. "That too."

"Okay, I'll reach out to her and schedule something." Raine pressed ahead. "It needs to be soon."

"Soon is good," Sommers agreed. "Looking forward to it."

Raine wasn't sure he was.

"Soon" meant it had to be on Abigail's terms. She wasn't about to adjust her schedule as a wealthy soon-to-be divorcée just to meet with the lawyer who was going to help her get there. Abigail wasn't going to come to him, so he, and Sommers, had to go to her.

But they drove separately.

Once his phone's GPS alerted him that he had reached the address Abigail had provided, Raine struggled to park his car between an unnecessarily large Land Rover with a vanity plate that read "QUEEN" and a wing-door Tesla SUV with a matte black paint job and black-tinted headlamps.

Rich people. Raine shook his head as he finished wedging his late-model Camry into place, leaving it a little slanted lest he bump into a luxury car while struggling to make his middle-class one perfectly parallel with the curb. Sommers was already standing on the sidewalk, waiting for him.

Raine stepped out of his car and glanced around. "Is this the place?"

"Oh, this is it," Sommers confirmed. "I do mostly commercial real estate, but a lot of my well-to-do clients ask for referrals to sell or buy a home. Madison Park is a very exclusive neighborhood. Very sought after. Exactly where I would expect someone like Abigail Willoughby to live."

But when Raine joined Sommers on the sidewalk, her eyes widened. "What happened to your face?"

Raine reflexively reached up to the healing cut. "You should see the other guy," he joked.

"Really?"

Raine frowned. "No, actually. The other guy is fine." He changed the subject. "Anyway, which one of these mansions is 4406 Larkspur Drive?"

"That one right there." Sommers nodded across the street. "The neo-Tudor with the iron fence around the perimeter."

As they crossed the street, Sommers gestured toward the Land Rover. "Thanks for not hitting my car, by the way. I'd hate to have to file an insurance claim against my partner."

Raine looked again at the "QUEEN" plate. He should have known.

The iron gate was locked, so Raine pressed the button on the intercom box bolted between its bars.

After a few moments, Abigail's voice came over the intercom. "Hello?"

"Hello, Ms. Willoughby." Raine spoke into the box. "It's Daniel Raine."

"And Rebecca Sommers!" she called past him.

"We're here for our appointment," Raine finished.

"One moment," came the reply, followed by an electric buzzing and the clank of the gate unlocking. "Please come to the side door. I'm having the front entry repainted today. Oh, and be sure to close the gate behind you."

Raine pushed the gate open, and they entered the grounds. The gate didn't have a spring on it to close automatically, so Raine slammed it shut behind them and assessed where to go next. The cement walk led directly to the front steps, but there was a path of stepping stones that split off just before the stairs and disappeared around the left side of the building. Raine and Sommers followed the stones and soon found themselves at the entrance to the kitchen. One of the kitchens, Raine guessed.

Abigail was waiting for them. She opened the door and welcomed them in with a wave of her arm. She was wearing a yellow floral-print dress, with billowing sleeves and an attached apron.

Very domestic, Raine supposed.

"Thank you for coming here to meet me," Abigail said. "I prefer to be home when there are workers in the home because, well, you know..."

Raine wasn't sure he did know other than to know that Abigail assumed people less well off than her were thereby automatically suspect of wanting to steal from her.

But Sommers replied, "Oh yes, of course. You can never be too careful." She gazed around the spacious kitchen, with its state-of-the-art appliances and view of Lake Washington through the adjoining parlor. "What a lovely home. Is this where you spend most of your time?"

"It is now," Abigail answered. "Truthfully, I didn't spend much time here after Jeremy and I were married. He had a couple of places downtown and the cabin on Whidbey Island, of course."

"Of course," Raine replied, barely managing to turn off the sarcasm before uttering the words. He guessed the "cabin" was larger than his house. Or rather, Natalie's house now, he remembered.

"So this was yours before the marriage?" Sommers continued. "I just love it."

Raine didn't have any strong feelings about the livability of the residence, but he was interested in its possible status as separate property not subject to the prenuptial agreement.

"Did you and Jeremy ever spend any time here as husband and wife? That could be important."

Abigail shook her head. "No, Jeremy never liked this place. Too bourgeois, he said. That's the main reason I'm here now."

"Because you want it to feel like it did before the marriage?" Sommers guessed.

"No, because this is the only place Jeremy didn't install a ridiculously elaborate surveillance system," Abigail explained. "He said it was to protect us against criminals, but it didn't take long for me to realize it was really so he could keep me under constant monitoring. He can't do that here."

Raine had no trouble believing that. The Jeremy Willoughby he had had the displeasure of meeting was very obviously a control freak. And that reminded him of why they'd come. "Can we sit down somewhere, Ms. Willoughby? We need to talk about the upcoming court date."

Abigail frowned slightly, but assented. "Of course. Come into the parlor. We can discuss matters over tea."

A tea service was already laid out on an ornate table by the window, affording a sweeping view of the water and Seattle's "Eastside" suburbs on the far bank. Raine hoped it wasn't green tea.

Abigail poured the tea and handed a cup of the mercifully black liquid to each of her guests. When Raine reached out for his cup, Abigail finally noticed the cut on his face. "Did Jeremy do that? I told you he would be upset."

"It wasn't Jeremy," Raine responded accurately, if misleadingly. He really didn't want to talk about it. "But yes, he did come to my office, and yes, he was upset. He is going to fight this vigorously. He's already hired one of the top law firms in town to represent him. They already served me with their notice of appearance and first set of motions. When we go to court next Wednesday, I expect it will be you and me on one side and Jeremy and six lawyers on the other. We need to be prepared."

Abigail lowered her cup slightly. "Oh, I don't intend to go to court, Mr. Raine. That's your job."

Raine sighed. He set his cup on the table. "I'm the lawyer, Ms. Willoughby, but you're the party. The petitioner, even. The judge will expect to see all the lawyers and all the litigants in the courtroom."

"Can't you just appear without me?" Abigail asked. "Have me sign a waiver of presence or something?"

"I suppose that is possible, Ms. Willoughby," Raine answered, "but it is strongly unadvisable. Not only could the judge interpret it as a lack of true interest in the outcome of the case, but it would deprive me of the ability to consult with you during the hearing, to help me answer any questions the judge might have about our proposed orders."

"I expected you to be able to anticipate any questions the judge might have, Mr. Raine." Abigail lifted an eyebrow at him. "Or did I overestimate you?"

Raine frowned. Abigail wasn't going to throw him into a wall, but she wasn't going to be an easy client either.

"Let me explain the importance of this hearing," Raine tried. "This is the hearing for temporary orders. The judge is going to make preliminary rulings on a whole host of issues, most importantly your access to bank accounts and properties. Now, you might think, with a name like 'temporary orders' that perhaps we can change things later and this hearing isn't all that important. You would be wrong. Because after the temporary orders are in place, they can only be modified by a showing of a substantial change of circumstances. That is a very high bar to clear, especially when the entire point of temporary orders is to freeze things in place prior to the trial. They're called temporary orders, but you need to think of them as first permanent orders."

"You've explained why the hearing is important, Mr. Raine." Abigail sniffed. "You haven't explained why my presence is."

"Think of it this way, Ms. Willoughby," Sommers jumped in. "Does Jeremy say things about you behind your back?"

Abigail's face crimped into a tight frown. "Yes, he does."

"Did you ever wish you could have been there to defend yourself and call bullshit on his lies?" Sommers followed up.

"Yes," Abigail confessed.

"Well, at this hearing, Jeremy is going to be there," Sommers explained, "and he's going to say things about you. So be there. Call bullshit."

Raine raised a finger. "Just don't use that phrase in open court," he cautioned.

Abigail took a long, deliberative sip of her tea. "What is it that we will be asking for?"

"Continued access to all personal and business financial accounts," Raine answered, "continued access to all residential and business properties, and a monthly spousal support payment."

"Obviously." Abigail nodded. Another sip. "And what will Jeremy be asking for?"

"No spousal support," Raine answered, "and to cut off your access to all accounts and properties. Maybe even this one."

"That would leave me with no money and nowhere to go." Abigail gasped. "Why would he think he would be entitled to all that?"

"The prenup," Raine and Sommers answered at the same time.

Sommers leaned back with an apologetic grin and gestured for Raine to continue.

"The prenuptial agreement," Raine repeated. "They are

going to argue that you won't be entitled to anything after the divorce, so you shouldn't get anything now."

"That is problematic," Abigail agreed.

"Yes," Raine confirmed. "You need to be there."

Abigail set down her tea. "Okay, Mr. Raine, I will be there. But you need to win."

6

Motions for temporary orders were heard by court commissioners, not judges. That was how the King County Superior Court handled family law matters. Trials, if it came to that, were heard by the actual elected judges, but all preliminary matters went first before a commissioner, or sort of assistant judge hired by the actual judges to hear the stuff they didn't want to be bothered with. The losing party could always petition a sitting judge for what was called a "revision", but those were rarely granted. Judges routinely overriding commissioners would undermine the very system they had set up. Raine knew he had one chance. Unfortunately he also knew the commissioner they drew and how badly that impacted that one chance.

Commissioner Eric Cassidy was everything wrong with the commissioner system. He had never faced the voters in an election, nor had he spent decades in the trenches as a family law attorney. Instead, his mommy was a judge on the Court of Appeals. He'd skipped those vetting processes to be appointed—that is, hired by the judges whose cases were reviewed by that same Court of Appeals—as a commissioner when he was only a year out of law school, and it only took that long because he'd failed the bar exam on his first try.

As Raine entered the family law courtroom that afternoon, he offered a friendly nod to the marshal who was assigned to stand sentry outside the courtroom just in case the judge issued a no-contact order or otherwise needed to separate the parties. Once inside, he scanned the gallery for his client, but she wasn't there yet. Her opponent was, however, surrounded by three lawyers of increasing age and equally moribund expressions. Raine didn't recognize any of them by sight, but that wasn't too surprising. They swam at different levels of the legal ocean. Langley Winterbottom was what some people called a "white shoe" law firm: mostly corporate law with high standards, high rates, and a high-rise office. The law firm of "& Raine" was more scuffed shoe: one lawyer, in a one-story office building, trying to win one hearing at a time. The good news was that the law wasn't supposed to care about how fancy the lawyers' offices were. The bad news was that Commissioner Eric Cassidy probably did. But the worst news was that Abigail Willoughby was late.

Jeremy nodded at Raine and whispered something to his lawyers. One of them peeled off and started to make his way across the crowded courtroom. They weren't the only case on the docket. Quite the contrary. The afternoon docket was filled with fourteen other hearings just like theirs, to decide on temporary orders that would quickly calcify into the presumptive final orders. Factoring in a fifteen-minute mid-afternoon break for the court staff, that averaged out to eleven minutes per hearing, five and a half minutes per side. The undersized commissioner's courtroom was filled with thirty lawyers and thirty parties getting divorced. Or, thanks to the attendance levels on their case, thirty-two lawyers and twenty-nine parties. One of those extra lawyers finished pushing through the crowd and approached Raine.

"Mr. Raine, I believe? My name is Howard Perkins. I represent Jeremy Willoughby."

Perkins was the middle of Jeremy's three lawyers, at least by age. He appeared to be in his early fifties, not too much older than Raine himself. His companions looked to be in their forties and sixties respectively. The oldest was probably the important one that Jeremy wanted representing him, the youngest was learning the ropes and carrying the briefcases, and the man in front of Raine was the one who was actually going to do the work. He had black hair slicked back from a clean-shaven face and wore a dark suit, white shirt, and red power tie. He didn't extend a hand to Raine.

"My client is prepared to enter into a deviation from the prenuptial agreement," Perkins advised, "if your client is willing to agree to our temporary orders and strike today's hearing."

Raine frowned slightly. He doubted the deviation was all that favorable to Abigail. Probably a small premium over what she was already going to get. Significantly less than she would receive if Raine was able to pierce the prenup.

"How generous of you," Raine replied. "Probably. I mean, I haven't seen the actual proposal, so it's hard to say. Also, it's a little late in the game for last minute settlement agreements. The commissioner will be out any second. You couldn't have sent this to me a few days ago?"

Perkins shrugged. "You know how it is, Mr. Raine. Clients rarely see clearly until they're standing before the judge."

There was a lot of truth to that, Raine knew. Perkins had obviously been around the courthouse block a few times. But so had Raine.

"And it leaves my client no time to really think about the

offer before having to make a decision about whether to accept it," Raine pointed out.

Perkins smiled. "There is that as well, yes." He glanced around the courtroom. "Speaking of which, where is Mrs. Willoughby?"

"I'm afraid she hasn't arrived yet," Raine admitted. "That will make it even more difficult to convey your offer, I'm afraid. Should we reschedule the hearing perhaps?"

Perkins's smile faded. "No. This offer is only available today. It expires when the judge takes the bench."

"Of course it does." Raine understood. "So what's the offer?"

"The amount she will receive under the prenuptial agreement," Perkins explained, "plus a lump sum equal to your hourly rate times the number of hours you've worked to date."

"My fees?" Raine clarified. "You want to buy me off so this goes away?"

"My client is prepared to offer one hundred and ten percent of the amount you are owed," Perkins expanded. "Deposited directly into any account you direct."

"Your client should be prepared to go fuck himself," Raine countered. "I'm not for sale."

Perkins chuckled at that. "We both know that isn't true, Mr. Raine. You aren't here out of the goodness of your heart. This isn't some pro bono case for a struggling single mother. You're here because you're getting paid. And you're getting paid with money generated from my client's businesses. I'm just offering to cut out the middleman. Or, in this case, the middlewoman."

At that moment, the middlewoman sailed into the courtroom.

"Daniel!" she called out, spying him amid the crowd. She had followed his advice and worn an understated navy suit.

"Did you know the courthouse has no valet parking? And with all of those dreadful homeless people living right outside?"

The sidewalks around the King County Courthouse were indeed filled with tents and other makeshift housing for a segment of Seattle's growing and intractable homelessness problem. There was also, indeed, no valet parking.

"I'm just glad you made it here before—" Raine started, but he was interrupted by the call of the bailiff.

"All rise! The King County Superior Court is now in session, the Honorable Commissioner Eric Cassidy presiding."

Perkins smirked at Raine. "Sorry, counsel. The offer has expired."

"What offer?" Abigail demanded, her head swiveling between her lawyer and the retreating figure of her husband's attorney. "Was there an offer? Was it a good offer?"

"It couldn't have been a good offer," Raine answered, "or they wouldn't have waited until the last second to offer it."

Commissioner Cassidy took the bench and smiled down at everyone. At least he was considered to be generally friendly. Some of the other less-than-qualified judges who had made it onto the bench could be defensive, even caustic, when confronted with lawyers who obviously knew more about the law than they did. Cassidy, in contrast, seemed to appreciate his good fortune in life and was just happy to be exploiting it for power and privilege, along with the pension and gold-plated health insurance. He might have no idea what he was doing, but he did it with a smile on his face.

"Good morning, everyone," he called out amicably. "Boy, we sure do have a full house this morning, don't we? Well, I won't waste any time, then. Most of you have lawyers, so I will assume they've already explained to you what we're doing today. The rest of you should just sort of pay attention so when we get to your case, you can know what to do too. All right then, do we have any matters that are ready? I see some attorneys from Langley Winterbottom are here. Are you folks ready?"

That wasn't good. Cassidy knew Raine's opponents. He and his appellate judge mother swam at that level of the ocean too. Cassidy wouldn't recognize Raine, not by face anyway. Probably not by name either. One of the downsides of being a general practitioner was not ever becoming a regular in any one area of law or with one set of judges. The judges who did a criminal law rotation got to know most of the prosecutors and public defenders. The judges who did a civil rotation got to know the plaintiff's personal injury bar and the insurance defense attorneys. And the family law commissioners got to know the lawyers who limited their practice to divorces and the like. Raine had appeared in front of all of them, but not any of them enough to be known.

"We are ready, Your Honor," Perkins replied. He stepped forward to the area directly in front of the judge's bench from whence the attorneys would deliver their arguments. He brought his client with him, positioning him to the outside, hands clasped formally in front of him, wearing an even nicer suit than Perkins.

Raine tugged lightly on Abigail's elbow. "Come on," he said. "We're first. Just stand next to me and look earnest."

"Earnest?" Abigail questioned.

"Honest," Raine translated. "Sincere."

Abigail frowned. "I know what it means, Daniel."

"This is the matter of Abigail Willoughby, petitioner," Commissioner Cassidy read from the pleadings he had spread out on the bench, "versus Jeremy Willoughby, respondent. We are here on the respondent's motion for temporary orders, I believe?"

"That is correct, Your Honor," Perkins confirmed. "I am

Howard Perkins of Langley Winterbottom, appearing on behalf of the respondent, Jeremy Willoughby. Present with me are attorneys Richard Winterbottom and Chase Gerber, also of Langley Winterbottom. We are ready and eager to proceed to the hearing on our motion for temporary orders."

Commissioner Cassidy smiled down at Perkins, nodding along as the lawyer spoke. Then, after a moment, he remembered himself and looked to Perkins's opponent.

"Good afternoon, uh, counsel," Cassidy said. "Could you please state your name for the record?"

That was judge-code for "I don't know/remember your name".

"Daniel Raine," he identified himself, "appearing on behalf of petitioner Abigail Willoughby. We are ready to proceed as well, Your Honor."

"Yes, Mr. Raine. Right." Cassidy pretended he knew Raine from any of the dozens of other lawyers from firms less significant than Langley Winterbottom. "Well, then, let's get to it, shall we? We have a lot of people here waiting for their turn at justice. We don't have all day."

Raine doubted justice could be achieved in the same arena as "we don't have all day", but the courts didn't necessarily equal justice. That was the system's dirty little not-so-secret. Not that justice could be elusive in criminal cases—everyone seemed to be learning that—but that it could be elusive in every corner of the courthouse, from innocent criminal defendants to uncompensated injured plaintiffs, to wives who had signed lopsided prenuptial agreements about to have access to even their own money frozen. At least if Perkins got his way.

"This motion for temporary orders was brought by the respondent, so I will hear first from Mr. Perkins," Commissioner Cassidy declared. "Whenever you're ready, Mr. Perkins."

Perkins thanked the judge, patted his client on the shoulder, then launched into his argument.

"America," he began—it was never good when the other side began with an appeal to apple pie and Chevrolet, Raine knew, "is the greatest nation in the history of the world for one simple, but overarching reason: freedom. Freedom to make choices. And the responsibility that comes with making those choices. For without responsibility, there can be no true freedom."

It was nonsense, blather even, but Cassidy was eating it up. No one believed in the meritocracy more than those with unearned status.

"In the case at bar, Your Honor," Perkins continued, "we can appreciate the importance of protecting our precious American freedom by holding our great nation's rugged individuals to the consequences of their choices. In this case, two adults met and fell in love. They made a choice to get married. Now, apparently, a choice is being made to end that marriage. But at the time of the marriage, even that unfortunate decision was anticipated. Those two adults entered knowingly, intelligently, and voluntarily into an agreement about how financial assets would be divided in the unfortunate event that the marriage was ever dissolved. Mr. Willoughby is not asking this court for anything other than the enforcement of that agreement. He is not asking for anything other than to hold the parties, both parties, to the consequences of their choices, just as our Founding Fathers intended."

Raine was actually a little impressed that Perkins had somehow managed to wave the flag in a divorce case. He'd seen it plenty of times in criminal cases when trying to convince a jury to actually hold the prosecution to the standard of proof beyond a reasonable doubt. Constitution, Bill of Rights, presumption of innocence, rah-rah, etc. Unfortunately, a glance up at Commissioner Cassidy confirmed he was impressed by it all too. A large grin had unfurled across his face, not unlike Old Glory herself.

"We fully expect," Perkins continued, "that the resolution of this case will include enforcement of the prenuptial agreement that Mrs. Willoughby chose to sign at the time she chose to marry our client. We also believe that Mrs. Willoughby expects this will be the outcome as well and may therefore act to pillage the accounts of our client prior to final resolution of this case at trial, which is still months away. It would undermine the purposes of the prenuptial agreement in this case, and all cases, and, dare I say, the American justice system as a whole, to allow a party who has contracted for a specific settlement to be allowed to plunder the other party's assets prior to enforcement of that settlement. It would be nigh impossible to claw back the stolen funds after they had been used for purchases and investments and who knows what else."

Nigh? Raine thought. He was less impressed with that. Cassidy still seemed enthralled by it all. Raine supposed Perkins's advocacy held more flourish than what the remainder of Cassidy's morning likely would entail.

"It is for that reason, Your Honor," Perkins began to sum up, "that we are asking the court to freeze Mrs. Willoughby's access to all of our client's accounts—personal, business, and otherwise—with the exception of a single account he will establish into which he will place the exact amount agreed upon in the prenuptial agreement. If Mrs. Willoughby chooses to use that money to wage her legal battle against her own previous choices and the natural consequences of those choices, then so be it. She is free to deplete that account in her quixotic attack on her own signature on that contract. But Mr. Willoughby's position must be protected pending that eventual and, quite honestly, foregone conclusion that Mrs.

Willoughby will receive not one penny more than what she agreed to nearly ten years ago, especially when those pennies justly belong to the man she is choosing now to divorce. Thank you."

Raine thought Cassidy might actually applaud, but instead he sat up straight, let out a satisfied sigh, then looked over to Raine. "Any response, counsel?"

"Yes, Your Honor. Thank you," Raine answered. He took a deep breath and launched into his argument, adjusting his prepared remarks slightly to address the flag-waving of Perkins's presentation. He just needed to add some patriotic buzzwords. "We agree with Mr. Perkins that the American justice system is the greatest ever developed in the history of mankind. And the cornerstone of that system is that every man, and woman, is entitled to their day in court. As Americans, our Constitution guarantees equal protection, due process, and a fair trial. Everyone knows about the First Amendment's right to free speech and the Fifth Amendment's right against self-incrimination, but our Founding Fathers were wise enough to include civil trials in the Bill of Rights as well. The Seventh Amendment to the United States Constitution enshrines the right of a trial for civil matters as well, civil matters like the one before Your Honor today. Ms. Willoughby is constitutionally guaranteed her right to a trial in the case she has brought to dissolve her marriage with Mr. Willoughby. And it is only right that the trial determines how the parties' assets are distributed. Until then, it is the duty of everyone involved in this litigation to safeguard the integrity of that trial, of due process and equal protection. It is the duty of all of us to ensure that issues are resolved fully and fairly and without prejudice to either party in advance of a full and fair hearing on all of the matters at issue in this litigation."

It was a bit much, Raine knew, but he wasn't wrong. Temporary orders were meant to keep things at the status quo until the trial could be held and the decisions made on the merits, based on sworn testimony of witnesses, not on the kisses and promises of paid attorneys. He remembered he should probably work that into his argument too.

"We are not here today to decide the merits of this case, Your Honor," Raine continued. "That is what the trial is for, and that day will come. All we are here for today is to make sure that things remain as they are pending the outcome of that trial. Prior to the filing of this dissolution action, both parties had full access to all accounts. While eventually, after the trial, those accounts will be divided, and arrangements will need to be adjusted, none of us know precisely what the final results of that trial will be, regardless of how confident Mr. Perkins acts today."

It was a slight jab, but one that prompted an indignant huff from his opponent. Raine accepted it and carried on.

"Accordingly, we are asking the court to deny the respondent's request for temporary orders locking my client out of the marital community's financial accounts. We expect a full and vigorous litigation of the validity of the prenuptial agreement, after which we will have a much clearer picture of the parties' financial situation. Until then, the court should refrain from doing anything that might jeopardize either side's ability to pay bills and generally maintain their standard of living. Thank you."

Cassidy wasn't smiling when Raine finished. He wasn't frowning either, but he seemed considerably less moved by Raine's argument.

"It seems to me, counsel," the commissioner began, again unable to recall Raine's name apparently, "that both sides are asking the court to guess who will win at the trial. Mr. Perkins assumes the prenuptial agreement will hold up, and therefore your client should be precluded from draining the accounts before that happens. You assume the prenuptial agreement will not hold up, so any draining of accounts would be appropriate."

"I'm not sure I would use the phrase 'draining the accounts', Your Honor," Raine protested. "Just maintaining the access she currently has."

"Yes, but to what end?" the commissioner challenged. "Why does she want access to the accounts if not to withdraw from them? One might argue that your very resistance to the temporary orders is evidence they are needed."

"I would argue that, Your Honor," Perkins put in. Raine threw a sideways frown at his opponent.

"I would disagree, Your Honor," Raine started to respond, but Abigail grabbed his jacket sleeve.

"I need access to that money," she growled in a low whisper. "You said you could get around that prenup."

"I said I would try," Raine reminded her.

"So do it," she hissed.

"I'm trying."

Abigail huffed, then looked up to address the commissioner herself. "May I say something, Your Honor?"

Raine's heart dropped. He needed her present for appearances and to answer questions, but the last thing he needed was for her to speak directly to the judge.

Cassidy grinned slightly. He was entertained. "Of course, ma'am. What would you like to tell me?"

"Your Honor," Raine interrupted, "I think it might be best if I could speak privately with my client before she says anything."

He was right. That would be best. But Abigail didn't care. Cassidy didn't either.

"I don't need to speak with you," she told Raine. She jabbed a finger past him at her husband. "I need to speak with him."

"Please address any comments to the bench," Cassidy cautioned her. "What would you like me to know?"

Raine sighed and took a half step back. He had tried to win. And now he was about to lose.

"I'd like you to know that Jeremy Willoughby is a sick, twisted, perverted son of a bitch," Abigail fairly shouted. "He took advantage of a young girl and tricked her into doing all sorts of terrible things she never would have done, including signing that stupid prenuptial agreement."

"You weren't that young, Abby." Jeremy cackled from the other side of his lawyer.

"And you weren't all that either, Jeremy," Abigail shot back. "Just because you had money, you thought people would do anything for you."

"You sure did a lot of things for my money." Jeremy leered at her. "At least at first."

"You know what, Jeremy?" Abigail jabbed that finger at him.

Don't say it, Raine thought.

He grabbed her arm. "Don't say it."

But she said it.

"Fuck you, Jeremy!"

The commissioner grabbed his gavel and pounded it on the bench. "That is enough, Mrs. Willoughby!"

"Fuck you!" she called out again, ignoring the judge. "And fuck your lawyers! And fuck that fucking prenup!"

Raine ran a hand over his face, then grabbed Abigail's arm again. "You're not helping. This is not helping us."

Abigail looked like she was about to tell him to fuck off too, but suddenly seemed to remember herself. She gasped and dropped her head into her hands.

"Has your client finished her outburst?" Cassidy asked from on high.

Raine could only nod. "I believe so, Your Honor."

"Good," Cassidy barked. "I am going to grant the respondent's motion for temporary orders. From what I have seen here this morning, there is a substantial likelihood the petitioner would act in a way that was not in the best interests of either party. I am directing the respondent to establish an account with funds equal to the amount stipulated in the prenuptial agreement, plus funds sufficient to cover the petitioner's attorney's fees for the balance of this litigation. I am hopeful this ruling may accelerate a negotiated resolution of this matter. Next case!"

The judge had just ordered Perkins's settlement offer. Maybe he should have taken it after all and avoided the drama. Then again, the drama was part of the allure of the profession. Still, he hated losing. Especially when it wasn't his fault.

Perkins turned and accepted a vigorous handshake from Jeremy and a pat on the back from his elder colleague. The younger one remained toward the back of the courtroom, guarding the briefcases. Raine put a tentative hand on the heaving shoulders of his own client. Her face was still in her hands, so he couldn't tell if she was crying or seething. In a way, it didn't matter. They were done and needed to vacate their spot at the bar for the next set of lawyers and litigants.

Jeremy exited the courtroom first, followed by his lawyers flocking behind. Raine waited a beat, lest they end up right on top of them in the hallway, then guided Abigail out of the courtroom.

"Let's talk outside," he said.

He expected a lot of that talking would be her yelling at him about the outcome, and him trying to be polite about blaming her for it.

It was a busy day at the courthouse—every day was busy at the courthouse—and the hallway was filled with other lawyers and litigants searching for that day in court Raine had pontificated about. That marshal was still there, trying not to look as bored as he obviously was. Abigail dropped her arms to her sides and looked everywhere except at her lawyer.

"We can appeal his ruling to a full judge," Raine started, hoping to skip the blame game and get right to solutions, however unlikely. "It's called a request for revision. I understand he didn't appreciate your outburst, but he's supposed to rule on the law, not emotion. We have five working days to—"

"This isn't over, Jeremy!" Abigail shouted past Raine at her husband.

Raine didn't want her to reignite her tirade, but he did appreciate that she had perhaps been listening to his explanation of the appeal process. "Correct. We can seek revision—"

"You lost, Abby!" Jeremy shouted back. He and his lawyers were huddled just a few yards away, on the other side of the courtroom door, and the marshal suddenly perked up at the developing conflict. "You will always lose against me! It's over!" He laughed. "You're not getting a dime!"

That wasn't technically true, Raine knew—the prenup provided for a decent, if inadequate, sum—but he understood Jeremy's point. So did Abigail. She disagreed. Loudly.

"Oh, don't you worry, Jeremy!" She started to march toward him, but the marshal intercepted her, placing himself between them. "I'll get what's coming to me! And so will you! Do you hear me, Jeremy? You're going to get what's coming to you!"

"Is that a threat?" Jeremy called out.

It sure sounded like a threat, Raine thought. As likely did the scores of bystanders who had stopped to watch the show.

"You need to stop talking, Abigail," Raine advised, but to no avail.

Abigail lunged toward Jeremy, forcing the marshal to lay hands on her to hold her back.

"It's a promise, Jeremy!" she screamed, pointing at him even as she struggled to free herself from the marshal's grasp. "It's a fucking promise! You're gonna get what you deserve, you pig, and I'm going to be the one to do it! I'm not going to let you get away with this!"

Raine ran his hands over his head and let out a long, deep sigh. There was no way he was going to win that revision now.

7

I t turned out that, despite Abigail openly threatening her estranged husband in front of a dozen witnesses, the marshal wasn't all that interested in arresting anyone. Too much paperwork, Raine supposed. The marshal just held on to Abigail until Jeremy exited the courthouse, laughing the entire way. As soon as the marshal released her, Abigail stormed out of the courthouse herself, without another word to Raine. Raine supposed he might be fired, but Abigail would have to actually communicate that to him. Until then, he was her lawyer. Which meant he wasn't quite finished with the hearing. He needed her signature.

Perkins had filed proposed temporary orders along with his motion for said orders. That was standard practice. Judges hated drafting their own orders. If they granted your motion, you'd better have an order prepared for them to sign. The orders had Perkins's and Jeremy's signatures on them at the time of filing. Cassidy added his signature after making his ruling to adopt them. Raine had planned to calm Abigail down out in the hallway, then go back inside the courtroom to sign the papers. Instead, she had stormed off, and he had been left to take the orders from the bailiff with a promise to get his client's signature and return them the next day.

Raine made his way back to his office. The rain had let up a bit; it was almost unnoticeable. He took the direct route to his office and gave Abigail a call. No answer. There was also no answer the six other times he called before quitting time.

Raine looked at the clock on his wall, at the orders on his desk, and at the clock again. He could try again tomorrow, he supposed. He stood up and grabbed his coat off the back of his door. He really didn't want to extend his workday by driving all the way out to Madison Park again, especially in rush hour. On the other hand... He looked back at the paperwork atop his desk. He wouldn't mind confirming whether he was fired. If so, he would have to return some of the retainer Abigail had paid, but not all of it, given the hours he'd already worked. Billing one more hour for driving out to her place to get a signature might hold off Rebecca and Hunter for an extra day or two after the rest of the money ran out. And besides, there was a good Greek place out that way. He could get the documents signed and be eating lamb shawarma by 7:00 p.m. He snatched the papers off his desk and set out for Chez Willoughby. Or maybe it was Chez Abigail, because it didn't look like they were going to be getting close to any other Willoughby assets. Not without a truly unexpected turn of events.

———

THE PARKING WASN'T MUCH BETTER than on his last trip to Abigail's. He was able to find a space he didn't have to spend ten minutes rocking his car into, but it was two blocks away. A light evening rain had returned on his drive over, the droplets dancing in the beams of his headlights. He pulled his hood over his head, tucked the orders inside his jacket, and hurried up the street to the iron gate of 4406 Larkspur Drive.

To Raine's surprise, the gate was open. Not all the way, but it wasn't latched; the gate rested against the iron frame of the fence. Raine took ahold of the gate, making sure it didn't lock, and pressed the intercom button embedded in it. He could hear the buzz when he pressed the button, but no further sound came from the intercom. He waited several seconds, then pressed the button a second time. Again there was the electronic buzz of his call, but again no reply. He waited a bit longer, then tried a third time. Still no response from within the house. He scanned the vehicles parked on the street to see if her car was there, but then realized he didn't know what kind of car she drove, and she probably had a garage anyway.

Raine took a moment to consider his options, but only a moment. He had driven all the way out there. He wasn't going to give up just because Abigail didn't answer the intercom. At least not when the gate was open. If it had been latched, he might not have had any choice but to grab some shawarma and try again tomorrow, but as it was, he could go up to that side door and probably catch Abigail in the kitchen with her AirPods turned up too loud. He wondered, as he pushed open the gate, whether she was listening to music or some true crime podcast. Those seemed to be all the rage lately. Raine didn't understand their popularity. Probably because he handled all-too-true crime cases himself. Once you've seen actual crime scene photos of a murder, the appeal of listening to someone else describe a case over a podcast lost a lot of its allure.

The rain was letting up, but it was supplemented by large drops of water dripping from the trees overhanging the pathway to the side of the home. Raine pushed his hood off, but kept the orders inside his jacket. It was bad enough they were going to be wrinkled when he returned them to the bailiff the next morning; he didn't need the ink to be smeared from raindrops. He was a professional, after all. At least that was what he told himself as he snuck up to a hidden entrance of someone else's home under cover of darkness.

When he reached the door, he raised a fist to knock, then noticed that door was also slightly ajar, separated from the doorframe by an inch or so. He went ahead and knocked, the force of his knuckles pushing the door a few inches farther open. No reply, which didn't surprise him as much as he thought it should have. It was silent inside the home.

"Hello?" he called out, pushing the door open all the way.

There was no response, of course.

Raine took a moment to assess his surroundings. The only noise was the sound of his own breathing. There was a strange smell in the air, faint but unmistakable. Raine couldn't quite place it, but it was familiar somehow, although not in a good way. There were no lights on in the kitchen, but there appeared to be a single table lamp on in the parlor where he and Sommers had taken tea with the lady of the house. His wet shoes squeaked as he crossed the kitchen. He hoped there wasn't anyone in the shadows listening. The hairs on the back of his neck were standing up, but he felt like it was for some reason other than the possibility of hidden assailants. There was something else afoot, he could sense.

He entered the parlor and scanned the dimly lit room. He almost missed it at first. The shoe at the far end of the couch. There were two things of note about it. The first was that it was a very nice shoe with a large gold buckle. The second was that it was attached to a very much not moving leg that disappeared behind the couch. Raine realized what the smell was.

Blood. There must be a lot of it, and it had been exposed to the air long enough to begin filling the home with its acrid scent. Raine set the crumpled orders on the coffee table and circled around to the far side of the couch, to confirm what the shoe and the stench had already told him:

Jeremy Willoughby was dead.

Not just dead, but murdered.

And not just murdered, but murdered inside Abigail's home.

"Fuck," Raine whispered through the hand he raised to cover his mouth. The comment was directed at both the scene on the floor before him and its import to his client and their case.

Jeremy lay sprawled across the floor between the couch and the fireplace, still dressed in the suit he'd worn to court that afternoon. He was on his stomach, arms splayed wide, and his face turned to the side, exposing a ghostly profile, the skin of his face blanched by the loss of blood. That blood had escaped from a very sizable, very open wound to the back of his head and had formed a large pool around his head and shoulders. It was about three feet across and appeared to have reached its maximum, judging by the surface tension and early signs of drying at the edges. Jeremy's heart had stopped beating shortly after he hit the floor, Raine surmised, so once gravity had extracted what it could from his head wound, the remainder of his blood stayed inside the body.

There was a sheaf of documents in Jeremy's hand, half soaked in blood. The still legible header read:

FINAL SETTLEMENT AGREEMENT

Raine frowned. Jeremy had come to bypass the lawyers and get Abigail to sign off on an even worse offer than Perkins had made to Raine that afternoon. And lying at the edge of the pool of blood was the object that had caused the head wound. It was a small abstract sculpture of some sort, a marble pyramid with a layer of jewels encrusted over most of its surface area. It was about a foot long and looked heavy. The sort of thing that would be displayed on the center of a table somewhere nearby. Also the sort of thing that would be easy to pick up and smash someone's brains in with. In fact, Raine could see hair and skin and quite possibly some of those smashed-in brains stuck in the cracks between the jewels.

Raine leaned a bit closer to examine the wound, taking care to keep his shoes out of the blood puddle. He hadn't yet reached the point where he was going to have to make a decision about what to do about the situation, but he knew he didn't want to leave his own bloody shoe prints behind. The wound was significant, the torn and split flesh exposing the bone of the skull underneath. In fact, it looked like it was several wounds on top of each other. Raine scanned the area immediately outside the blood pool and noticed the telltale speckle of blood on the bricks of the fireplace. Raine had seen enough crime scene photos over the years to know what blood spatter looked like, and what it meant. Whoever had snatched the statuette off whatever table it had been displayed on and struck the first blow to the back of Jeremy's head—the one that sent him sprawling off the couch—had followed up with several more frenzied strikes to his head, casting off blood against the fireplace with each rise and fall of the statuette, until Jeremy stopped moving—and probably a blow or two after that. Then they dropped the statuette and fled, not bothering to close the door or the gate behind them.

Jeremy had been sitting on the couch, head down, reviewing the documents clutched in his now-dead hand. He hadn't expected the blow that sent him to the floor.

That first blow had been unplanned, an emotional

outburst. The killer had grabbed the nearest weapon and lashed out.

The subsequent blows were more premeditated. The killer had decided in those moments that Jeremy couldn't be allowed to get up again.

The killer was someone who knew Jeremy. Someone Jeremy was willing to turn his back on. Someone Jeremy could make that upset that quickly. Someone who had reasons, at least in the moment, to make sure Jeremy Willoughby died on that floor.

On Abigail's floor.

It was hard to draw any other conclusion. The police certainly wouldn't. They weren't known for drawing hard conclusions when easy ones were offered up on a jewel-encrusted marble platter.

Raine knew Abigail wasn't in the house anymore. No one was except Raine, and Jeremy, after a fashion. Raine decided it was time to leave as well. He remembered to retrieve those unsigned orders from the coffee table, if only to use them to pull the kitchen door mostly closed again without leaving fingerprints. He repeated the process with the iron gate, then made his way across the street to make two phone calls. The first was an anonymous call to 911 after blocking his number. The second was to Rebecca Sommers.

"Danny! How are you? Long time no private investigating. Do you need me again?"

"Yes," Raine confirmed with a nod to himself. "I'm definitely going to need you again the next time I talk to Abigail. This next conversation is not one I want to have alone."

"Okay," Sommers answered. "When?"

"Soon, I suspect," Raine said. He could already hear sirens approaching.

"Um, okay. And where?" Sommers asked. "Your office or her place again?"

"Neither of those places, I'm afraid," Raine responded.

"Where, then?" Sommers inquired.

"I'm pretty sure our next conversation with Abigail Willoughby," Raine answered, "will be in the King County Jail."

8

The King County Jail was two blocks up the hill from the courthouse. In a way, it was an upgrade. There were no homeless encampments, and they did offer a sort of valet service, if you counted riding in the back of a police car. Somehow, Raine didn't think Abigail would appreciate the improvement.

He had waited outside Abigail's home long enough to watch, from a distance, as the police arrived, then went inside the residence. He wasn't looking to be a witness in a murder case, especially not one where his client was sure to be the prime suspect. He just made sure no one else went inside before the police. That way, they would see exactly what he saw. His observations would be duplicative. At least that was what he was going to say if the cops ever figured out he had been inside, and tracked him down for a statement and an explanation.

In the meantime, he decided to spend the evening back at his office. He didn't much like his new divorced-dad apartment, so he was in no rush to go home for the night. Plus, Sommers wanted to get the full scoop on what he had seen.

He could hardly blame her, but again, he wasn't having that conversation in his sad little studio apartment. He grabbed shawarma for two and met her at the "Law Offices of & Raine." He had just witnessed a dead body firsthand, but he was still hungry.

"What the hell happened?" Sommers asked even as he walked up to the front door. Her QUEEN-mobile was parked illegally in a loading zone directly in front of the office building. He guessed she had a good feeling for when the cops were actually out enforcing parking infractions. Likely not while half the department was dealing with a murder in Madison Park. He wished he'd thought to park there too.

"Not outside," he said. She stepped aside, and he unlocked the office door. They both went inside, and Raine turned on the lights again. There was something unsettling about an office after dark. Like they were trespassing on whatever usually happened when everyone had gone home for the night.

Sommers closed the door behind them and locked the deadbolt. "Okay. We're inside. What the hell happened?"

"Someone murdered Jeremy Willoughby," Raine answered. "Come on, let's eat in the conference room. I'll grab a couple of sodas from the fridge."

"Maybe something stronger?" Sommers suggested.

"Better not," Raine cautioned. "We could be driving to the jail any minute."

"You think Abigail murdered him?"

"I think the cops will think she did," Raine answered. "Me? I don't know."

"So you really think she could have done it?"

Raine disappeared for a moment to the office kitchenette, then returned with two cans of soda. "Of course. What kind of lawyer would I be if I weren't open to every possibility?"

"Abigail's lawyer?" Sommers proposed. "Shouldn't you be defending her, not accusing her?"

"I'm not accusing her of anything," Raine replied. He pulled two to-go containers out of the food bag and slid one over to Sommers. "And I can defend her whether she did it or not."

"Can you really?" Sommers challenged with a cock of her head.

Raine considered for a moment. He nodded. "Of course."

Raine's phone rang at that moment. He frowned at the dinner he hadn't taken even one bite of yet, then sighed and answered the call. He had a feeling who it was.

"Law office of Daniel R—"

"Daniel!" It was Abigail. "They arrested me, Daniel! They think I murdered Jeremy. I swear I didn't, but they wouldn't believe me. I didn't murder Jeremy. I didn't murder anyone. I could never. And certainly not Jeremy. He's my husband, for God's sake."

Raine nodded. That was about what he expected her to say when she called. "Are you at the jail yet?"

"Why, yes. Yes," Abigail confirmed. "They told me I could call my lawyer, so I didn't know who else to call. You're still my lawyer, aren't you, Daniel?"

"Of course I am, Abigail," Daniel assured her. "Don't say anything to anyone. Rebecca and I will be there in fifteen minutes."

"But, Daniel—" Abigail protested.

"Fifteen minutes," Raine repeated. "Don't say anything."

Abigail agreed, and Raine hung up.

"Fifteen minutes?" Sommers questioned. "The jail can't be more than five minutes from here."

"It's not," Raine confirmed before taking a bite of his dinner. "But I'm hungry."

MOST JAILS HAD SET VISITING hours, outside of which visitors couldn't meet with an inmate, but those restricted visiting hours didn't apply to attorneys. Or their investigators. It was closer to twenty minutes later when Raine and Sommers entered the lobby of the King County Jail and checked in with the officer at the reception desk. It was another ten minutes before another guard came and got them from the lobby, to lead them back to an interview room to meet with their client. By then, Abigail had been stripped of her street clothes and outfitted in red jail scrubs. Red meant high security. All accused murderers were high security. Even the ones with perfectly manicured nails and no criminal history.

"Daniel! Rebecca!" Abigail called out as she spilled into the other side of the meeting room. She was separated from them by a wall of plexiglass, but they could hear one another through the circle of holes drilled into the center of the partition. "What is happening? This is a nightmare!"

"It is a nightmare," Raine agreed. She was going to need a lot of reassurance. He could offer some, but not as much as she was going to want. "But there's a process, and I'm going to help you through it."

"We're going to help you through it," Sommers amended.

But Raine shook his head. "No, I'm going to help you through this, and Rebecca is going to help me. I'm the one who knows how the court system works, how it really works, so I'm going to need you to listen to me, and I'm going to need you to trust me. Both of you."

Abigail looked hesitantly between Raine and Sommers, who herself looked tentatively at Raine. But neither of them said anything in protest.

"Your husband is dead," Raine began. "Murdered. Inside your home."

"How did you know that?" Abigail asked. "The police wouldn't even let me inside when I arrived home. They arrested me immediately."

"Just listen," Raine told her. "Your husband was murdered inside your home, and you are the prime suspect, in case that wasn't already obvious by the fact that you are now sitting in jail. In fact, your presence here suggests that you are not only the prime suspect, you are likely going to be the only suspect. They are going to start building a case against you, and they are going to charge you."

"But I didn't do it!" Abigail protested. "I'm innocent."

"That is going to become increasingly irrelevant," Raine answered. "I need you to understand that. It doesn't matter that you're innocent."

"This is the crappiest pep talk I've ever heard," Sommers put in.

"It's not a pep talk," Raine said. "It's real talk. Your husband was bludgeoned to death in your home hours after you threatened him in front of dozens of witnesses."

"Bludgeoned?" Abigail gasped. "I could, I could never do that to Jeremy."

"Unfortunately, that's one of the most likely ways you could have done it," Raine explained. "You're too much smaller than him to strangle him, and he would have over-powered you if you'd tried to use a knife as well. A gun would have worked if you're a good shot, but it wasn't a gun. It was a heavy statuette to the back of the head. Exactly what his estranged wife would do when he turned his back on her."

"I didn't do it!" Abigail shrieked.

"Won't they look at other suspects?" Sommers questioned. "They can't just jump to the most obvious conclusion."

Raine shook his head and grinned. "They can, and they

will. They aren't going to mess up their case by going and looking for any evidence that might cast doubt on it."

"But someone must have seen something," Abigail said. "The real killer, I mean."

Raine nodded. "That's our best hope. Please tell me you have surveillance cameras somewhere at that house."

Abigail's face dropped. "No. No, I told you. That's why I went there. Because there weren't any cameras."

"Not even outside?" Raine ventured.

Abigail shook her head. "No. No, I'm sorry, Daniel."

Daniel smiled at her. "Don't be sorry, Abigail. Be strong. This is going to be very difficult."

"But you're going to help me, right, Daniel?" Abigail pleaded. "You can do a murder case too, right?"

Raine nodded. "I can do a murder case."

He didn't want to, but there wasn't going to be any more work to do on the divorce case.

"It won't be cheap, though," Daniel cautioned. A first-degree murder retainer was going to approach six figures, and the Bar Association allowed criminal fees to be nonrefundable and collected in full up front. Patrick McCollum had needed a payment plan. Abigail Willoughby wouldn't.

"How will I pay you?" Abigail almost wailed. "That judge said I couldn't access our joint accounts anymore!"

Raine grinned slightly. "That order was never entered," he explained. "And it won't be now. That case is over."

"The divorce case is over?" Abigail asked.

"Of course," Raine confirmed. "The husband is dead."

"And my accounts aren't frozen?"

"No," Raine answered. He knew there might be one more hurdle to jump regarding those accounts, but it wasn't the time to bring it up. Not when he was about to close the deal. "The temporary orders were never entered, and first thing in the morning I will file a motion to formally dismiss the divorce case. Then we can focus one hundred percent on the criminal case. That is, if I'm hired for that?"

"Oh yes, Daniel, you're hired," Abigail confirmed. "Whatever it costs. Whatever it takes. I need you, Daniel."

Raine nodded. "I know. Now, listen up. Here's the plan."

The only chance Abigail had to avoid being charged with the murder of her estranged husband was if she had an iron-clad alibi for the time of the murder or if the real killer had left behind some clue as to their identity. Of course, that assumed Abigail wasn't the real killer. As it was, however, no evidence of either of those things appeared to have surfaced, judging by the fact that Abigail had not been released.

If they went ahead and charged her, the arraignment would be scheduled for 1:00 p.m. the next day. The court held arraignments in the afternoon so that the prosecutors would have time to review reports in the morning and decide whether there was enough to charge a given suspect. They would all have to wait until the next day to learn whether the prosecutor decided there was enough to charge Abigail.

9

"Murder in the first degree." Raine frowned at the complaint handed to him by the prosecutor. Her name was Emma Nakamoto. Raine had seen her around the courthouse but didn't know her by name. Kind of how the judges knew him. She was about forty, with long black hair and a soft expression. Resting nice face. That was too bad. The jury was going to like her. "That's disappointing."

"What did you expect, manslaughter?" Nakamoto asked. "She beat his damn head in with a marble statue. Oh, that reminds me, it's not just murder in the first degree. There's also a deadly weapon enhancement. Adds three years."

Raine's frown deepened. "Doesn't seem like a lot, since she's facing twenty-five to life."

"Every little bit helps," Nakamoto said. "Are you ready to do the arraignment? The guards have transported all of the in-custody defendants to the holding cells. We can call yours first if you're ready."

"Yes, I'm ready," Raine confirmed. "But are you sure you aren't jumping the gun a bit here, uh, can I call you Emma?"

Nakamoto shrugged slightly. "I guess. Dan, right? Nice to meet you."

She extended a hand, and Raine shook it, increasingly disappointed at the affability of his opponent. He needed an overzealous persecutor, not a likable public servant.

"Seriously, though," Raine continued, "have you even had time to consider other suspects? I mean, who's to say Abigail Willoughby really murdered her husband?"

"The jury," Emma answered. "At the trial, anyway. Until then, I guess it's me. And I've reviewed the entire case file. There's really no doubt it was her. Her fingerprints were even on the murder weapon. I had the lab guys compare the latent prints on the statuette with your client's booking prints this morning. Clear match."

Raine was disappointed to hear that, but not unprepared. "Of course her fingerprints were on it. It happened in her home. Everything in there has her fingerprints on it."

"You know, Dan"—Nakamoto grinned at him—"saying 'the murder happened in my client's home' is maybe not the defense you think it is."

Raine supposed there was some truth to that.

"I'm just saying," he continued, "that maybe you should hold off filing any charges for a few days, maybe a week or two. Make sure you're sure before you charge someone with murder in the first degree."

"With a deadly weapon enhancement," Nakamoto reminded him. "So give your crazy rich client enough time to book a flight to some tropical island with no extradition treaty with the US? No, I don't think so, Dan."

"You really think she would do that?" Raine asked, trying to sound like he didn't also think Abigail might do exactly that if she got a chance.

"Actually, I don't," Nakamoto answered, "but not because

of her. Because of me. Now, let's get this arraignment on the road. I've got other cases, as I'm sure you do."

He did have other cases, but none as important as Abigail's. And his effort to short-circuit the arraignment having failed, the battle was about to be joined. "Fine. Let's do this."

"Willoughby!" Nakamoto shouted at the guard from across the courtroom. Then, in a more standard volume, she informed the bailiff, "We're ready for the judge."

The bailiff nodded and picked up the phone. A few moments later, the judge came out to the bailiff's bellow: "All rise! The King County Superior Court is now in session, the Honorable Lawrence Billingsley presiding."

Raine nodded at their draw of judge. Billingsley had been around long enough to know what he was doing, but not so long that he didn't care anymore. He had been a prosecutor before becoming a judge, so that wasn't ideal, but his reputation since he'd taken the bench was that he was fair despite his background. Raine sure hoped so.

"Are the parties ready on the matter of the *State of Washington versus Abigail Willoughby*?" Billingsley asked formally despite having already been advised of as much by his bailiff.

"The State is ready," Nakamoto answered sharply as she stepped forward to the prosecutor's spot at the bar. "Emma Nakamoto for the State."

Raine followed suit, to the defense side. "The defense is ready as well, Your Honor. Daniel Raine appearing on behalf of the defendant."

Nakamoto nodded to the guard at the door to the holding cells, who in turn opened the door with a loud clank. Abigail was waiting just inside and was escorted to stand next to Raine by a second guard, who remained positioned behind her for the hearing. It was a bit much, Raine thought. The in-custody arraignment courtroom was perfectly secure, with the gallery and public entrance safely on the other side of a glass partition with a locked door in the middle of it.

Also in the gallery were several news cameras, also safely excluded from disrupting the proceedings. Raine supposed he shouldn't be surprised to see them. Jeremy Willoughby was rich enough to be a story in town. It just wasn't going to help his case any to have the media running reports of Abigail being charged with his murder, no matter how many times they mumbled the word "allegedly" when they described what the prosecution said she did to her husband.

Although the security arrangements kept the reporters out, they were actually designed to keep the inmates in, but one look at Abigail was enough to know she wasn't going to escape, let alone hurt anyone. A night in jail had not done her good. During their meeting the previous night, she had managed to maintain some of her swagger despite the institutional setting and clothing. That afternoon, however, she looked haggard. Her hair was unkempt. She had been given some basic cosmetics, but it was nothing compared to her usual look. And her eyes were dulled. Raine wondered if she'd slept at all.

"How are you doing?" he asked her in a whisper when she came up next to him.

"You have to get me out of here, Daniel," she whispered back. "I can't stay in here. I'm not made for this."

"I'll do my best, Abigail," Raine answered, "but I'm going to need you to stay calm. No more outbursts. That's what got us here in the first place."

Abigail just frowned in agreement.

"Now, the first thing will be the arraignment," Raine explained. "I will enter a plea of not guilty for you. Then we will talk about conditions of release."

"Conditions of release?" Abigail asked.

"Bail," Raine translated.

"Ah yes, bail," Abigail answered. "I would like to post bail."

"I would like that too," Raine assured her. He turned his attention to the judge.

"You may proceed, Ms. Nakamoto," Judge Billingsley directed.

"Thank you, Your Honor." She handed some papers to the bailiff. "At this time, the State is filing one count of murder in the first degree, with a deadly weapon enhancement, against the defendant, Abigail Jane Willoughby. We would ask defense to acknowledge receipt of the complaint, waive a formal reading, and enter a plea."

It was Raine's turn. "The defense acknowledges receipt of the complaint, Your Honor. We waive a formal reading of the charges and ask the court to enter a plea of not guilty."

"A plea of not guilty will be entered," Judge Billingsley proclaimed. And that was the arraignment. "Would the parties like to be heard regarding conditions of release?"

Another formal, but silly question. Of course they would.

"Yes, Your Honor," Nakamoto answered first. The prosecution always got to go first. Ostensibly, that was so the defendant could have the last word, but more often than not, in Raine's experience anyway, it only enabled the prosecution to win the judge over before the defense got to say word one. "Standard bail in a murder one case is typically one million dollars. In this case, the State is going to be asking the court to set bail at ten million dollars."

"Ten million?" Raine couldn't help but ask aloud.

He was supposed to wait his turn to speak, but the judge seemed to share his surprise, so rather than scold Raine, Billingsley questioned Nakamoto.

"Ten million dollars?" the judge asked. "Why such a high bail, Ms. Nakamoto? Does the defendant have criminal history I am unaware of? Something out of state perhaps?"

"No, Your Honor," Nakamoto admitted, "but she has significant financial resources, and the State believes one million dollars will be insufficient to keep her in custody pending the trial. Our fear is that given the severity of the penalty she is facing and her access to financial resources, she will be tempted to flee the country. Most defendants are not in a position to do that. Ms. Willoughby, however, is."

"I'm not sure I should raise someone's bail just because they can probably post it," Billingsley ruminated.

"I would disagree, Your Honor," Nakamoto responded. "Pursuant to Criminal Rule 3.2, bail serves two purposes. The first is to ensure the defendant returns to court, because they will receive the money back if they appear for every court date. The second purpose is to protect the public by keeping a dangerous defendant in custody. That second purpose only makes sense if the intent is to create a bail that is prohibitively high, thereby keeping the defendant in custody and the community safe. Here, the court should take the defendant's financial circumstances into account and impose a high enough bail to ensure both her future appearance and the safety of our community. Thank you."

Billingsley was actually nodding along a bit by the end of Nakamoto's argument. She did have a point, Raine supposed. But so did he.

"Any response, Mr. Raine?" the judge invited.

"Yes, Your Honor," Raine replied. "I am going to ask the court to release Ms. Willoughby on her own recognizance."

Billingsley's eyebrows shot up almost as much as they had at Nakamoto's request for ten million dollars.

"Now, I realize that is a bit of an ask," Raine acknowledged, a hand raised toward the judge, "but Ms. Willoughby has absolutely no criminal history. More importantly, she is presumed innocent, and she vigorously denies the allegation that she murdered her husband."

"Wasn't she in family court yesterday afternoon with her husband?" Judge Billingsley interrupted. "I heard something about an adverse ruling and maybe some threatening language?"

News travelled fast in the courthouse. Raine forced a seemingly calm smile onto his face. "Well, yes, Your Honor, there was a hearing yesterday, and as often happens in family law proceedings, things did get a little heated, but only for a moment. Getting upset in divorce court is common, even expected. Murder is not. The defense will be fighting this untrue accusation to our utmost ability, but for us to do so, I need Ms. Willoughby to be out of custody so that we can meet and discuss the case, prepare our defense, and secure the acquittal she so justly deserves. We cannot do that if she is held in custody because the prosecutor has been reading too many dime-store novels and thinks a woman of Ms. Willoughby's stature and reputation would flee rather than fight for her day in court."

"No need for the personal attacks, Mr. Raine," Judge Billingsley cautioned. "We're all just doing our jobs here."

Raine immediately regretted the swipe at Nakamoto. He was still in Perkins mode. He needed to switch to Nakamoto mode. The jury would like her even more if he was a jerk to her.

"My apologies, Your Honor," Raine offered. "I just meant to say that Ms. Nakamoto's concerns are without basis. She is imagining a worst-case scenario and asking the court to act accordingly. I, on the other hand, am asking the court to remember that, under our Constitution, Ms. Willoughby is presumed innocent. Allow her to be released on her promise to appear, and we can guarantee you that she will appear. She will appear to fight, and she will appear to win. Thank you."

Billingsley frowned slightly as he chewed his cheek.

"May I respond?" Nakamoto asked.

But the judge shook his head. "No need, Ms. Nakamoto. I believe I've heard enough. You want me to keep her in jail pending the trial because she murdered her husband. Mr. Raine wants me to let her out because she didn't. I'm supposed to guess what the outcome of the trial will be somehow and then make my decision based on that. But I have to say, that sounds backwards to me."

Raine also thought it was backwards to hold someone in jail while they were presumed innocent, but he didn't interrupt the judge to say so. It was rarely a good idea to interrupt a judge, especially when they were making a ruling.

"I note the first thing you said, Ms. Nakamoto," Billingsley continued. "You said the bail for a first-degree murder case was usually one million dollars. I agree. That does seem to be the usual bail amount on such cases, and I don't see any reason to deviate from that in this case."

Raine frowned, but decided to call it a win. Abigail could post that now that the temporary orders from the divorce case were no good.

"I do that in part," the judge continued, "because I think you may be mistaken as to how easily Ms. Willoughby will be able to reach her assets."

"The divorce case was rendered moot by the murder, Your Honor," Nakamoto said. "The family court doesn't have jurisdiction over her finances anymore."

"I can confirm that's true, Your Honor," Raine put in. "I filed a motion to dismiss the dissolution proceeding this morning."

"Yes, you did," Judge Billingsley agreed. He pointed at the computer monitor to one side of the bench. "In fact, I confirmed as much while the two of you were talking. It looks like Ms. Willoughby lost the battle but won the war. She lost the temporary orders, but the case has been dismissed, and those orders with it."

"I'm sorry, Your Honor. I'm confused," Nakamoto said. "If that case has been dismissed, then there's nothing to prevent Ms. Willoughby from posting the one-million-dollar bail and fleeing."

Raine wanted to agree with Nakamoto, but he realized what the judge was talking about. What he was about to do. What Raine feared he might do.

Nakamoto was a specialist. She was a prosecutor. She only did criminal law, and she only did it from one side. But Raine was a generalist. He did a lot of different types of law, and while that could sometimes be a disadvantage— Nakamoto likely knew more about the Sentencing Reform Act of 1984 off the top of her head—there were other times when it was an advantage. He knew a little about a lot. Judges were generalists too. They were expected to know a lot about a lot. And if Billingsley knew what Raine knew about the intersection of criminal law and probate law, then that bail was going to be a lot harder to post than Nakamoto realized. It was the issue Raine hadn't raised with Abigail the night before. He had hoped it wouldn't get raised at the bail hearing either.

"The family court can no longer restrict Ms. Willoughby's access to her and her late husband's accounts," Judge Billingsley explained, "but I can. Under Revised Code of Washington Title 11.84, a murderer cannot inherit from their murder victim. While I can imagine some circumstances where the cause of death might be contested, RCW Section 11.84.140 states very clearly that a criminal conviction for murder is conclusive evidence for the purposes of the murder inheritance statute. If Ms. Willoughby is convicted of the murder of her husband, she will inherit nothing from him, and his estate will pass to whomever the secondary beneficiaries might be."

"Might I suggest we allow the Probate Court to handle such matters, Your Honor?" Raine tried. "We're just here for an arraignment and a quick bail hearing. One million dollars sounds very fair, Your Honor. Thank you. I think you can move on to your next case."

Judge Billingsley smiled down at Raine. "I appreciate your efforts, Mr. Raine, but I'm afraid I cannot allow a situation to exist wherein your client could—and if she is truly guilty, very likely would—liquidate the victim's estate prior to her conviction."

It was the temporary orders hearing all over again.

"What is happening?" Abigail tugged on his arm. "Why is he talking about wills and estates? Am I getting out or not?"

Not, Raine realized.

"Therefore, in addition to setting bail at one million dollars," the judge concluded, "I will also enter an order requiring that any withdrawals or other transactions involving Ms. Willoughby and the assets of her or her late husband must be approved by Mr. Willoughby's own business accountant, who shall be made a trustee and will therefore carry a fiduciary duty to protect and preserve the assets in question."

Nakamoto looked confused but pleased.

Raine was the opposite of both of those things.

"What just happened?" Abigail asked again for clarification. "Am I going to be allowed to post bail?"

Raine cared about that, of course. He was paid to care. But there was a related problem.

"What's the name of Jeremy's accountant?" he asked.

"Desmond Mitchell," Abigail answered. "Are you going to talk to him about paying my bail?"

"Yes," Raine told her. He didn't say the other part out loud: *After I talk to him about paying my fee.*

Raine departed the courtroom, intent on visiting Mitchell as soon as possible. The gaggle of reporters he'd spied before the arraignment had other ideas.

"Mr. Raine! Mr. Raine!" one of them called out as she ran toward him in the hallway outside the courtroom. She had perfectly styled hair and a royal blue blazer, her microphone awkwardly extended as she jogged the corridor. "It is Raine, isn't it?"

Raine stopped and turned back to face his pursuers. He wasn't interested in trying the case in the media, but the eventual jurors, whoever they might be, might be watching the news that night. If he could help blunt the narrative of "estranged wife murders ex-husband", that could only be a good thing.

"Yes, Daniel Raine," he confirmed. "I represent Ms. Abigail Willoughby."

"Why did she do it?" The reporter jabbed the microphone in Raine's face as the trailing cameraman stopped and pointed the camera at him.

Raine knew the answer to that question. "She didn't. That's why we pled not guilty."

"But surely she was involved somehow," the reporter insisted. "The murder happened inside her own home."

Before Raine could address that, which was good since he hadn't figured out yet quite how to address it, another reporter shouted out a different question from the pack behind the blue-blazered woman. "Is it true she won't inherit anything if she's convicted? Is that how you're being paid?"

Raine also knew the answer to any questions about how he was paid. "I don't answer questions about business arrangements."

But it reminded him that he had better things to do than answer questions designed to enflame rather than elucidate.

"I'm afraid I can't stay and answer questions," he announced to a response of disappointed groans. "But I will say this: Abigail Willoughby is innocent, and she looks forward to her day in court. Thank you."

It wasn't much, but it would have to be enough. Kind of like what Raine needed to extract from Desmond Mitchell.

10

Desmond Mitchell worked directly for Jeremy Willoughby. Or he had, anyway, before the latter's untimely death. Mitchell was in-house, not contracted from an independent accounting firm. Raine wasn't sure why, but he found that unexpected. Sommers, less so.

"Somebody like Jeremy Willoughby probably had a dozen accountants," Sommers opined the next morning as she and Raine rode the elevator to the forty-fourth floor of the Columbia Tower, Seattle's tallest building. "Outside ones to keep the investors happy, but an in-house one to know the real numbers."

"Are you suggesting Willoughby was committing fraud?" Raine questioned.

"Don't be absurd," Sommers scoffed. "I'm simply saying that investors deserve outside audits, but the owner deserves an honest, discreet, and loyal accountant whom he can trust with the most intimate details of his business. An insider, who knows not to talk to outsiders."

"Like lawyers," Raine pointed out. "And real estate agents, I suppose."

"Exactly," she agreed. "But maybe his loyalty to Jeremy will transfer to loyalty to Abigail."

"Seems unlikely," Raine opined, "since she murdered him."

"I thought you said she was innocent," Sommers replied.

"She said she was innocent," Raine clarified, "not me. But I'm her lawyer either way. If I get paid, that is."

"I like getting paid," Sommers agreed.

The elevator announced its arrival at the forty-fourth floor with a *ding*, and Raine and Sommers exited into the lobby of Willoughby Enterprises. Or one of its subsidiaries, at least. Willoughby Accounting, maybe. It was unclear. There was just a very large gold *W* behind the receptionist at the otherwise all black entry.

"Good morning," the receptionist greeted them. She was a young woman with her hair pulled back into a tight pony-tail and thick-rimmed glasses on an oval face. Her clothes were as black as the décor. "May I help you?"

"I certainly hope so," Raine replied affably, trying to over-come the moribund environment. "We have an appointment with Desmond Mitchell."

The receptionist's thin-lipped expression didn't change. She offered only an, "Ah," as she looked to her computer screen. "Mr. Raine?" she confirmed after a moment.

"And Ms. Sommers," Sommers put in before Raine could answer. "We're partners."

The receptionist looked flatly at Raine. He offered a half grin and shrug in return. "Yeah, we're partners," he conceded.

"Delightful," the receptionist replied without any indica-tion she really thought that. "Have a seat. I'll let Mr. Mitchell know you're here."

There were several black chairs surrounding a black table

positioned exactly so they couldn't see any sunlight from any windows on the floor.

"Thanks for bringing me along, by the way," Sommers said once they were seated. "I'm starting to think maybe you do think of me as your partner."

Raine wasn't interested in exploring his thoughts about their relationship right then. "I think you could be useful in this conversation. I imagine Willoughby's assets are pretty complex, bordering on impenetrable. I don't want to overlook a chance to get paid because I didn't understand all the lingo."

"As long as I get paid too," Sommers reminded him.

"You aren't getting paid if I don't," Raine told her. "If I'm not her lawyer, you're going to need to find a different way to be there when all of the assets transfer to her. And that won't happen at all if she's convicted."

"So I'm professionally invested in the outcome of a murder trial." Sommers laughed to herself. "Whoever would have thought that, huh?"

Raine was used to being professionally invested in the outcomes of trials. "I hope Mitchell doesn't keep us waiting too long."

"You don't like small talk?" Sommers ventured.

"I don't like not knowing if I'm going to get paid," Raine responded. "I could be doing other things right now."

"Me too, Danny," Sommers counseled, "but sometimes you have to make time."

Raine narrowed his eyes at the platitude, and its deliverer, but before he could say something unpleasant that he would probably regret later, Desmond Mitchell emerged from behind the wall with the golden *W*.

"Mr. Raine? Ms. Sommers?" he greeted them. "I'm Desmond Mitchell."

He was mostly what Raine had expected given his name

and profession. Thin, balding, glasses, a nervous posture, shirt and tie but no jacket. The only thing surprising was his height. He must have been at least six feet six. Looking up at him gave the impression of looking up at a scarecrow in a cornfield. If that scarecrow were an accountant, that is.

Raine stood up and shook Mitchell's long-fingered hand. "Thanks for meeting with us, Mr. Mitchell. We'll try not to take up too much of your time."

"I would tell you not to worry about that," Mitchell replied as he turned and led them back toward his office, "but in truth, I appreciate it. Things are crazy right now. No one is sure what to do now that Mr. Willoughby is dead. There is just a lot of confusion about all of the various businesses and how everything fits together. And I'm the one who's supposed to know all of that."

"Do you?" Sommers inquired.

"Of course I do," Mitchell snapped, "but that doesn't mean I want to spend all day on the phone explaining it to everyone else."

"Sometimes you get to do it in person," Raine quipped.

"Oh, I hope you aren't going to ask me to explain how everything fits together, Mr. Raine," Mitchell cautioned. They had reached his office. "I could tell you... but then I'd have to kill you."

It was a joke, Raine realized after a moment. Nothing like a little murder humor after a murder. "Ah. Yes. Very funny. And no, we're not here to learn all that. We're just here to talk to you about releasing some funds for Abigail to use."

Mitchell frowned. "For bail, right? Look, I know you're just a couple of lawyers doing your job or whatever, but I'm not particularly eager to hand over bail money to the person who murdered my boss."

Sommers raised a finger. "I'm not actually a lawyer. I'm a private eye."

"Investigator." Raine rolled his eyes slightly. "She's my investigator. And I understand what you're saying, Mr. Mitchell, so why don't we put the question of bail money aside for a moment and talk about the question of legal fees? Ms. Willoughby is going to need to be able to pay me, but the only way to do that is for you to release those funds."

Mitchell just stared at Raine for several seconds. His eyes were very deep set, Raine noticed, and so dark brown as to be almost black.

"Everyone needs to get paid, Mr. Raine," Mitchell finally said. "I won't stand in the way of that. I'll just need to see a copy of the fee agreement, and I will make sure the funds are properly transferred to your business account."

That was easy, Raine thought. "Thank you, Mr. Mitchell."

"Call me Desmond," he insisted.

"Okay. Thank you, Desmond," Raine said. "Now about Ms. Willoughby's bail money—"

"I'm not sure I can be as helpful with that, Mr. Raine," Mitchell interrupted. "It's one thing to make sure Ms. Willoughby is able to pay for her defense. It's another to fund it directly by helping her get out of jail."

Raine narrowed his eyes at Mitchell. "Paying me is probably more directly helpful to her than posting her bail."

Mitchell shrugged. "It's not about helping or not helping Ms. Willoughby. It's about how it looks to the board of directors. I can line item 'legal fees' and no one will look twice at it, but 'bail money'? That is not one of our usual expenses, Mr. Raine. I can assure you I will get questions about that. I like my job very much, Mr. Raine. I would prefer not to put it in jeopardy."

Raine sighed. That made some sense. *Damn it.*

"Especially since she probably did it, right?" Sommers probed. "Would it change your mind if we could show you she's innocent?"

Mitchell shook his head. "Oh, it's nothing like that. I don't think she did it."

"You don't?" Raine was surprised.

"Abigail? Murder Jeremy? Oh, no." Mitchell waved the idea away. "There are so many better suspects than Abigail. She loved him, the silly girl. But Jeremy had a lot of enemies. You don't get to be as rich as him without being, well, a ruthless asshole. And ruthless assholes accumulate enemies. I can think of at least three different people who would be more likely to murder Jeremy than Abigail."

"Who?" Raine asked. That could be just the information he needed.

"Well, let me see." Mitchell glanced at the ceiling as he counted off his suspect list on his fingers. "His son. His first wife. Hell, I think our receptionist out there wanted to smash his head in too. But if I had to pick the most likely suspect, I would say it's the person who will benefit the most from his death."

"I think that's Abigail," Sommers pointed out.

"No, not her," Mitchell said. "Well, maybe she does benefit the most. I'm not sure. I should look into that. But no, I mean who will benefit the most from Mr. Willoughby's businesses suddenly being without a leader? Who is best positioned and most motivated to take advantage of the chaos that is sure to follow?"

"I don't know. Who?" Raine asked.

"David Smith," Mitchell answered.

"David E. Smith III," Sommers replied knowingly. "Hunter just sold his condo in Belltown. He's almost as rich as Willoughby."

"Not even," Mitchell scoffed.

"Smith owns a tech company too," Sommers explained. "He didn't start it the way Willoughby did, but he took it over and made it grow like crazy. He was probably Willoughby's main rival."

"No probably about it," Mitchell said. "In fact, Mr. Willoughby had spies inside Smith's company. He said Smith was stealing our trade secrets. Maybe Smith murdered Mr. Willoughby to protect his secrets."

It was thin, but Raine appreciated the effort.

"We will look into that," Raine said. "I'm glad you think it was someone other than Abigail. So does that mean you'll figure out a way to free up the bail money?"

"Oh, no, definitely not," Mitchell said. "I'm sorry, but posting her bail is just not a risk I can justify to my superiors. She may not have done it, but she's going to be convicted. My God, Jeremy was murdered inside her home. Of course she's going to be convicted."

11

The trip to Desmond Mitchell wasn't a complete failure. Raine got paid, and they had a list of suspects. Still, Abigail wasn't going to be happy to hear that she was going to be staying behind bars for the time being.

"I'm sorry." Abigail choked back a scream. "He said what?"

They were in a meeting room at the King County Jail again. It was a different cubicle, but you would hardly have known it. Same bifurcated setup. Same yellowed plexiglass. Same red jail jammies.

"He said he couldn't authorize the bail money because it wasn't a good risk," Raine tried to explain.

"He thinks you're going to be convicted," Sommers added.

"But I'm innocent," Abigail protested. "Doesn't that count for something?"

"The prisons are full of innocent people," Raine replied.

"Again, Dan, you really need to work on your pep talks," Sommers scolded.

"Well, not full," Raine qualified, "but there are innocent

people in prison. The system doesn't always work. We have to be realistic about that if we're going to have any chance of winning."

"If you say so," Abigail said. "But what about now? I haven't been convicted of anything yet. I am still presumed innocent, right? Why am I being held in jail if I'm supposed to be presumed innocent?"

Raine grimaced and rubbed the back of his neck. "Yeah, that's another part of the system. About seventy percent of people in jail in the US are actually being held on bail awaiting trial. You're presumed innocent at the trial, but for everything until then, you're pretty much presumed guilty."

"That's outrageous!" Abigail huffed.

"That's America." Raine shrugged. "But we have a plan."

"To fix the system so innocent people stay out of jail until and unless they're convicted?" Abigail asked.

Raine actually laughed out loud at that. "Oh, no. I have no way to fix something that fucked up. No, I mean about getting your bail money. We have a plan for that."

"What's the plan?" Abigail asked.

"It's actually the same plan for defending you at trial," Sommers added. "It was my idea."

Raine cocked his head at his "partner". "It most certainly was not. Not the part about the defense at trial anyway. That's my job. You just kind of realized it might change Mitchell's mind too."

"What's the plan?!" Abigail yelled. Jail was getting to her. She was wearing her hair pulled back now, and the dark roots were already showing. The institutional makeup had caused her skin to break out, so she was wearing just light lipstick and mascara. She was probably about to start gaining weight too, Raine knew. Jail food was basically ninety-five percent carbs.

"If you didn't do it," Raine explained, "that means someone else did."

"Obviously," Abigail growled.

"So we need to find that someone else," Sommers said.

"That also seems obvious," Abigail grumbled. "I'm paying you for this? Funny how you managed to convince Desmond to pay you, but not post my bail."

"We're working on it," Raine assured her. "But we're going to need some background from you to know where best to start. Desmond suggested three possible suspects: Jeremy's son, Jeremy's first wife, and some guy named Smith who is some sort of business rival."

"David Smith?" Abigail asked. "Oh, no, I don't think it was him. Jeremy hated him, but I don't think it was returned. That was just a business rivalry. You don't murder someone over business. That's, well, bad business. You can't compete from behind bars."

Raine supposed there was some truth to that. They would need to prioritize their approach.

"So who should we start with?" He asked her advice. "The son or the ex-wife?"

Abigail frowned as she considered. Truthfully, Raine thought she looked better with less makeup, the dark bags under her eyes from sleeping with one eye open notwithstanding.

"Lucas hated Jeremy," Abigail said finally, "but he's a wimp. I can't see him having the guts to attack his father. Plus they haven't spoken for years. I don't know why he ever would have been at my home with Jeremy."

"You know, that raises another question we're going to need an answer for," Raine interjected. "Why was Jeremy in your home that evening?"

"And where were you?" Sommers added.

Raine suppressed an irritated sigh. He was getting to that.

In the meantime, he needed Abigail to answer one question at a time.

"I have no idea why Jeremy was in my home," Abigail insisted. "As for my whereabouts, I wasn't at home."

"We know you weren't at home," Raine said. He went ahead and pursued that topic after all. "Where were you?"

Abigail hesitated. "I believe I was driving home at the time of the murder. When I arrived home, the police were already there. I had no idea what was happening. There were five or six police cars, all with their lights flashing, and my front gate was blocked by crime scene tape. When I approached an officer to ask what was going on, I explained who I was, and he immediately arrested me. Rather roughly, too, I might add. I'm a relatively small woman. He didn't need to handle me like a common criminal."

"He didn't treat you like a common criminal," Raine told her. "He treated you like you were a murderer, which is actually a pretty rare type of criminal."

"Where were you driving home from?" Sommers kept her eye on the ball.

"I was just out," Abigail said. She looked pointedly at Raine. "It had been a very disappointing afternoon in court, and I had gotten rather upset. I needed time to calm down."

"Where?" Sommers wouldn't give up.

"Here, there, everywhere." Abigail threw her hands up. "I was driving around, all right? By myself."

"Well, I would have preferred hearing that you spent the afternoon with a dozen witnesses, handing out food to the poor or something," Raine said, "but we can work with this. We can verify you were away from the house with your phone's GPS and cell tower pings."

But Abigail shook her head slightly. "I didn't have my phone with me."

That's strange, Raine thought. Everyone had their phone with them all the time, it seemed.

"What do you mean you didn't have your phone with you?" Sommers asked for him. "Where was it?"

"It was at the house," Abigail admitted.

"At the house?" Raine threw his hands up. "So your phone data is going to show that you were in the house when Jeremy was murdered."

"Why was your phone in the house?" Sommers asked.

"I didn't want Jeremy to be able to track me," Abigail said. "He's very controlling. Oh, Daniel, you saw how he treated me at that hearing. Always talking down to me. Always acting like he was better than me. He treated me like a possession, not a wife. I know he used to track me because he confronted me one time about where I had been. I couldn't figure out how he knew until he told me it was my phone. So after that, if I wanted to go somewhere without him knowing, I would leave my phone behind."

Raine pinched the bridge of his nose, but then nodded. "Okay. That's not great, but I think we can spin that in a way that the jury understands. Maybe we should just go with battered wife syndrome. Say you did it, but he deserved it."

"Daniel!" Abigail screeched. "I'm not going to say I murdered Jeremy when you know very well that I didn't."

"Sorry, I'm just brainstorming," Raine defended. "No idea is a bad idea, right?"

"That's a bad idea," Sommers told him.

Raine pressed on. "So how long were you driving around by yourself, with no phone or other way to prove it?"

"I don't know how long," Abigail answered, again rather unhelpfully. "Long enough for Jeremy to go to my house without my permission and get murdered by someone else who was in my home without my permission. It was actually a very significant invasion of my privacy, but no one seems to care about that."

Raine suppressed another sigh. He did not, in fact, care about that. But he knew he needed to pretend like he did.

"Of course we care, Abigail," he consoled. "That's why we want to find out who really did this. Well, that, and to get you acquitted."

"And get your bail money," Sommers added. "If we can get some evidence that one of these other people is the real culprit, maybe that will change Desmond's risk analysis, and maybe he'll get the board of directors to authorize the money."

Abigail's expression lifted. "Do you really think so?"

"It's our only choice," Raine answered. "If we don't give the jury the real killer, they'll convict you."

"And you'll never get out," Sommers said. "Who should we talk to first?"

Abigail took a long, deep breath, held it for a moment, then exhaled. "Talk to Bethany. She never got over Jeremy, and she always blamed me for their divorce. She thinks we had an affair while they were still married. We didn't, but she never believed me. If there's anyone who hated both of us enough to murder him and frame me, it's Bethany Carter-Willoughby."

12

Bethany Carter-Willoughby had become something of a recluse after her divorce from Jeremy Willoughby, at least judging by her address and how long it took Raine to find it. In fact, it was Sommers who had to find it. All of the usual tricks a real investigator would have used came up empty: driver's license records, voting records, credit report records. All of those returned to a post office box at the main post office downtown. When all of the usual paths came up empty, Sommers had a hunch that Bethany had taken up residence in Seattle's most exclusive, and reclusive, condo tower. Knowing which haystack to look in, Hunter and her team back at her office were able to locate the needle, to wit: the purchase and sale agreement for a unit on the thirty-third floor, bought by a "B. D. Carter".

But there was a reason she had bought there.

"How does anyone get in here?" Raine asked, looking at what should have been the front entrance to the condo tower, but noticing that the very locked door had no handle on the outside.

"They don't," Sommers answered. "All of the residents

park underground in a secured private lot, then take the elevators directly to their units. There is no public entrance."

"What about this?" Raine pointed at the unmarked door.

"Think of that as an exit," Sommers suggested. "Building codes require street-level ingress and egress in case of an emergency, but they don't require a way for the public to just walk in. Not in this neighborhood."

Raine glanced over his shoulder at their surroundings. It wasn't as bad as around the courthouse, but it was definitely not a place you would want to find yourself after dark. Instead of groupings of tents and cardboard shelters, there were individual homeless people sleeping in doorways and the alley behind the building. "I guess I can understand that. But how are we going to get inside?"

"How do you get anything done in this town, Danny?" Sommers smiled at him. She pointed at the figure walking toward them from the other side of the secure glass. "Connections."

A moment later, the unhandled door opened, and a professional-looking woman stuck her head out. "Rebecca! What are you doing here? Please come on in."

Raine looked at Sommers. "They know you?"

"I sold half the units in this building, Danny," Sommers chirped. "Of course they know me."

"I don't know why you're standing outside my building, though." The woman put a hand up at Raine's chest to stop him from entering. "And I don't know you. Is he with you, Rebecca?"

"Yes," Sommers confirmed. "He's my assistant."

"Assistant?" Raine scoffed. "I thought we were partners."

Sommers laughed at that. "In your world, we're partners. In mine, you're my assistant. Now, come on. Jackie can't keep this door open forever."

Raine felt like he probably fit their definition of that, but he fell in line behind Sommers and entered the building. Jackie closed the door securely behind them.

Raine had to tell himself not to let his jaw drop at the absolute splendor of the lobby. In comparison to the cold, damp conditions of the homeless people outside, it was almost sickening. Certainly striking. A vaulted ceiling floated above three roaring fireplaces and a collection of leather and velvet couches and chairs. There were even some of those "fainting couches" with the rolling back and single armrest. Raine could picture a bloated Roman senator being fed grapes by a gaggle of servants. As it was, however, there was no one else in the lobby save the three of them.

"What are you doing here, Rebecca? Are you going to be selling another one of our units?" Jackie asked excitedly. She had brown hair pulled back into a loose bun and wore a blue suit over a cream shell. Reading glasses hung around her neck although Raine thought she was too young to need them just yet. They were probably just to complete her look, he suspected.

"Actually, Jackie," Sommers answered, "I need a favor."

Jackie's smile faded. "You know I can't compromise the privacy of any of our residents, Rebecca."

"Of course not," Sommers agreed. "And I would never ask you to compromise your professional standards just because I was responsible for making sure this investment actually worked out for the builders rather than becoming another mostly empty condo tower in the sketchier part of Belltown. But no, please, I would never ask you to compromise the privacy of the residents I already know live here because I sold them their units and kept you employed."

Jackie took a moment; then her smile returned with a laugh. "Rebecca, I always did like you. You cut right through the bullshit."

"That's the only way to get these people to spend their money." Sommers returned the laugh.

"What do you need?" Jackie asked.

Raine was feeling very third wheel, but he knew third wheels needed to keep quiet sometimes.

"Bethany Carter-Willoughby," Sommers answered. "We need to get a message to her."

"It's just Bethany Carter now," Jackie said. "She dropped the Willoughby. I think she might finally be over him."

"That's why we're here," Sommers said. "Jeremy Willoughby is dead."

Jackie's eyes flew wide. "What? When? How?"

"He was murdered." Raine finally spoke up. Wheels needed grease sometimes too, or something. "Just a couple of days ago."

"Oh my God." Jackie raised her hands to her mouth. "Who did it?"

"That's why we're here, Jackie," Sommers said. "I can't explain everything. It's kind of top-secret private-eye stuff. But we need to talk with Ms. Carter."

Top-secret private-eye stuff? Raine suppressed an eye roll.

"Oh wow." Jackie put her hand to her mouth again. "Really? Are you doing that now too?"

Sommers raised a cautionary hand and offered a knowing nod. "I can't really talk about the details, Jackie. Just know that it's important. My ability to sell any more of these luxury residences could depend on it."

Not to mention Abigail Willoughby spending the rest of her life behind bars, Raine thought. But that wouldn't be a helpful squeak.

"What do you need me to do?" Jackie asked.

"Please let Ms. Carter know that we're here to talk to her about Jeremy," Sommers instructed. "I'm sure she's already heard the news. We have some additional information that she might be interested in."

That was probably true, Raine supposed, although he wondered how all of this would play out once it was revealed that they represented the person accused of murdering Jeremy.

Jackie just frowned at him for a moment, then looked again to Sommers. "Let me see what I can do. Wait here."

Raine had no objection to that. There were no actual servants with grapes, but there was an overstuffed chair right in front of one of the fires. He made a beeline to it and relaxed into the warm leather.

"I hope you appreciate what I'm risking by doing this," Sommers said in a hushed tone as she sat down on a small couch next to him.

"I appreciate that you're enjoying yourself," Raine observed. "And I imagine you'll manage to maintain your relationship with Jackie no matter how our conversation with Bethany Carter goes."

"I might even improve it." Sommers grinned.

"I expected that was the plan," Raine told her. "Rebecca's number one client is always Rebecca."

Sommers didn't argue with that. She didn't try to defend it either. She just smiled and leaned back on the couch to await Jackie's return.

They didn't have to wait long. Jackie appeared a few minutes later, hands folded in front of her and a serious expression on her face. "Ms. Carter would like to speak with you."

Raine pushed himself, somewhat reluctantly, out of his chair. Sommers popped to her feet. "Thank you, Jackie. I'll explain everything later. Maybe over dinner at the Met?"

"Canlis?" Jackie countered.

Then together, they both agreed. "Altura."

Raine had never been able to comfortably afford to eat at the Metropolitan Grill or Canlis. He'd never even heard of Altura.

Jackie led them to the elevators and flashed her security badge to open the doors of the unit waiting at the lobby level. She leaned inside and flashed the badge again, then pressed 33. "Ms. Carter is expecting you. You can go directly to her door. It's unit 3301."

The elevator doors closed, and they rushed straight to the thirty-third floor. When they stepped off, they were greeted with refreshingly cool air and a pleasant scent. Vanilla, Raine thought. Or maybe cinnamon. He wasn't sure, but he imagined it was probably pretty nice to come home to that every day. He was starting to think he didn't have any idea how the other half lived.

They made their way to unit 3301. There were only four doors on the short hallway. Every unit was a corner unit. Of course.

Sommers knocked three times, a sharp staccato, then stepped back to center herself in front of the peephole. She fluffed her hair and raised her chin. Raine took a step away lest his grizzled bulk ruin the first impression Sommers was crafting. After a few moments, the door opened, and they were face-to-face with Jeremy Willoughby's first wife.

Bethany Carter was probably a decade older than Abigail. Her hair was a natural gray, cut simply at her shoulders. She wore light makeup and a comfortable outfit that reminded Raine of both pajamas and an evening dress.

"Ms. Carter?" Sommers started the introductions. "My name is Rebecca Sommers. This is Daniel Raine. He's an attorney, and he represents Abigail Willoughby. She is charged with murdering your ex-husband, Jeremy."

Blunt. Raine wasn't sure how Carter might react, but he expected more of a reaction than they received.

"Oh," Carter said. "Well, come inside, then. I'll start some tea."

Carter's condominium rivaled the lobby in its grandeur. Floor-to-ceiling windows offered a panoramic view of Elliott Bay and Mount Rainier. The furniture and art were straight out of a design magazine. White furniture, colorful artwork, a stack of well-worn novels on a table near the fireplace. Raine and Sommers waited for Carter to emerge from the kitchen, then followed her lead for the seating. Carter sat in the center of the large couch. Raine and Sommers took seats in the chairs opposite.

"So you want me to help the woman who stole my husband and then murdered him?" Carter began. "That's quite the ask."

"I can't speak to how your marriage with Jeremy ended," Raine responded, "but Abigail didn't murder Jeremy. She's innocent."

"Did she tell you that?" Carter scoffed.

"Well, yes," Raine admitted.

"And so now you're looking for other suspects," Carter deduced. "I'm flattered that you would think me capable of a feat of such ferocity and passion, but I lost my passion many years ago. When Jeremy divorced me for that young—well, let's just say for Abigail, I received a very nice divorce settlement. We didn't have a prenuptial agreement. We got married because we were in love. The money came later. I have managed to establish a very comfortable life up here above the city. I have no interest in climbing back down into the mud with the likes of Jeremy and Abigail Willoughby."

"Can you tell us where you were when Jeremy was murdered?" Raine went ahead and got right to it. Carter seemed like she could take it.

Carter smiled. "Where were you on the night of June seventeenth, eh?"

"Something like that," Raine allowed.

"I was here," Carter answered. "Alone with my books."

Raine looked at Sommers, who returned his puzzled expression. "We didn't tell you what night it happened," Sommers pointed out.

"It doesn't matter," Carter answered. "I'm here every night."

"You wouldn't happen to have any witnesses, would you?" Raine ventured.

"Probably," Carter answered. "Go ahead and tell me which night it was, and I can tell you who was with me that night."

Raine's eyebrows rose.

"Don't look so surprised, Mr. Raine," Carter admonished. "I may be divorced and old, but I'm not dead. I have several gentlemen friends I see on a regular basis. It's likely one of them was here that night. Although..."

"Although what?" Sommers said.

"What time did it happen?" Carter asked.

"Between six and seven," Raine answered.

"Are you sure?" Carter tested.

"I'm sure," Raine confirmed.

Carter frowned. "Well, then, I'm afraid I don't have an alibi after all. I don't receive my callers until after eight. I'm not one for small talk."

Raine could appreciate that. Glanced around the condominium again. Sometimes it wasn't just what people said, it was how they said it. And where. Bethany Carter had moved on. If she was going to bludgeon Jeremy to death, she would have done it years ago.

"Have you spoken with anyone else about the case?" Raine needed to ask. He didn't want to be surprised by new information when she undoubtedly testified at Abigail's trial. "Reporters, perhaps?"

Bethany laughed. "Oh, Mr. Raine, I don't live here so that I can be bothered by reporters. I assure you, any conversations I have had about the death of my late husband have been minimal and superficial. Much like ours now."

Raine nodded. He could take a hint. "Perhaps we should be leaving, then. We appreciate your time. And thanks for the tea."

Carter seemed indifferent, but Sommers had one more question.

"Why did you say Abigail 'stole' Jeremy away from you?"

Carter grimaced slightly at the memory. "Because I came home one night and found him fucking her on our bed."

"Oh," Raine said.

"Indeed," Carter agreed. "I believe that's what you lawyers call proof beyond a reasonable doubt. Please give her my regards."

Raine and Sommers took their leave then. No badge was needed to call the elevator to depart. On the way down, Raine summed up their visit.

"Well, now we know Jeremy's ex-wife doesn't have a verifiable alibi," he said. "And we know Abigail lied to us."

13

Raine wasn't surprised to learn that Abigail had lied to them. In fact, he would have been surprised if she hadn't lied to them. All of his clients lied to him. The personal injury clients lied about their injuries. The bankruptcy clients lied about their finances. The divorce clients lied about their spouses. But the criminal clients were the worst. They lied about everything. Raine had a working theory that the greater the jeopardy a client was facing, the more they would lie to their attorney, out of fear that the lawyer wouldn't work as hard if they knew the client was guilty. But Raine knew his clients were usually guilty. That's why they got caught. Abigail might be the exception that proved the rule. Or she might just be another example of it. Either way, Raine was going to need to have an awkward conversation with her.

Speaking of awkward conversations, it was the night of Jordan's first basketball game of the season. That meant a night in a middle school gymnasium, rooting for a group of thirteen-year-olds to actually make a basket. He and Natalie were committed to "co-parenting", which apparently meant sitting next to her at the game to cheer on their boy. Not that Raine minded. It wasn't like he didn't miss her.

"Dan," Natalie said when he appeared on the bleachers next to her, "you made it."

"Of course I made it," Raine replied. "I've always come to the kids' games. The divorce doesn't change that."

He hadn't seen her since signing the divorce papers. She looked great, as always. He wished he didn't like seeing her again so much.

"I meant you made it on time," Natalie clarified. "You weren't always on time."

Raine supposed that was true. He sat down next to her and squinted across the gym at their boy on the opposite sideline. "Is he starting?"

Natalie gave him a lopsided frown. "What do you think?"

Jordan was good enough to make the team, but he had never been good enough to be a star. His strengths were defense and rebounding, not scoring. Scorers were starters.

"Oh well," Raine said. "As long as he has fun."

That would end up being debatable. Jordan didn't play much in the first half and almost none in the second half except for the last twenty-three seconds, garbage time after the game was already lost. He finished with three shots, no points, and no rebounds. Not his best game.

Raine was proud of him anyway. That was his son out there, giving his all.

During the long stretches of the game where Jordan wasn't playing, Raine tried to make conversation with Natalie.

"How's Jason?"

"How's work?"

"Any upcoming travel plans?"

And finally, because he just couldn't stop himself, "Seeing anyone?"

Natalie responded monosyllabically to all of them except the last one, which prompted her to say, after a very long, very loud sigh, "Stop talking, Dan. Please just stop talking."

After the final buzzer, the coach pulled his team into the corner for the post-game breakdown while the parents all stood up and made their way down the bleachers and onto the court to await their kids. "He played pretty well, right?" Raine asked.

Natalie shook her head. "Don't, Dan. The coach barely put him in the game at all. He's going to feel bad enough as it is."

"I just want to be supportive."

"He won't see it that way," Natalie said. "Just don't say anything."

Jordan made his way over to his parents. Or rather to his mom, whom he was staying with while they worked out the final details of the residential schedule.

Raine raised his hand for a high five. "Way to go, Jordan. Better luck next time."

Jordan looked at his father's hand and very definitely did not high-five it. He looked at his mom. "Can we just go?"

Natalie pulled her car keys out of her purse and handed them to Jordan. "You can head out to the car, honey. I'll be there in a minute."

Raine could only watch as his younger boy retreated from the gym, and him. "What did I say?"

Natalie shook her head. "You never did know."

"What does that mean?" Raine demanded.

But Natalie just gave him a lopsided smile and another shake of her head. "It's good you came, Dan," she said. "Next time, we don't need to sit together."

That stung, maybe more than Jordan not wanting to give him a high five. Or talk to him. Or be seen with him.

"Tell Jordan I'm proud of him," Raine asked of her. "Even if he hates me."

"You're his dad, Dan," Natalie replied. "He'll always love you. But sometimes, whether it's fair or not, he's going to hate you too."

14

Jeremy Willoughby's son hated him, Abigail said. Maybe he was the one who smashed that marble statuette into the back of his father's head. Raine wasn't worried about Jordan or Jason doing that to him—at least not yet—but he could see how a strained relationship could quickly turn to an explosive one under the right circumstances. It really depended on what type of person Lucas Willoughby was, and there was only one good way to find that out.

"Again?" Sommers sighed into the phone when Raine called her. "I'm having fun and all, but I have a real job too, you know?"

Raine did know. She rarely failed to mention it in any of their conversations. "I just figured you'd want in on this one too," he answered, "but if you want to take a pass, I'm pretty sure I can talk to Lucas alone. I don't think I'll need you to sweet-talk me past security."

"Where does he live?" Sommers demanded.

"Does that matter?" Raine wondered.

"Yes," Sommers answered without elucidation. "Just tell

me the address."

Raine checked the address he had located for Lucas Willoughby. "Uh, let's see. It's 4731 Rainier Court South."

"Nope," Sommers snapped. "Out of my area. You can handle it alone."

"Are you sure?" Raine asked. He was starting to enjoy her company.

"Am I sure that I don't want to put my real job on hold to visit a squalid artists' co-op?" she asked rhetorically. "Yes, I'm sure."

"How do you know it's a squalid artists' co-op?"

"How do you know what evidence rule to cite when you make a hearsay objection?"

"It's my job to know," Raine answered.

"Exactly," Sommers returned. "Let me know if he says anything of value."

"Value to the case?" Raine questioned. "Or value to you?"

"I think you know the answer to that, Danny," Sommers chirped. "Bye."

Raine did know the answer to that. He was a little disappointed. He'd grown to enjoy having someone to bounce ideas off of, even if they weren't a lawyer. Or maybe because they weren't a lawyer. On the other hand, he didn't mind a little alone time as he drove south from his office toward the squalid artists' co-op Lucas Willoughby called home.

In the event, it wasn't actually squalid. It wasn't far above that though. It appeared to have once been a post office or similar government building, probably first converted to condos and then, when that failed, converted again to "Co-Operative Housing and Studio Space" per the graffitied sign by the side of the road. The building itself was also marked with graffiti, although Raine wondered whether it was the work of street hooligans or resident artists. Some of it was actually rather impressive. Some of it, not so much. Probably like the collection of artists who lived there. Lucas's unit was number 17. All of them appeared to have doors that opened directly onto the sidewalk, a feature at once simple and dangerous. Raine circled the building until he found the door with the number 17 painted on it. Nothing artistic about the numbers, just black stencil. It was off the main roadway and featured no graffiti, lending weight to the street hooligan theory. He knocked on the door and stepped back to await its opening.

It was a little after 10:00 a.m. when Raine arrived, and he had no illusions that a community of artists might be mostly still asleep at that hour, so he was surprised to hear movement inside immediately after his knock. It consisted of things moving and/or breaking and a voice, although he couldn't quite make out the words. Its tone was either surprised or annoyed. Maybe both. He was about to find out.

There were several locks on the door. Raine listened as each was unlatched in succession, and the door swung slowly open to reveal who Raine assumed must be Lucas Willoughby. He was tall and lanky, almost gaunt, with messy black hair, a five-o'clock shadow seven hours early, and a grubby T-shirt and jeans on. His feet were bare. "Hello?" he greeted his guest, his eyelids heavy but the eyes under them focused on his unexpected visitor.

"Lucas Willoughby?" Raine asked in confirmation. "My name is Daniel Raine. I'm an attorney. I'd like to talk to you about your father's death."

Lucas took a moment to let all of the words register. "You're my dad's attorney?" They didn't quite register fully, it appeared.

"No, I'm *an* attorney," Raine replied. "I represent your stepmother, Abigail Willoughby."

Lucas took another minute, then started nodding. "Yeah. Abby. She's cool."

Raine was agnostic on the issue. "Can I come inside?"

Lucas thought for several moments, then pulled the door open all the way and stepped to the side. "Yeah, sure. Come on in, man. Sit anywhere."

As inviting as that sounded, it actually presented Raine with a challenge. There didn't appear to be a flat surface in the apartment that wasn't covered in something, whether it be clothes, dishes, paint supplies, or the green-eyed cat that was eyeing him from the pile of sheets on the floor that was probably Lucas's bed. Raine settled on a chair that seemed to have the fewest number of things on it, none of them likely to stain his suit. Lucas dropped onto the bed and started petting the cat, which responded by closing one eye in pleasure but keeping the other one on Raine.

"Am I the first person to come to talk to you about this?" Raine suspected from the state of the apartment. "No reporters have stopped by or anything?"

"Nah, nothing like that," Lucas confirmed. "Or if they did, I didn't hear them knock."

Raine could believe that.

"So what do you want to talk about, man?" Lucas asked. "I'm kinda surprised Abby killed my dad, but I'm kinda not. Like, she's a sweet lady, but he's a complete asshole. So I wouldn't think she could do something like that, but then I could kinda see her doing it to him. You know?"

Raine did know, actually. That was a very fair and reasonable summation of the problem he faced. Nakamoto could use that observation as her opening statement.

"Well, Abigail is pretty adamant she didn't do it," Raine said.

"Oh." Lucas nodded. "Well, that's probably good."

"Yeah," Raine agreed. "So now we're just trying to figure out where everyone else was the night your father was murdered."

It took a moment for that comment to land. Lucas narrowed his eyes slowly. Raine wondered what substance he was on and whether it was left over from last night or fresh that morning.

"Wait," Lucas said finally. "Are you asking me where I was when my father was murdered? Like, I'm a suspect or something?"

Pretty much, Raine thought to himself. But he knew better than to say that.

"No, not like that," he insisted. "We're just trying to piece everything together about that night. The police are going to come here eventually and ask you all the same questions. You might as well tell me first."

Raine wished that were true. The police should be interviewing every person with the slightest motive, but they had their suspect. Case closed and delivered to the prosecutor's desk, nice and tidy with a bow on top.

"Do you have an alibi for that night?" Raine asked.

"An alibi?" Lucas laughed. "Like, people who were with me when my dad got offed or whatever?"

"Yeah, like that," Raine confirmed.

Lucas shrugged. "I don't know. Probably. I live here because we're all artists, and it's, like, super social, you know? We're always hanging out and helping each other and sharing ideas and stuff. I'm sure I was with somebody, either here or there, although we were all probably high. That might not help, huh?"

"Depends on what the cops think, I guess," Raine answered.

Lucas leaned forward, disturbing his cat's reverie. "Dude. Really? The cops are gonna come here?"

"Dude," Raine assured him, "really."

Lucas looked around his dwelling and suddenly seemed to sober up. "I should probably clean up, then, huh?"

He stood up and started pulling things off those chairs and tables, although in no discernible order. Raine stood up too. The cat glared at him accusingly.

"Pardon me for saying so, Lucas," Raine said, "but you don't seem very upset that your father is dead."

Lucas stopped his random tidying. His arms fell to his sides, and he frowned, but only slightly. Then he dropped whatever fabric he had in his hands—clothes? towels? art rags? Raine didn't know—and gestured for Raine to follow him. "Come see this."

Lucas stepped over the various piles on the floor, and Raine followed his footsteps, like the Christmas carol about that king and the footprints in the snow. Around the other side of some shelving piled with paint and other art supplies Raine couldn't possibly have identified was an enormous canvas, five feet by five feet. On it was painted an absolutely captivating scene of trees and animals and sky and stars. It was really very good. Raine felt a little bad at being surprised.

"You painted this?" He pointed at the composition. "It's really good."

Lucas smiled. "It's not done yet, but thanks. I'm liking where it's headed."

Raine stepped closer. It was filled with a series of static vignettes captured in the nooks and crannies of the scenery. Men and women, children and pets, doing the mundane and the ephemeral. It was like a novel, a series of novels, disassembled and reassembled, waiting for the viewer to piece the story back together again. And happily so. Raine couldn't take his eyes off it. "It's not done? What more could you add? There's already so much."

"And there's so much more to add," Lucas answered. "You can't see what's not there, but I can."

Raine liked that.

"That's how it is with my dad," Lucas said.

Raine cocked his head. "What do you mean?"

Lucas gestured around his apartment/studio. "This is me. This is who I am and what I do and what I love. And you know what's not here? My dad. My dad never understood this. He never understood me. He wanted me to run his company someday, but I'd rather cut my eyes out than do that, and I'm a visual artist, man. So he cut me off." Lucas frowned in thought for a moment. "He even wrote me out of his will. He thought if I didn't have money, if I didn't have him, I'd come crawling back and beg to live the life he wanted for me. That was almost five years ago. Five years, man. Five years without him in my life, and I'm doing fine."

Lucas pointed at the painting. "What do you think I should add?"

Raine scanned the painting, looking for something lacking. He couldn't find anything. "I don't think you need to add anything."

"What's missing?"

"Nothing."

"Exactly," Lucas said. "My father stopped being a part of my life years ago. Why would I need to get rid of him if he was already gone?"

Raine could hardly argue with that logic. He took his leave of Lucas Willoughby and paused outside to collect his thoughts.

Lucas didn't do it. Raine was convinced of that. As much as he could be convinced anyone didn't do it, given that he wasn't there when it happened. But Lucas made an excellent point. Why would he murder someone who was already completely out of his life? It didn't make sense. There were other people with better motive, means, and opportunity. Abigail Willoughby, for example.

Emma Nakamoto certainly thought so.

15

The criminal case was proceeding forward regardless of Raine's efforts to find another viable suspect. It was time for the pretrial conference, the court date between the arraignment, where the prosecutor told you what you were accused of, and the trial, where the jury told you whether you did it. The pretrial conference was an opportunity to see whether the case could be resolved by way of a plea bargain. Most criminal cases settled short of trial— over ninety percent. Part of that was because most people charged with crimes did in fact commit those crimes. Generally speaking, the system wasn't supposed to prosecute innocent people. It did, of course, but it wasn't supposed to. But when it did, it could be hard to reach a plea bargain.

"She didn't do it," Raine began the negotiations. Not a lot of room for movement.

"I can prove she did," Nakamoto countered.

Pretrial conferences took place in a large conference room outside the actual courtroom, and there were dozens of them scheduled at the same time. The room was filled with prosecutors and defense attorneys, most with multiple cases, negotiating cases like speed dating, rotating to the next opposing counsel every few minutes with a deal worked out, a promise to talk more, or a decision to end negotiations and confirm the case for trial. Raine could tell where he and Nakamoto were going to end up.

"Convincing twelve people too stupid to get out of jury duty isn't the same as proving it," Raine said.

Nakamoto cocked her head. "I'm pretty sure it's exactly the same. That's what proving it means."

"Okay," Raine admitted, "but it doesn't mean she did it. The prisons are full of innocent people. Do you really want to be responsible for adding another?"

Nakamoto frowned at him. She listed off her case on her fingers. "The victim was murdered inside your client's home. She threatened him that afternoon. She wasn't going to get anything out of the divorce that she filed. He showed up with a final settlement agreement for her to sign, which was even worse than the prenup. But with him dead, she stands to inherit everything. And she has no alibi. Tell me again why I should think she's innocent?"

"Because she is?" Raine tried.

"And you know that how?" Nakamoto challenged. "Because she told you? Come on, how many clients have you had lie to you? Better yet, how many clients have never lied to you? Zero, right?"

It was pretty close to zero, Raine knew. Especially the criminal clients. But he wasn't going to admit that. Better to change the subject, back to her weaknesses rather than his.

"Look, your entire case is circumstantial," Raine said. "No one saw my client there. Her so-called threats were generic at best and hours earlier. Any fingerprints and DNA don't mean anything because it was her home. She denied it when she was arrested, so you don't have a confession. It's all speculation. You have no witnesses who can actually say she did it. You have no direct evidence whatsoever."

"And we both know the judge will tell the jurors," Nakamoto recited the jury instruction, "'The law does not distinguish between direct and circumstantial evidence. One is not necessarily more or less valuable than the other.'"

That was exactly what the judge would tell the jurors. Raine was impressed by her ability to cite the pattern jury instructions from memory. "Yeah, but the reason the judge has to tell them that is because no one really believes it," Raine countered. "Are you telling me you wouldn't rather have a witness who saw my client commit the murder? Or better yet, two witnesses? How about three? And if you want that, so does the jury. The law may not distinguish between direct and circumstantial evidence, but people sure do."

Nakamoto frowned. "You're not wrong, but I expect the jurors to follow their instructions. Especially when there's no evidence to the contrary, circumstantial or otherwise. Have you looked at the discovery we sent you? The will? That final settlement agreement in the victim's cold, dead hand? If that divorce had gone through, she would have gotten nothing. But he hadn't changed his will yet, so now she stands to get everything."

"If I win the trial," Raine pointed out.

"Which I will prevent," Nakamoto boasted. "I assume your client doesn't have an alibi, or you would have told me already."

"She has an alibi," Raine insisted. "Of course she has an alibi because she didn't do it, which means she was somewhere else."

Nakamoto raised an eyebrow. "Is it a verifiable alibi? Or just I was alone somewhere else with no witnesses to confirm that."

Raine shrugged slightly. "More in the no-witnesses cate-

gory, but it's still an alibi. You put on nothing but circumstantial guesses and innuendos, then all I have to do is put her on
the stand to say she didn't do it, and I win."

"You put her on the stand"—Nakamoto smiled at the
prospect—"and I get to cross-examine her. When I'm done,
the jury will think she killed her husband and three more
people besides. I'll destroy her."

Raine sighed. He knew that was probably accurate. Innocent or not, Abigail wouldn't hold up well under a withering
cross-examination by a seasoned prosecutor. If she couldn't
adequately explain her whereabouts at the time of the
murder to her own attorney and his fake investigator, how
would she do it when pressed by the prosecutor? The answer
was, she wouldn't. At least not yet. He was going to have to
prepare her because trial was seeming increasingly likely.

"Look, let's cut to the chase," Raine said. "What's the
offer? Can you offer a manslaughter? That's seven years. I
may be able to talk her into that."

Nakamoto laughed. "Maybe, but you're not going to talk
me into it. This is a clear murder one. Did you read the
autopsy report? The medical examiner was able to identify at
least seven different strikes to the back of his head. There
may have been more, but the flesh was too lacerated and
deformed by that point. That's premeditation."

"That's passion," Raine countered. "Fear. Instinct. The
opposite of premeditation."

"Tell it to the jury," Nakamoto told him.

"I guess I'll have to," Raine conceded. "She's not pleading
to murder one."

"What about murder two?" Nakamoto offered. "I'll admit
it could have been a crime of passion. But it was still intentional. That's murder two. If she's willing to plead to that, I
can offer that."

"That's twelve to fifteen years, right?" Raine was familiar

with the sentencing guidelines but didn't have them quite memorized.

"Right," Nakamoto confirmed. "I can offer murder two, high end, fifteen years."

Raine shook his head, more to himself than to her. "I can't plead her to fifteen years. She didn't do it."

"You keep saying that," Nakamoto said, "but you're not giving me any reason to believe you."

"Aren't you the one who's supposed to prove she did it?" Raine challenged. "Not the other way around?"

"Look. It's Dan, right?" she double-checked before launching into whatever she was about to say.

"Right." Raine confirmed his name. It was a sign of how well he'd avoided criminal work lately that the prosecutors didn't know his name.

"Look, Dan," Nakamoto said, "I'm willing to be open-minded about this. I don't want to prosecute an innocent person, but you have to give me something. I admit the evidence is circumstantial, but it's pretty damn good circumstantial evidence, and we both know the law says circumstantial evidence is enough. If you want a better offer, if you want a dismissal, then give me something. Anything. You haven't done that. Not yet. And until you do, I can't offer anything better than pleading guilty to murder. Otherwise, we're going to trial."

Raine frowned slightly, but he knew she was right. "Give you a reason to dismiss," he repeated, "or take my chances at trial."

"I'm afraid so," Nakamoto confirmed. "And honestly, I don't like your chances at trial."

Neither did Raine.

At that moment, they were interrupted by another attorney who had begun standing over them like a patron at a crowded restaurant waiting for a table to open up. "Hey,

Emma, are you going to be much longer?" she asked. She held up an armful of files. "I've got a few cases I need to talk with you about, but I have to get going soon. I've got a meeting I need to get to."

Nakamoto nodded up at the other attorney. Raine thought he recognized her as one of the public defenders. The number of files in her arms supported that conclusion.

"I'm almost done here, Janet," Nakamoto said. "Gimme like two minutes."

Janet stepped back, and Nakamoto returned her attention to Raine. "Do you have anything for me?" she asked again. "Anything at all?"

Raine had to shake his head. "Not yet," he admitted.

"Then let's confirm it for trial," Nakamoto said. "If she really is innocent, I hope you come up with something before then."

"Me too," Raine agreed. "Me too."

16

Raine decided it was time to talk to Abigail again. Maybe another week in jail had jogged her memory about her alibi. And it was probably time to confront her about lying to him. The lie had been about the overlap between her relationship with Jeremy and Bethany's. That was personal and perhaps embarrassing, so he could forgive it, but it evidenced an ability to lie to him. He wouldn't be doing his job if he didn't explore the possibility that she had lied about other things as well. In fact, he hoped she had. He needed a better alibi than "I was driving around by myself without my phone".

Raine took out his own phone. He was willing to meet with Lucas without a witness, but not Abigail. Not when the entire point of the meeting was how she might be a liar.

"Rebecca Sommers, executive Realtor." Raine was actually starting to like the sound of that.

"J. Daniel Raine, executive lawyer." He tried it on for size. "Or maybe executive attorney. Which sounds better?"

"Hanging up on you is sounding pretty good right now," Sommers answered. "Do you actually need something?"

"I need you to sit in on a come-to-Jesus talk with Abigail Willoughby," Raine explained. "I need to confront her about why she lied to us, and find out what else she's lying about. The prosecutor isn't offering any deals, and we're running out of time."

There were a few moments before Sommers replied, "Let's grab dinner first. I have a reservation at my club tonight. Let's discuss options over dinner."

It was Raine's turn to hesitate. Was she asking him out? "Uh, options? The only option I'm proposing is confronting Abigail."

"I know," Sommers replied. "That's why we should discuss options. Seven o'clock. Rainier Bay Club. The table is under my name."

Sommers didn't give Raine a chance to respond. She hung up, and that was, apparently, that. Raine looked at his phone, then shoved it in his pocket. He hoped she was paying.

THE RAINIER BAY Club had views of neither Mount Rainier nor Elliott Bay. Instead, its panoramic windows faced Lake Union, the small lake situated between Lake Washington and Puget Sound, of which Elliott Bay was a part. Raine had never been to the Rainier Bay Club. In fact, he wasn't sure he'd ever even heard of it. It appeared to be affiliated in some way with a nearby marina, but Raine was one of those Seattleites who never owned a boat. He had taken to heart the advice that the only thing better than having a boat is having a friend who has a boat, and Mike Hawkins had a nice boat. So there was a chance they had moored nearby on one of those sunny afternoons of summers past. But he had never been inside. He was sure of that as he stepped up to the maître d's podium.

"Good evening, sir," the maître d' greeted him. He was

younger than Raine, dressed in a pressed white shirt and pants, with a black belt and shiny shoes. He seemed like a nice fellow, but then Raine supposed he was paid to seem that way. "Welcome to the Rainier Bay Club. Are you a new member?"

Raine appreciated the polite way in which the maître d' informed him he didn't really belong, in several ways. Raine's work shoes were definitely not as polished as the greeter's. But he supposed they all had jobs to do, and Raine wasn't going to begrudge someone else doing his.

"I am not," Raine confirmed. "I'm meeting a member for dinner. Rebecca Sommers?"

The maître d' smiled at the name. "Ah, Ms. Sommers. Yes, of course. She said she was expecting a guest this evening." He called out to a waitress near the bar. "Zoë, please show our guest to Ms. Sommers's table."

Ms. Sommers's table was centered in those panoramic windows, on a platform elevated two elegant steps from the rest of the restaurant. Hers wasn't the only table on the platform, but it sure seemed to be the most important. Sommers had her back to the view, as if she'd seen it a million times already, and smiled as Raine approached.

"Danny!" she called out. "You made it."

Raine suddenly felt underdressed, which was difficult to do in Seattle. He'd opted to keep on his suit, but lose the tie. None of the other men in the club were dressed any better than that, but he could feel that their clothes were more expensive than his. He also noticed most of them had turned to watch him step up on the platform and be greeted with a kiss on the cheek by *the* Rebecca Sommers, executive Realtor.

"Fancy place," he observed. "Fancy greeting, as well."

Sommers grinned as they sat at the table. "I know fancy, Danny. And I know what it can stir up." She pointed to a glass of brown liquid over ice already set in front of him. "I took the liberty of ordering you an old-fashioned."

Raine couldn't complain about that. "Thanks," he said, reaching out for the drink. "So why are we here exactly? This couldn't have been a phone call?"

"Phone calls are dreadful, Danny," Sommers answered. "And far too private. Sometimes, you need to be seen."

Raine glanced around the dining room again. They were definitely being seen. He was accustomed to being the one everyone was looking at when he was delivering a closing argument. But not in his current setting. He wasn't accustomed to anything in his current setting.

"Seen by whom?" he asked over a sip of his old-fashioned. It was excellent.

"By the sort of people who already know who I am, but might not know who you are," Sommers answered. "The sort of people who want to find out."

Raine frowned slightly. He sensed the evening might drag on, especially if Sommers insisted on playing riddle of the Sphinx. He decided to try to move things forward. "Fine. Whatever. Now, tell me why you don't think we should confront Abigail yet. If she lied about when she started her relationship with Jeremy, she's probably lied about other things. I'm still not satisfied with her explanation of her whereabouts at the time of the murder. If we can't lock down a credible alibi, the jury will convict her no matter who else we point the finger at."

Sommers nodded along. "So what did she lie about again?"

"About when she started up with Jeremy," Raine repeated.

"Mm-hm." Sommers nodded. "Having sex with a married man?"

Before Raine could reply, one of those other men in the

club, the ones with the more expensive clothing, stepped up to their table.

"Rebecca, you look lovely this evening," the man said. He was tall and muscular, with swept-back black hair, a neatly trimmed beard, and absolutely glowing skin. "I don't believe I've had the pleasure of meeting your dinner companion," he asked without actually looking at Raine.

Raine extended his hand. "Daniel R—"

"This is Daniel," Sommers interrupted. "No need for last names tonight. He's my guest. That's all you need to know right now, Bradley."

Bradley accepted the admonishment with a tightened smile. "Of course, Rebecca."

"What about you, Bradley?" Sommers asked. "Are you dining alone tonight?"

Bradley's smile loosened up a notch. "No," he fairly admitted. "I am here with someone as well. But I just had to say hello to you and your escort for the evening."

"Well, thank you for doing so, Bradley," Rebecca answered. "Please give my regards to your guest as well."

Bradley took his leave then, and Raine cocked his head at Sommers. "Escort? Does he think I'm a gigolo?"

"Don't flatter yourself, Danny." Sommers chuckled. "He just wanted to intimate that without saying it. We both know you'd be younger and wearing tighter clothes if you were a paid escort."

Raine frowned downward at his clothes and inward at his age.

"Everyone knows everyone here," Sommers explained. "So when we see someone we don't know, well, we just have to know."

"That seems juvenile," Raine observed.

But Sommers shrugged slightly. "I think it's useful. It's

always useful if you know what the currency is, so long as you have some."

"I'm your currency?" Raine ventured.

"Again, don't flatter yourself," Sommers chided. "It's not you per se. It's the fact that no one knows who you are. It's the information that's the currency. And I'm about to use it to trade for the information we need." She looked up at the next man approaching their table. He was even younger and more handsome than Bradley. "Cameron! How are you, you disreputable thing?"

"Rebecca darling," Cameron replied. He leaned down and kissed Sommers on the cheek, just as she had done to Raine. "You seem to have a different date every night. It's wonderful to see you this evening. You always light up the club."

So Cameron didn't come out and ask who Raine was, and Sommers rewarded him with the information anyway. She gestured across the table. "This is J. Daniel Raine. He's a very important local attorney. This is a sort of business dinner."

Cameron reached out to shake Raine's hand. "A pleasure to meet you, Mr. Raine. Do take care of our Rebecca, won't you?"

Raine was pretty sure Sommers was taking care of him, not the other way around. "Of course," he answered.

Cameron glanced quickly around, then leaned in and lowered his voice. "Is this about that unpleasantness I heard you were involved in, dearest?"

Raine supposed someone probably had heard about her working with him on the case. It wasn't like it was a secret, and these people seemed to like to talk.

But Sommers shook her head slightly, sending her hair bouncing. She looked especially put together that evening, which was saying something. "Not that unpleasantness, no. A different unpleasantness, I'm afraid."

Cameron looked again to Raine. He shrugged. "Kind of

comes with the job," Raine said. "No one needs a lawyer until it gets to the point that they need a lawyer."

Cameron forced a smile that was really more of a grimace. "Of course. Well, enjoy your dinner, Rebecca. You too, J. Daniel." And he departed.

"Why did you tell him my name but not the first guy?" Raine asked.

Sommers grinned. "There's a hierarchy to everything, J. Daniel. Bradley doesn't rate. Cameron does. And now they will talk to each other and learn that as well. Cameron will take it as a compliment. Bradley, as a challenge."

Raine nodded. "Can we just go with 'Dan', by the way. I thought I didn't like 'Danny', but 'J. Daniel' is even worse."

Sommers laughed. "Let's go with 'Daniel' tonight, I think. After that, 'Dan' will be fine." She raised her gaze and motioned for a waiter to come over. "We'd better get our dinner ordered before our next inquisitor arrives, or we'll never eat."

Raine glanced around, and sure enough, several of the patrons at the surrounding tables were looking their way, curious about Rebecca Sommers and her unknown dinner guest.

"Does this always happen when you eat here?" he asked.

"Only when I bring a new man here," Sommers answered. "Everyone likes fresh meat. Except the old meat."

The waiter was a young man who also seemed to know Sommers. She ordered the salmon and recommended the beef tenderloin to Raine. By then Raine would have been willing to eat the plate, so he didn't argue. He ordered it rare, hoping that might get it to the table a few minutes earlier. As the waiter receded, the next visitor approached.

He was an older gentleman, probably well into his sixties judging by the wrinkles, but with the physique of a younger, athletic man under his designer clothes. "Rebecca, you know

I get jealous when you come around with some new young buck and don't even say hello."

Sommers offered her hand to the man. He took it and kissed it.

"Daniel, this is Montgomery Carmichael," she introduced. "Montgomery, this is Daniel Raine. He's a—"

"He's an attorney," Montgomery finished. "Yes, I heard."

Already? Raine was surprised.

"You're not in any sort of trouble, now are you, my dear?" Montgomery raised an eyebrow at her. "You know I'd do anything to help you. Anything at all."

"I do know that, Monty," Sommers answered, putting a hand on his arm. "And I may come ask for your help after all. But for right now, Mr. Raine is in my very capable hands."

Raine started at the unexpected placement of who was in whose hands. Montgomery simply laughed at it.

"I'm sure he is," he said. "I'm sure he is. Well, it was a pleasure to meet you, young man. Treat our Rebecca well tonight, or I daresay you'll have more than just me to answer to."

Montgomery departed, and Raine leaned forward. "They all think we're on a date, right?"

"Right," Sommers confirmed. "That's exactly the point."

"But we are not on a date, right?" Raine followed up.

"Oh, good Lord, no." Sommers waved the notion away with a scowl. "I hate to keep saying this, but don't flatter yourself. You're bait, Dan. You're not the main course."

Raine couldn't help but wonder who among the assembled might end up being that main course, but he found himself relieved to be just bait. Sommers wasn't his type, and he was pretty sure he wasn't hers either.

"So who are we trying to reel in?" Raine asked, keeping up the metaphor.

Sommers smiled and nodded at the man coming up the steps. "Him."

He was thin and young and a little on the shorter side. Raine guessed he was barely old enough to order the drink in his hand. He had blond hair cut into a fade on the sides and back, with a loose mop in the front that fell almost into his eyes. He was the only one in the club, other than the waiters, to be wearing a tie, and its silk was so shiny, it seemed to glow on its own. His mouth remained a thin line, but his eyes almost burst with a smile as he reached the table.

"Ms. Sommers," he began formally, "I just wanted to pay my respects. And also to your companion, whom I don't believe I've ever met."

"This is Daniel Raine," Sommers said. "He's an attorney. We are working on a murder case together."

Raine noted the sudden candor. He must rate higher than Cameron.

"Dan, this is Evan Childress," Sommers introduced him. "You can tell him anything."

Raine shook Evan's hand. "Do I have to?"

"Only if you want me to tell you something in return," Evan answered. "May I join you?"

He didn't wait for Sommers's "of course" before pulling out one of the two empty chairs at their table. "You piqued my interest, Rebecca. Teasing those other boys like that. I knew it was important, but I must admit, I didn't know it was 'murder' important. Are you branching out from real estate, or just resorting to more aggressive ways of getting properties to market?"

"Maybe a little bit of both," Rebecca returned. "It's quite the sordid tale. Shall I tell you about it?"

"About how Abigail Willoughby murdered her husband after she lost everything in the divorce she so unwisely set into motion?" Evan asked with a wink. "Oh, yes, please do."

"You know all that?" Raine asked. Then he remembered to add, "Also, she didn't murder him. Someone else did it."

Evan raised an incredulous eyebrow. "Who else would have access to her home in order to commit that murder, Mr. Raine?"

Raine frowned. "I know that part looks bad, but—"

"No, Dan." Evan reached out and placed a hand on Raine's arm. "I'm asking you. Who else would have access to her home?"

Raine had to admit, that was a good question. "Well, Jeremy, obviously," he began, "since he was murdered inside her home."

"Yes, obviously," Evan allowed. "What about her lover?"

It was Raine's eyebrows that rose that time. "Excuse me? Her lover?"

"Evan knows everyone and everything in this town," Rebecca explained.

"Everyone and everything worth knowing, that is," Evan clarified.

Raine considered for a moment. "You didn't know me."

Evan took a moment, then burst out laughing. He patted Raine on the cheek, then turned to Sommers. "Oh my God, Rebecca, he really is darling."

"He has his moments," Sommers allowed.

"No, Dan, I didn't know you," Evan explained. "I know Rebecca. You're ancillary."

Raine wanted to protest, but he had been feeling pretty ancillary since he'd arrived at the Rainier Bay Club.

"Who is her, uh, lover?" Raine asked, hesitating at the word. "Assuming she even had one."

Abigail cheating on Jeremy was not going to be a good fact for him. It was just one more motive to get rid of her husband. Although, the fact that she filed for divorce suggested a willingness to rid herself of him nonlethally.

"Well, she tried hard not to let anyone know, of course," Evan began.

"Of course," Rebecca agreed solemnly.

"But no one can keep everything hidden forever," Evan continued. "That's the tragedy of it all, really, wouldn't you agree, Dan?"

Raine shook his head at whatever Evan was intimating. "Let's cut to the chase. Who was Abigail fucking?"

Evan gasped and threw wide eyes at Sommers.

"Allegedly fucking," Raine qualified.

Evan laughed. "Always the lawyer, eh, Dan? Okay then. Are you sure you want to know? I don't think you're going to want to know."

"I probably don't," Raine agreed, "but I need to know. Professionally, that is."

Another grin from Evan. "Professionally. Of course."

Raine was about to lose his patience when the waiter arrived with their entrees. Evan glanced at Raine's rare tenderloin, the juices filling the plate. "You know they'll cook that for you if you ask them to, right?"

"Name, Evan," Raine said. "Give me a name."

"Okay, Mr. Raine, I'll tell you who your client's secret lover is," Evan relented. "David Smith."

Raine squinted at him. "I don't know who that is."

"Yes, you do," Sommers reminded him. "He was Jeremy Willoughby's primary business rival. That's what Desmond told us."

"The accountant?" Raine recalled. "Okay, I remember that. So Abigail was fucking her husband's business rival, and you think she gave him a key to her place. Is that the theory?"

"It's not a bad theory," Sommers opined.

"Except that no one except Evan here had any idea of it." Raine jabbed a thumb at their tablemate. "There's, like, seven layers of hearsay there. It's not like I can call him as an expert on high society infidelities."

"I am an expert on high society infidelities," Evan insisted.

"I don't doubt that," Raine allowed. "But that's not a generally accepted area of expertise. It won't pass the Frye test."

"The what?" Sommers squinched her face at him.

"Lawyer joke, never mind," Raine dismissed her question. "I'm not excited about putting my client on the stand to say that she didn't kill her husband, it was probably the guy she was having a secret affair with."

"So don't have her say it," Sommers suggested.

"I'm not using Evan," Raine repeated. "The only other person would be—"

Oh, he realized. "David Smith."

"Exactly." Evan crossed his arms. "I will leave you two to your schemes now. It was nice to meet you, Mr. Raine. Rebecca, it's always a delight."

He stood up and gave Rebecca a parting kiss on the cheek, which Rebecca returned with a squeeze of his arm.

"It's speculation at best," Raine grumbled when they were alone again. "And she's going to deny it when I confront her with it. No judge will allow me to try to prove an affair by calling two witnesses, both of whom will deny it."

"Don't confront her yet," Sommers counseled. "Confirm it first."

"How?"

Sommers grinned. "David Smith."

Raine finally set down the silverware he'd been using to shovel his meal into his face. "You think some super-rich businessman is going to admit to having a motive for murder?"

"Well, not if you phrase it that way," Sommers admonished. "But he might admit to besting Jeremy Willoughby in yet another arena. Make it a brag instead of a confession."

Raine sighed through his nose. He gestured at the throng of men still circling their table. "Why all the theatrics? Why not just tell me you thought Abigail was having an affair?"

"I didn't think that," Sommers insisted. "I just knew Evan would know. But he wouldn't tell me unless he wanted something from me."

Raine glanced again into the crowd but couldn't spy Evan Childress. "What does he want from you? Seems like he's the one with all of the information."

Sommers smiled broadly, red lips glistening from the light of the crystal chandeliers, and leaned forward, sending a strand of platinum curls bouncing across her sequined neckline. "Information isn't the only currency, Dan."

Raine thought for a moment. "Him?"

"Why not?"

"Um, I just kind of got the feeling"—Raine struggled—"you weren't really his type, if you know what I mean."

"I'm not sure I do." Sommers made him say it.

"It just sort of seemed like I might be more his type," Raine said.

Sommers shook her head and laughed. "You do think very highly of yourself, don't you?" She reached across the table and tapped his nose with a finger. "I like that."

"Ms. Sommers," Raine cautioned, "people are watching. This is how rumors start."

"The rumors already started, Dan," Sommers replied. "That's why you're here. To stir up rumors and jealousy and make the weaker sex crawl to me with offers of information and delight."

Raine looked around the club once more. "Not me, right?"

"Not you, Dan," Sommers confirmed. "You're not my type. But my type is in that crowd there, and one of them will happily take your seat at my table when you've finished your meal."

Raine nodded. He knew they wouldn't be collaborating anymore that night.

"So we visit David Smith first thing tomorrow?"

"Tomorrow is fine," Sommers agreed. She glanced around the ballroom and smiled. "But we'd better make it the afternoon."

17

The elevator doors opened to the top-floor offices of NWTech, David Smith's primary business. NWTech was engaged in software applications of some sort that Raine didn't find particularly interesting or understandable. The office was located at the top the Century Square Building on the edge of Westlake Square, a once vibrant upscale shopping plaza in Seattle's downtown core that had more recently turned into another sketchy public space, housing some of the spillover from the homeless tent encampments a block away on Third Avenue.

Sommers placed a gentle hand on Raine's chest. "Pretend you don't know me."

"What?" Raine questioned. "Why?"

"Trust me," Sommers advised with the slightest of smiles.

Raine was willing to do that. She had more than earned his trust by then.

Sommers gestured for him to exit first. He did so and made his way up to the receptionist's desk to ask to see David E. Smith.

"Do you have an appointment?" the receptionist inquired

with a raised eyebrow. She was in her thirties, with thin black hair pushed back over her ears, little to no makeup, and a simple navy suit. The lobby matched her appearance: practical and minimalist. The NWTech logo on the wall behind her was the only décor. The chairs were a dark gray fabric. There were no magazines on the single glass coffee table.

Raine definitely did not have an appointment. Had he called to make an appointment, Raine felt certain the answer would have been no.

"Hello. I represent Mr. Smith's mistress who is accused of murder, and I was hoping he might confess to the crime himself."

"I do not have an appointment," Raine admitted. "It's a time-sensitive matter that only recently came to my attention. I thought it best to come straight here and see if Mr. Smith might be available."

"Mr. Smith is rarely available," the receptionist answered. "And never for walk-ins."

Raine sighed. "Could I try to book an appointment, then?" he tried. "Sometime soon? Maybe even later this afternoon if he has something available? I don't need much time."

"Mr. Smith takes his meetings in ten-minute intervals," the receptionist informed him. "I could see if there might be an opening sometime in the next few days."

"Thank you," Raine answered. Ten minutes wasn't likely to be enough time, but it was easier to overstay your welcome once you were inside.

"Can I get your names, please?" the receptionist asked, spying Rebecca standing behind Raine.

"Daniel Raine," he answered.

"Rebecca Sommers," she added, "but we're not together."

The receptionist smiled approvingly. "The Rebecca Sommers?"

Sommers smiled. "Yes." She beamed. "In fact, I believe I

may have helped Mr. Smith find this particular office location."

"What can I do for you, Ms. Sommers?" the receptionist asked, turning her attention fully away from Raine.

"Well, I'm also here to get an appointment with David"— Sommers frowned slightly—"but it's actually a reschedule. Mr. Smith didn't show for our previous appointment. He's not the type to miss a business appointment, I wouldn't think, so I fear"—she pointed at the receptionist's screen—"it might have been a scheduling error."

Raine found himself slightly annoyed at being pushed aside, but he was also curious to see where Sommers was going with it all.

The receptionist looked appropriately concerned that she might have made a mistake with her boss's calendar. "What day were you supposed to meet with him?"

Sommers took a moment to pretend to recall. "It was three weeks ago. A Wednesday. At six p.m."

The time of the murder, Raine knew. He couldn't help but smile.

The receptionist clicked her mouse a few times, then shook her head and looked up. "No, I'm sorry, Ms. Sommers. There was no appointment at that time. Mr. Smith had that entire evening blocked out as personal time, from four to eight o'clock."

"Personal time?" Sommers questioned. "Couldn't that include a meeting with me?"

The receptionist shook her head. "No, that means he is alone and not to be disturbed for any reason."

"So he wasn't just at some dinner with a friend," Sommers confirmed, "or off at a tech conference on Portland with a hundred witnesses?"

"Witnesses?" The receptionist frowned at the choice of word.

"Colleagues," Sommers corrected. "He wasn't with anyone, I mean?"

The receptionist's frown deepened. She looked again at Raine and then back to Sommers. "Are you sure you two aren't together?"

"I am very sure," Sommers replied first. "Does this gentleman look like the sort of person I would spend time with?"

Raine threw her an insulted glance, but didn't say anything.

"And speaking of my valuable time," Sommers continued, "it appears I've spent enough of it here talking with you. I'll just contact David directly and see why he stood me up, with no witnesses to corroborate his story, no less. Good day."

With that, Sommers turned and headed for the elevators.

Raine stepped forward again. "So can I schedule an appointment now?"

The receptionist scowled slightly and returned to her data entry without replying directly.

"You know, if Mr. Smith isn't available right now, I could come back later today," he offered.

The receptionist displayed a tight smile and a raised index finger. "If you could give me just a moment, Mr. Raine?"

Raine sighed and crossed his arms. "Yes. Of course."

He turned away and glanced around impatiently. It wasn't going exactly to plan so far, but it hadn't completely derailed yet either. That would take a few minutes while the receptionist clacked away at her keyboard.

"I'm afraid I can't schedule an appointment for you, Mr. Raine," the receptionist finally announced.

Raine frowned. "What about early next week? I'd rather do it sooner, but if it's in the first part of the week…"

"No, I mean I can't schedule an appointment for you ever,"

the receptionist clarified. "We always screen anyone who requests to meet with Mr. Smith, which I just did while you were waiting. It was fairly simple to find you online, determine that you're an attorney, then run your name through the court's website to see what active cases you are attorney of record on. You represent Abigail Willoughby, who is accused of murdering her husband, Jeremy Willoughby. Jeremy Willoughby also happened to be a competitor of Mr. Smith. I found that concerning, so I messaged our COO, and she determined that you will not be allowed to meet with Mr. Smith. Ever."

Raine wasn't sure what to say.

"I can also see the cases you were a party on," the receptionist continued. "Congratulations on your recent divorce."

"Wow," Raine said, burying the sting her comment shot through him. "That was unnecessary."

The receptionist shrugged indifferently.

"Anyway, how do you know I'm here to discuss the Willoughby case?" Raine demanded.

"The fact that you asked that question instead of telling me what other case you're here on," the receptionist replied, "answers your question."

Raine knew he'd lost, and he didn't feel much like adding to that loss by throwing a fit about it and still losing. He thanked the receptionist and made his way back to the elevator bank. Sommers was already gone. She was waiting for him in the lobby.

"Well, that didn't go well," Raine said as he stepped off the elevator.

"Speak for yourself," Sommers answered. "I confirmed David E. Smith III doesn't have an alibi for the time of the murder."

"That was pretty good work," Raine had to admire. "I just wish we could have confronted him with it personally to see what he would say. Just because he wasn't at work doesn't mean he was with Abigail."

"Or murdering Jeremy," Sommers added, "but those are both possible now."

"True, and we can still confront Abigail about it," Raine suggested. "We could even tell her Smith confirmed their affair and see how she reacts."

"You'd lie to your own client?" Sommers questioned.

"She lied to me," Raine defended as they reached the lobby and the elevator doors opened. "Might serve her right. And anyway, it would only be to see how she reacts. If she confessed to it, then I'd tell her the truth."

They had crossed the lobby and exited without realizing they were on the Third Avenue side of the building. Third Avenue had long been a problem area for downtown Seattle, especially at the intersection of Pike Street, just a few blocks up from the fabled Pike Place Market. Even before swaths of downtown had turned into tent cities, people had crossed the street to avoid the throng of the mentally ill and/or drug addicted at intersection of Third and Pike, and Raine and Sommers had just walked right into the middle of them.

Raine understood that homelessness was a complicated problem with complicated causes and no easy solutions. He had read the *Johnson v. Grants Pass* and *Martin v. Boise* cases, even if only out of professional curiosity, since no homeless person charged with public vagrancy could ever have afforded to hire him. He knew he didn't have the answers, and complex problems required complex solutions. But none of that mattered when confronted with a six-foot-four homeless man wrapped in a dirty blanket and staring down at them with angry eyes and a large object half-concealed in his hand.

"Shit!" Raine called out. He instinctively grabbed for Sommers's hand, but she yanked it away.

"I don't need your help," she scolded. "Just keep your head up and walk fast."

It was good advice, but Raine suspected it might prove inadequate. The man they were confronted with upon their exit from the building didn't seem focused on them after all, or on anything for that matter. He continued to stumble up the street, oblivious to them. But they were hardly invisible with their nice suits and quickened gait.

The afternoon rain had stopped, but the water had pulled the stench of urine and inadequate industrial cleaner from the sidewalk. They just needed to turn the corner and get one block east to Westlake Plaza, then one more block to Fifth Avenue, where the stores were nice again and the people on the sidewalks were mostly tourists. Raine would have preferred to cross Third before turning right, but the light was against them, so he made space and pushed Sommers ahead of him behind what everyone in town knew was the single worst bus shelter in the city. The crowd didn't part exactly, but they made their way through with minimal contact. They just needed to get past the alley and hope they timed it to get a WALK signal across Fourth Avenue.

He never saw the punch coming.

18

The blow was definitely to his head. It sent Raine reeling forward and onto his hands and knees, into a puddle of the aforementioned water, urine, and cleaner. It seemed to have landed against his right ear, because he couldn't hear anything out of it. The constricting tunnel vision also threatened to drop the rest of him into that puddle, but he managed to maintain consciousness even as the world around him spun and lurched. When he was able to look up again, he saw a man grabbing Sommers by the wrist. He wasn't as large as the man whom they had first encountered upon exiting the building, but he was bigger than Sommers, and he was shouting something about angels and demons. Raine pushed himself to his feet and stumbled toward them. Sommers looked like she was about to try some fancy jujitsu leg sweep or something, but Raine took advantage of the man's divided attention, likely exacerbated by whatever chemicals were in his blood, and stepped between them to punch the man as hard as he could directly in the center of his face.

The flesh beneath Raine's fist gave way, and the man crumpled to the ground.

Sommers pushed Raine away. "I didn't need your help!" she shouted at him.

"I didn't do it to help you," Raine growled at her, standing over the bleeding man, chest heaving. "I did it because he fucking hit me first."

The man pushed himself up enough to scramble away into the alleyway, leaving a trail of blood to join the rain and urine. Raine watched after him with a primal satisfaction, but then began to feel the pain in his hand from its encounter with another person's skull. He shook it, sending more blood and water to the ground. He suddenly realized what he had done.

"Goddamn it." He stomped a foot into a puddle as he turned a tight, angry circle. "I didn't want to hit some poor homeless guy."

"He hit you first, remember?" Sommers said. Then she looked at the stunned crowd at the bus shelter, who were becoming less stunned and more angry that one of theirs had been sent to the ground. "Come on. We need to get out of here."

Raine tucked his throbbing hand under his armpit and followed Sommers's lead, half-running to the intersection with Fourth Avenue and crossing against the light, which simply was not done in Seattle.

"What the fuck!" Raine called out once they were on the other side of the traffic from any would-be pursuers. The pain in his hand had momentarily distracted him from the pain in his ear. That moment passed. "I can't fucking hear out of my ear. Damn it. What the hell was that about?" Then, "Aw, shit, I hope he's okay."

"Fuck him," Sommers replied. "He deserved it. And he would have gotten worse from me if you hadn't stepped in."

Raine wasn't sure he believed either of those things. It was starting to rain again. He welcomed the chance to rinse some of the fight off himself, even at the expense of his suit. "The city really needs to do something about this. You can't have random violence in the middle of..." He trailed off.

"The middle of downtown," Sommers finished. "I know. Do you have any idea what's happened to property values on Third Avenue in the last decade?"

"Random violence," Raine repeated. He couldn't have cared less about property values on Third Avenue. "Holy shit. What if that's what it was? What if it wasn't someone Jeremy knew? What if it wasn't someone Abigail let in? What if it was just some random crazy guy who walked into an open house and attacked the person inside?"

"In Madison Park?" Sommers scoffed. "Unlikely."

"But not impossible," Raine insisted.

"You'd better hope that's not what happened," Sommers said. "We'll never find the killer if it was some random homeless man who got lost in a good neighborhood."

Raine knew that was true. He also knew the jurors, whoever they were, would have to walk through a gauntlet like they had just traversed to get into the courthouse every day. "We might not have to. We can blame the entire thing on an unidentified violent maniac, the kind the mayor and the city council refuse to take off the streets. The jury will be the type of law-abiding people who actually respond to their jury summons. They'd eat that up."

Sommers looked like she wanted to argue. She didn't.

"It might work," Raine continued, nodding as the drizzle picked up and started to mat down his already slickened hair. "Let's call it plan B."

"What's plan A?" Sommers asked, pulling her collar up against the shower.

"That all depends," Raine answered, "on what Abigail tells us when we call her a liar."

He ran a hand over his hair and looked unapprovingly at whatever combination of fluids was left on his palm. "I need to clean up. Meet me at the jail in two hours."

19

Raine still didn't feel clean when he arrived at the jail. Not physically and not emotionally. He regretted lashing out like that, and he hoped the man got the medical aid he needed. On the other hand, he still couldn't hear out of his right ear.

"Feeling better?" Sommers asked as he stepped up to her in the lobby.

Raine shrugged. "Doesn't matter. Let's just talk to Abigail and get this straightened out once and for all. I need to know what to tell the jury when I give my opening statement. 'My client was just kind of missing for a few hours at the time of the murder' isn't going to sound very good."

"It'll probably sound better than 'She was cheating on her husband with his business rival'."

But Raine shook his head. "No, that would be better. It might be morally bad, but it's an alibi. I'd rather have her with someone who can verify her whereabouts."

"Even if her whereabouts were under him?" Sommers quipped.

"Anywhere but standing over Jeremy with a bloody pyramid in her hand."

Raine walked over to the reception desk and provided the guard with his bar card. Sommers stepped up and provided her ID as well. A few minutes later, the door to the insides of the jail opened up, and they were escorted to the visiting area. A few minutes after that, Abigail entered from the other side of the plexiglass.

She was looking better than the last time they had seen her. People could get used to a lot of things, and jail was no exception. She appeared less gaunt, likely from having gotten used to the food, and she had figured out a way to keep herself groomed using what supplies she was provided. Her eyes held an appropriate amount of concern given the circumstances, but the abject terror of their first meeting behind glass was long gone.

There were a few ways Raine could play the encounter. He could start with small talk to warm her up, ask about that jail food and if there were any good books in the jail library. He could jump in with an update about the case, explain what was left to do before trial and what their trial strategies might be. That would be a good segue into why your attorney should be fully, and accurately, informed. Or he could just get right to it.

"You lied to me," Raine began. His voice wasn't angry, but it was firm.

Abigail's eyebrows knitted together. "About what?"

That was the question asked by a person who either hadn't lied at all, or had lied about more than one thing. Raine told her as much. "And since I know you lied at least once, I also know you lied more than that."

"What did I lie about?" Abigail demanded. She crossed her arms. "And why would I lie to my attorney?"

Raine answered the second question first. "You would lie

to your attorney for the same reason everyone lies to their attorney. You want me to do my absolute best for you, but you're afraid if I know the whole truth, I might not try quite as hard."

Abigail shifted slightly in her seat. She looked away.

"What you lied about," Raine continued, "what I know you lied about is when you and Jeremy began your relationship. It wasn't after his divorce. His ex-wife caught the two of you in a compromising position."

"Fucking," Sommers translated.

Raine grimaced. "Thanks."

Abigail sighed and let her arms fall to her sides again. "Okay, fine. I lied about that. I'm not proud of it, but I didn't think it mattered. It just shows how much I loved him, right?"

"That's one way to spin it," Sommers allowed.

"Which is kind of my point," Raine explained. "Let me spin it. Whatever the truth is, I can spin it. If I spin the truth, I'm being a lawyer. But if I spin a lie and it gets exposed as a lie, well then I'm just a liar. And you're going to be a convicted murderer."

Abigail frowned, but nodded.

"So what else did you lie about?" Raine forged ahead.

Abigail cocked her head. "I mean, that's it." It almost sounded like a question.

"I know you lied to me about more than that," Raine reminded her. "I'm just not sure about what. That's kind of the problem with lies. But let me take a guess. You weren't alone, just driving around at the time of the murder, were you?"

Abigail didn't answer immediately, which was an answer in itself.

"If you were with someone, that's an alibi," Raine explained. "Even if it was someone you shouldn't have been with."

"Even if it was David Smith." Sommers cut to the chase.

"David?" Abigail gasped. "Oh, no. No, I wasn't with David."

The way she said his name made Raine think she was lying. Or at least Evan Childress hadn't been.

"Look." Raine leaned forward onto the small shelf in front of the partition. "I know that when you lied to us about starting up with Jeremy while he was still married, you were trying to protect yourself and him. You didn't want people to think you were the type of person who would sleep with a married man. And you didn't want people to think Jeremy was that type of married man. That's all perfectly under-standable. Protecting yourself is the main reason people lie. It's why everyone lies to their lawyers. They want their lawyers to do the best job possible to protect them. So I get it if your instinct now is to protect yourself again and to protect David Smith. But honestly, I don't care if you're the type of woman who would sleep with a married man while you're still married to a different man. And I sure as hell don't care what kind of man David Smith is. But if you're lying now to protect him or to protect yourself, you have to understand that you're doing the exact opposite. It's not protecting your-self to let yourself get convicted of murder and spend the rest of your life in prison. Right now, in the circumstances you find yourself in, protecting yourself means telling your lawyer the absolute and complete truth about where you were that night, even if it was underneath David Smith."

Abigail took a long deep breath and leaned back in her chair. She exhaled through the hand she raised to her mouth as she looked Raine dead in the eye. She took that hand from her mouth and pointed directly at him. "Fuck. You."

Raine's eyebrows shot up. "Excuse me?"

"Don't you dare try to tell me what kind of woman I am," Abigail snarled. "You don't know me. You don't know what

I've been through or who I am. You don't know what it's like to be a woman, and you don't know what it's like to be pursued and used and abused by powerful men."

Raine supposed that was all true. The initial adrenaline rush of being called out faded quickly. He was just glad she was talking. So he shut up.

"Yes, fine, Jeremy and I started up before he got divorced," Abigail admitted, "but I didn't know that, did I? He lied to me. He told me they were already separated and everything was done except the final paperwork. Turned out he hadn't even told her he wanted a divorce. I'm not sure he even did, except that when he got caught, she wanted one. So, for me, it was the truth. I didn't knowingly sleep with a married man. And it's the same with David. Yes, I know him. Yes, I like him. Yes, maybe in a different life it would have been him I fell for instead of Jeremy. But that life is long past. You want to know where I was when Jeremy was murdered? Do you?"

"Yes." Raine nodded. "That's exactly what I want."

"I wasn't with David, but I wish I were," Abigail almost shouted. "I wanted to be with someone who wanted to be with me, and apparently that wasn't Jeremy. Do you know how mortifying it was to have to go to that hearing? To lose that hearing? To listen to my husband say not only was he okay with a divorce, but he didn't want me to get anything from it? I don't think I even really wanted a divorce. I just wanted him to notice me, to think he might lose me."

"You filed for divorce," Sommers questioned, "as a bargaining chip in your relationship?"

"Seems a bit extreme," Raine agreed.

"Yes. No. I don't know." Abigail shook her head. "I didn't think he would be so okay with it. I wanted him to fight for me. I wanted him to beg me not to leave him."

"For what it's worth"—Raine rubbed the mostly healed

cut under his eye—"he did try to convince me to drop the case."

"But that's just so like him." Abigail threw her hands up. "Fix things behind my back instead of just talking to me. If he'd asked me to drop it, I would have. That's what I really wanted, I think. But then he didn't. He was fine with it. He was more than fine with it. He was laughing. He laughed at me. In front of everyone."

She was sliding back into her motive for the killing. Not helpful. Raine redirected her. "So where were you?"

Abigail shook her head again and laughed, a dark, sad little laugh. She wiped her nose with the back of her hand. "You want to know where I was? Fine. Everyone thinks I'm this strong beautiful rich woman."

Humble, too, Raine thought.

"But I'm only human," she continued. "I waited all afternoon for Jeremy to call me and tell me he wanted to reconcile. But he never did. And suddenly my house felt so big and empty, yet so small and suffocating. I was so angry at him. I was so angry at myself for wanting him to call. I just had to get out of there. I didn't leave my phone behind because I was afraid he would track me. I left it behind because I was afraid if he called and asked me to come back, I would. In an instant. And then what power would I have? My life would be over. He'd own me like he owns everything else. I didn't want him to ask me to live like that. Because I knew I'd say yes."

"Where were you?" Raine prodded.

"I drove to Gas Works Park," Abigail finally explained. "I used to go there when I was a little girl with my parents. I loved the comparison of the rusty old gas works and the shiny new skyscrapers across Lake Union. I would go there sometimes when I was younger and just needed time to myself. So I went there again. I didn't even get out of my car. I just sat there and cried. By myself. I cried until I was done. Done crying. And done with Jeremy. For good."

"Then you went back home," Raine surmised, "and the police were there."

"And they arrested me for murdering my husband," Abigail finished. "I didn't. I don't even wish I had. I was hurt, but I wasn't angry. Not really. And certainly not enough to kill him."

Raine rubbed a thoughtful hand over his chin. It wasn't great. But it was believable. That would have to be enough.

"So you weren't with David Smith?" he asked one more time.

"No," Abigail barked. "Stop asking me that. He's not my alibi."

"Good." Raine nodded. "That means you're not his alibi either."

Abigail frowned at Raine. "Are you going to claim David did it?"

"It's not my job to prove who did it," Raine answered. "That's the prosecutor's job. But if there's someone else with motive and no alibi, that makes her job harder. So I need you to be honest with me one more time, Abigail. Did David Smith have a motive to kill Jeremy?"

Abigail hesitated. That was Raine's answer.

Sommers asked the next logical question. "Did David have a key to your house, Abigail?"

Abigail declined to answer that question as well. "David has become a good friend," she allowed, "but he would never have hurt Jeremy."

Raine demurred. "I guess we'll let the jury decide."

RAINE AND SOMMERS came to a stop in the center of the cement plaza outside the entrance to the jail. It was meant to be a pedestrian-friendly mini-park, but it turned out that very few people wanted to hang out in front of a jail. The rain had stopped again, but a darker patch of the gray sky was heading their way. Still, Raine wanted to take a moment and let things settle into his mind.

"Do you believe her?" Sommers asked him. She too had one eye on the approaching clouds.

"That she was down at Gas Works Park crying in her Benz while her husband was murdered?" Raine frowned. "I'm not sure. But it was quite the performance. I hope she can repeat it on the stand. The jury might just buy it."

"You think she was with Smith?" Sommers supposed.

Raine frowned. "I did when we got here, but now I'm not so sure. I feel like I gave her the out to tell us. I mean, she has to understand that cheating on Jeremy isn't anywhere near as bad as murdering him."

"I kind of thought she'd realize what you were suggesting and go along with it," Sommers said. "Even if she wasn't with him, she should say she was. If he denies it, well, of course he denies it. He's married too. It's probably the only time you'd believe someone's alibi when the alibi witness says they weren't together."

Raine nodded slightly and smiled at his partner. "You're exactly right. So let's make that happen."

20

The final hearing before the trial was called the readiness hearing. As its name suggested, it was when the attorneys appeared before the judge to confirm that the parties were ready to begin the trial. It was a fast, formal hearing with the defendant present, even if in jail garb and shackles. There was little time for any sort of substantive conversation with the prosecutor. So Raine ambushed her in a courthouse hallway the day before. He could look up attorneys on the court's website too. Nakamoto had a pretrial on a different case that morning. Raine waited on a bench outside in the hall until she exited the negotiating room, on her way back to her office. Or so she thought.

"Ms. Nakamoto!" Raine called out as he stood up. "Emma!"

She turned to see who had called her name. When she saw Raine, she frowned.

"Do you have a moment to talk about the Willoughby case?" he asked.

"Don't we have readiness tomorrow?" she replied. "Can't we talk then?"

"Not really," Raine answered. "It'll be too late then."

Nakamoto took a moment, then sighed and stepped over to Raine. "Fine. Too late for what?"

"Too late for you to give my client the benefit of the doubt and consider another suspect," Raine answered.

"Who?" Nakamoto asked.

"David Smith," Raine answered, not without some flair. As much as those two words would allow, anyway.

Nakamoto stared at him for a beat. "I don't know who that is."

"Yeah, it's a pretty common name," Raine allowed. "David E. Smith III is another rich tech magnate. He was Jeremy's chief rival—in more ways than one."

Nakamoto took another beat, then pinched the bridge of her nose. "Look, Raine. You seem like a nice enough guy. I don't have anything against your client either. But I have a job to do, and Abigail Willoughby isn't my only case. If you've got something to tell me that I might actually care about, then please, I'm begging you, just tell me. I really don't have time for riddles."

"She was fucking him," Raine said. "They were having an affair. That's why Smith killed Jeremy. Jealous lover. Classic motive."

Raine didn't actually know that for sure, but it was a good story. He didn't need it to be true. He needed Nakamoto to think it might be true.

"They were getting divorced," Nakamoto pointed out. "Why not just wait until it was final? Or don't wait, fuck all you want, and let it become final on its own. I'm not seeing the motive."

"Well, I'm not saying it was a smart thing to do," Raine countered, "but murder is usually a crime of passion, right? It's rarely cold and calculating. It's losing it and smashing someone over the head with the heaviest object within arm's reach."

"That object was inside your client's home," Nakamoto pointed out. "Why would her new boyfriend be at her house with her estranged husband?"

"Maybe they were trying to air everything out," Raine suggested, "and things went sideways."

Nakamoto narrowed her eyes at Raine. "So your client was there? Is she willing to make a statement against this Smith guy?"

"Oh, no, she wasn't there." Raine waved the idea away. "She was down at Gas Works Park, crying her eyes out."

Nakamoto took a moment. "So what you're telling me is your client wasn't there, her new boyfriend confronted her soon-to-be ex-husband, in her house, she doesn't know why either of them were there, and the boyfriend killed the husband, but she didn't see it and can't provide any evidence to support it or help me convict him. Is that about right?"

Raine had to nod. "Yes."

"And this guy I'm supposed to charge with murder with no actual evidence," Nakamoto continued, "David E. Smith III. He's one of Seattle's richest and therefore, I assume, most powerful men?"

"Yes, I would think that's correct," Raine confirmed.

Nakamoto put a finger to her lips and nodded a few times before responding. "I realize I told you I needed a specific person to consider as a possible other suspect, so this is probably my fault. What I meant was *actual* evidence of a *credible* suspect. Not guesswork based on a weak motive and no witnesses. I hope you realize I don't want to convict your client of murder if she didn't actually do it, but you are giving me absolutely no reason to think anyone but her did it. You'd be better off claiming it was some random burglar who got surprised that someone was in the house and panicked."

"That's plan B," Raine admitted.

"Great." Nakamoto laughed. "You do that. Meanwhile, I'm going to answer ready tomorrow. Because I am. I'm ready to convict your client of murder. I hope you're ready for that too."

21

The readiness hearing went about as well as Raine expected, which was to say, it didn't go very well at all. The good news was that there wasn't much to decide at such a hearing, and therefore there wasn't much that could go wrong. But what there was to go wrong, did.

The hearing was scheduled again in the Criminal Presiding Courtroom, again with a dozen or more other cases also on the docket. Raine was there early. Nakamoto showed up shortly after him. The judge took the bench. Abigail was brought in from the holding cells again, and again she was wearing jail garb. She wouldn't get to dress in regular clothes again until the trial, when everyone would pretend to the jury that she wasn't being detained pretrial despite the presumption of innocence because the judge thought she was probably actually guilty and was afraid she would flee.

And Sommers was off doing her real job.

"The next matter is the *State of Washington versus Abigail Willoughby*," Judge Billingsley announced. He was still on his rotation in the presiding criminal courtroom. He wouldn't be the trial judge. That would be determined at the readiness hearing as well, assuming both sides were ready. "This matter is on for readiness. The trial is scheduled to begin next Monday. Ms. Nakamoto, is the State ready for trial?"

"The State is ready," Nakamoto confirmed.

"Mr. Raine, is the defense ready?"

Raine took a moment to look at Abigail. It didn't really matter if she was ready. He was. "Yes, Your Honor," he answered. "The defense is ready."

"Good," Billingsley said. "As I said, the trial is scheduled to begin next Monday. The parties are to report at nine a.m. to Judge Patel's courtroom."

Raine's already low mood dropped further. Patel was a former prosecutor who got himself appointed to the bench by sucking up to every important person he could find and promising to be the fair-minded judge everyone would want him to be. Raine could have admired the ambition, but once Patel reached his goal, he reverted to form and became almost an extension of the prosecutor's office. Patel wasn't going to order the jury to find the defendant guilty or anything quite that extreme, but Raine wasn't going to have any of his objections sustained either.

"Are there any other matters to be addressed before we call the next case?" Judge Billingsley asked.

Raine didn't have any. Unfortunately, Nakamoto did.

"There is one matter, Your Honor." She raised a professional hand toward the bench. She held a notepad in her other hand, outlining the argument she was about to make. "Mr. Raine informed me yesterday that he intended to introduce 'other suspect evidence' in the case, and it would be the State's position that such evidence is inadmissible. The law in Washington State dates back to at least 1932 in the case of *State v. Downs*, wherein our State Supreme Court ruled, and I quote, 'before such testimony can be received, there must be such proof of connection with the crime, such a train of facts or circumstances as tend clearly to point out someone besides the accused as the guilty party.' *Downs* and subsequent cases require, before such proffered evidence may be admitted, specific facts showing that the specific other suspect actually committed the crime. Speculation is insufficient."

Judge Billingsley frowned slightly at Nakamoto. "I'm sorry. Who is this alleged other suspect?"

"David E. Smith III," Nakamoto answered.

There was a quiet murmur through the lawyers and civilians gathered in the courtroom, but Raine was distracted from it by his client's very much not quiet demand, "What?!"

"David Smith?" Billingsley questioned. "The tech guy?"

"Yes, Your Honor," Nakamoto confirmed. "Mr. Raine informed me yesterday that there was a preexisting, well, relationship between the defendant and Mr. Smith, and that he believed Mr. Smith might be the person responsible for the murder. I asked for specific evidence to support this allegation, but he was unable to provide any. That being the case, Your Honor, he shouldn't be allowed to suggest it to the jury either."

"What the hell did you tell her?" Abigail demanded.

"I told her you didn't do it," Raine whispered back. "Was I incorrect about that?"

Abigail didn't answer. But Billingsley wanted an answer from Raine.

"Mr. Raine, is this correct?" the judge asked. "Did you make those statements? And do you intend to claim Mr. Smith was the true killer without any actual evidence to support that allegation?"

Raine took a moment. Trials were large, unwieldy things. They were organic, alive even. Once they started, they could and would go in directions no one anticipated, or directions that were anticipated and planned against but followed anyway. Raine didn't have enough information at that point to point the finger at Smith in open court, but that door could be opened quickly by the right answer from the right witness at the right time, maybe even days or weeks into the testimony. Raine didn't need to win anything right then; he just needed to avoid losing.

"I have no intention of introducing any evidence at trial that would be barred by the evidence rules or the case law," Raine answered carefully. "My negotiations with Ms. Nakamoto yesterday were nothing more than that: negotiations between lawyers, literally in the hallway. I understand the difference between such freewheeling hallway conversations and the strictures required for the formal presentation of evidence in a criminal trial. I would have thought Ms. Nakamoto understood that as well."

It was a calculated decision to throw a quick dig at his opponent at that moment. Divert attention from his allegedly ill intentions to her own failure to grasp the difference between negotiations and trial.

"Given the facts of this case, Your Honor," Raine continued, "any claim by the defense that Ms. Willoughby was not the killer is inherently a claim that someone other than her committed the crime. The defendant's death could not have been an accident or suicide. He was murdered by someone. We say that someone was not Ms. Willoughby. Logically, then, it must have been someone else. But I can and will assure this court right now that I will not introduce, or seek to introduce, any speculative evidence of any specific other possible suspect. If at some point I believe the evidence supports the introduction of specific other suspect evidence, then I will first seek the permission of Judge Patel to elicit such testimony."

He left unspoken the part where they all knew Patel would deny any such request, no matter how strong the evidence. But knowing that would be Patel's ruling gave Billingsley enough space to avoid ruling himself.

"Given Mr. Raine's representations that he does not intend to accuse Mr. Smith in his opening statement or anything like that," Billingsley said, "I believe this is an issue best handled by the trial judge, when and if it arises."

Raine was satisfied with that ruling. So was Nakamoto, it seemed from her expression. She had wanted to scare Raine off from, as Billingsley said, accusing David Smith in his opening statement. It didn't mean he couldn't do it later, but he was going to need the right people to say the right things. Raine looked at Abigail. Her expression was still one of anger. Raine wasn't going to be able to count on her saying it either. Plan B was starting to look like plan A, but the good news was that Nakamoto was so focused on keeping out evidence of Smith, she might forget to address the random homeless burglar angle. Trials had their own ebbs and flows. The attorney who could best ride those waves was usually the one who came out on top.

"If there is nothing further," Judge Billingsley declared, "the matter is adjourned until nine a.m. Monday morning."

Nakamoto hurried out of the courtroom, and Abigail, still upset, was only too glad to be escorted away by her jail guards. Raine took a breath. Trial was confirmed, finally. His client was innocent, probably. There was nothing left to do but to spend the weekend preparing his opening statement and hoping there were no more surprises before Monday morning.

22

R aine spent most of the weekend at his office. He was working on the trial, and he didn't much like his apartment anyway. There wasn't anything wrong with it particularly, but it wasn't the home he had shared with, then lost to, Natalie. It was a studio, which just reminded him he hadn't even found a place yet where his boys could spend the night. He needed to make that a priority. Right after the trial. He hoped.

But his hopes weren't faring too well right then. He had also hoped for no surprises over the weekend, but when he finally locked up his office late Sunday evening and headed toward his car, the only vehicle left in the lot behind the building, lit, poorly, by a single streetlamp on the next block, he was very much surprised by the three large men who stepped out of the shadows to cut off his path.

"Daniel Raine?" the one in the middle asked. The other two just stood there. They were all about the same size, smaller than Raine individually, but more than a match for him combined.

Each of them was dressed in black, and Raine couldn't

really make out their faces, backlit as they were from the distant streetlamp. They outnumbered him, and they had him cornered. He might get his ass kicked, but he wasn't going to be a coward about it.

"That's me," he confirmed. "How can I help you fine gentlemen on this dark night?"

"We're here on behalf of Mr. David Smith," the man in the middle continued.

Oh great, Raine thought. He was about to get roughed up by some rich asshole's goons. Again.

"I don't think beating up Abigail Willoughby's lawyer is going to make Mr. Smith look very innocent," Raine offered. "Just my two cents."

"Beating up?" the man in the middle stammered. "What? No. No."

He stepped forward, and Raine could finally make out his face. He didn't recognize him, but he was at least a decade older than Raine.

"I'm Duncan Mayfield," the man said. "This is Robert Jacobs and Elliott Anderson. We're attorneys for Mr. Smith."

"Attorneys?" Raine cocked his head.

"Yes. Here." Duncan Mayfield thrust a document at Raine. "This is a cease-and-desist letter. Mr. Smith learned that you were defaming him by suggesting that he was responsible for the murder of Jeremy Willoughby, and further that he was involved in an illicit relationship with Mr. Willoughby's wife."

"Abigail," Raine said, accepting the paper. "My client."

"Yes, yes," Mayfield agreed with a dismissive wave. "Regardless, you are hereby directed to refrain from any further defamatory statements under threat of civil action."

Raine looked down at the letter, but he couldn't make it out in the darkness. "You realize anything an attorney says in court is immune from a claim of defamation, right? I mean, you guys are big-shot lawyers from a firm that's probably charging Smith more for being here tonight than I charge all my clients in a year. You must realize this document is worthless."

"We realize that there are exceptions to every rule," Mayfield replied. "And where there aren't exceptions, we can ask the court to craft them. We also realize, as I'm sure do you, that Mr. Smith will be able to afford such litigation far longer than you and your solo practice ever could. If you wish to remain in business and not waste every penny defending a defamation suit funded by one of the deepest pockets in Seattle, you will keep Mr. Smith's name out of your mouth and out of your case. Is that understood?"

Raine looked again at the letter. He understood. He just didn't care.

He pushed his way between the street gang of lawyers and held the cease-and-desist letter aloft as he walked to his car.

"Thanks for dropping by, boys," he called out over his shoulder. "Now I know I'm onto something."

23

J udge Patel, in addition to being a prosecutor in a robe, was also a stickler for punctuality. Fortunately, Raine was aware of that. As the saying went, a good lawyer knows the law, but a great lawyer knows the judges. Raine got to Patel's courtroom at 8:45 a.m.

Nakamoto walked in a few minutes later. They exchanged greetings, but no small talk. Small talk was for distraction, and neither of them wanted to be distracted when the trial was about to start. Or at any point during the trial. And probably not afterward either, since one of them was going to lose and would hardly be in the mood to talk to the other about the weather or the Seahawks.

Abigail arrived next, only a few minutes before 9:00 a.m. The almost late arrival was a passive-aggressive way for the guards—that is, the government—to minimize the time a defendant has to speak with their attorney. She was again in handcuffs and surrounded by those guards, but she was dressed in an impeccably tailored suit. The guards undid her handcuffs, and she stood before Raine once again, the picture of a free woman. But they'd shoot her if she ran for the door.

"I still wish you hadn't dragged David's name into this," Abigail began, "but I understand why you did it."

Trial had a way of sharpening one's focus. It was the final act. If they lost, Abigail was going to die in prison.

"It didn't work anyway," she observed.

"Never say never," Raine counseled. "We haven't even started our case yet. There's plenty of time to smear everyone you've ever known and loved."

"Even Jeremy?"

Raine nodded. "Especially Jeremy."

Any further conversation was cut short by the call of the bailiff. "All rise! The King County Superior Court is now in session, the Honorable Rajesh Patel presiding."

Raine and Abigail were already standing. Nakamoto rose sharply to her feet. And Patel floated into place above them, black robes swirling. "Please be seated," he instructed. The job didn't seem to be aging him. His hair was still jet black, and there were few if any wrinkles on his medium brown skin.

Everyone sat down, and Judge Patel continued, "We are here on the matter of the *State of Washington versus Abigail Jane Willoughby*. Are both parties ready to begin the trial?"

Nakamoto stood up first. Lawyers always stood when addressing the judge, and prosecutors always answered first. "The State is ready," she confirmed.

Raine stood up next. Abigail started to follow him to her feet, but he stopped her with a gesture of his hand. "The defense is ready as well, Your Honor."

"Good," Patel responded. "Now, before we get started picking a jury and all of that, I want to make several things clear. First and foremost, this is my courtroom. Some prosecutors get used to running things in those high-volume courtrooms where they decide which cases to call next, but I am telling you right now, no prosecutor will be running things in my courtroom. And certainly no defense attorney ever will."

Of course not, Raine thought, but without changing his neutral facial expression.

"When I make a ruling, do not argue with me," Judge Patel continued. "If I choose to explain my ruling, it's a professional courtesy to you, not an invitation for further debate. If you argue with me, I will end my explanation. If you continue to argue, I will hold you in contempt. Your remedy is on appeal, not with me. I'm not one of those judges who rules for whoever gets in the last word. I am the last word. Is that understood?"

"Yes, Your Honor," Nakamoto stood up again to answer. "Of course, Your Honor."

Raine took a moment to stand again, offering the only response he could utter out loud. "Yes, Your Honor."

"Good," Patel said again. Raine expected to hear that word a lot whenever anyone agreed with the person whom, under law and procedure, everyone had to agree with. "Next, let me tell you how we are going to proceed today and for the rest of the week until we have a jury selected and sworn in..."

There were always housekeeping matters to be handled before the trial could actually begin. In a murder trial, it could take days to sort them out. Picking a jury alone could take a week or more. Most judges invited input and preferences from the attorneys.

But not Judge Patel. He told the lawyers what they were doing and didn't even end with an, "Is that understood?" Probably because one of them could say no and start advocating their position despite the judge's attempt to avoid exactly that.

So court would be in session from 9:00 a.m. to 5:00 p.m., with a one-hour lunch break, and two fifteen-minute breaks in the morning and afternoon, mostly to provide a rest for the court reporter's hands. There would be one hundred potential jurors. They would be questioned en masse. Each attorney would get to address the potential jurors for thirty minutes at a time, alternating. Challenges for cause would be brought up as soon as the potential bias became apparent. There would be twelve regular jurors and four alternate jurors. The alternate jurors would be designated in advance, but not told that they would be excused just before deliberations, lest they pay less attention than they should.

"And one more thing," Patel added after listing out the procedures he would be imposing, "Ms. Nakamoto has tried several cases in front of me, and of course we were once colleagues in the Prosecutor's Office."

Of course, Raine thought again. It was going to be a long trial.

"But I don't believe you've appeared before me previously, Mr. Raine."

Raine stood up. "I have not, Your Honor. I am looking forward to it, I can assure you."

Patel frowned slightly at Raine's comment. "We'll see about that. In any event, whenever I see a lawyer on my docket who's never appeared before me before, I ask around to see what I can learn about that lawyer and his case. One thing I learned, Mr. Raine, is that you may have plans to suggest or even name other possible suspects in this case, without having any evidence of such people being in any way actually connected to the crime charged. I want you to understand that I will not allow that to happen."

Raine wasn't surprised that Patel had spoken with Billingsley. But he was a little disappointed. Not at being called out; that was part of the job. But because he was in fact hoping he could try to sneak just that sort of accusation into his case. He had to. If he didn't give the jury an alternative suspect to Abigail, they would have no alternative verdict to guilty.

"My client has entered a plea of not guilty, Your Honor," Raine answered. "She did not commit the crime, and I am going to tell the jury that in my opening statement. Logically then, someone else must have done it. That being said, I understand the law and will not name a specific other suspect until and unless there is evidence to support such an accusation."

Patel frowned again, but nodded. "Have you ever read the *Downs* case, Mr. Raine? *State v. Downs*, the case that established that rule in Washington?"

"I'm sure I have, Your Honor," Raine replied, unsure whether he ever had, "but the details escape me at the moment."

"It's a great case, Mr. Raine," the judge replied conversationally. "One of those old-timey cases from back when Seattle was a small frontier town, not much more than the jumping-off point for people seeking their fortunes in Alaska. Like those old cases about when the police can search you. We use them for drug cases now, but in those days, the cops were searching people for gambling dice. Dice! Isn't that great?"

Raine nodded. "Great, Your Honor."

"And the *Downs* case was like that too," Patel went on. "There was a burglary where a safe was cracked, and this Downs guy did it, but his lawyers wanted to tell the jury that this other guy, who everyone called 'Madison Jimmy', was in town, and Madison Jimmy was a well-known safecracker, so maybe he did it. I love that this guy's name was 'Madison Jimmy', and I love that anyone could be 'a well-known safecracker'. Do you know any well-known safecrackers, Mr. Raine?"

"I do not, Your Honor," Raine admitted.

"Right. Neither do I," Patel answered, "and I've been doing this for decades."

Raine noted that by saying "this", Patel had combined being both a judge and a prosecutor, and that he didn't appear to appreciate their being any difference between the jobs.

"The court didn't let them tell the jury that Madison Jimmy, the well-known safecracker, was in town that night, Mr. Raine," Judge Patel continued, "and you don't get to tell them that either."

Raine considered making a quip about having no plans to accuse Madison Jimmy of Jeremy Willoughby's murder, but thought better of it. "Understood, Your Honor."

"Good," the judge said yet again. "I'll be watching you. We all will."

That last comment landed strangely for Raine, and he instinctively looked around the courtroom to see who else might be watching for references to Madison Jimmy. Trials weren't usually heavily attended, even murder trials, despite what one might see on television or in the movies. Usually the only people willing to sit through that long of an endeavor were the family of the victim, but Abigail was seated at the defendant's table, Lucas had cut ties with his father years earlier, and Bethany wasn't going to leave her luxury condo for days on end over the memory of the man who cheated on her. Raine didn't expect to see anyone other than maybe a random public defender or junior prosecutor interested in perhaps learning something from watching a trial, but those sorts of observers were unlikely to start appearing until it was time for opening statements. Even the reporters would wait until then. So Raine was surprised to see, when he scanned the courtroom, a single person seated in the very back row, who averted his eyes when Raine spotted him. He was an older man in a nondescript suit, with thinning gray hair fighting a losing battle atop his pink head. Raine wondered who he was, but wasn't going to get the chance to ask him. Judge Patel was still talking.

"I'm glad you understand, Mr. Raine," the judge went on. "Any violation of that order will result in a finding of contempt and you joining your client in the King County Jail. Is that understood?"

No one liked being threatened, but Raine was distracted enough by the man in the back of the courtroom to simply offer a quick acquiescence. "Of course, Your Honor. Whatever you say, Your Honor. Thank you, Your Honor."

And they were off. Judge Patel followed his plan. They began with motions in limine—the simple evidentiary and procedural motions that didn't require testimony, such as excluding witnesses during the testimony of other witnesses —and moved on to the questioning and selection of the jury. It took a week and a day, and for all of it, Abigail sat attentive and silent at Raine's side, dressed in a different stylish but tasteful suit with perfectly matched shoes each day. And for all of it, that unnamed balding man sat in the back of the courtroom in the same nondescript suit and dark tie. At the end of that week and a day, they had a jury, and Raine had had enough.

Judge Patel swore in the sixteen people in the jury box and sent them home for the day, to return the next morning for opening statements. When the jurors had left, the judge excused the parties and retired to his chambers himself. The guards handcuffed Abigail and escorted her back to her cell for the night. Nakamoto gathered up her things and hurried out without a word to her opponent. And Raine left his things on the defense table to confront the man in the back before he could exit the courtroom.

"Excuse me, sir." He reached out an arm to block the

doors. "Could you tell me who you are and what your interest in the case is?"

The man was several inches shorter than Raine. His suit was actually nicer than Raine had assessed from a distance. It was just old. The man's shoes matched: they looked like they had originally been expensive but had earned their value through years of shining and re-shining. He needed a fresh haircut.

"I could," the man answered in a voice deeper than Raine had expected, "but I won't."

"Why not?" Raine demanded.

"I don't answer to you," the man explained. "Now, if you'll excuse me—"

"Who do you answer to?" Raine pressed.

The man smiled. "If I told you that, then I'd be telling you those other things as well, now wouldn't I?"

Raine could hardly argue. That was why he'd asked.

"So unless you plan on physically restraining me," the man said, "I will be leaving now."

Raine hesitated, then stepped aside, and the man exited the courtroom. Raine frowned and took a moment. The bailiff and the court reporter had also left the room. He was alone.

He pulled out his phone and pressed the contact. "Hello? Rebecca? I've got a real private-eye job for you."

24

When they reconvened the next morning in Judge Patel's courtroom, promptly at 9:00 a.m., the man in the back of the courtroom wasn't there. Raine wondered whether Rebecca had actually managed to identify the man and, in so doing, scared him off. Raine was looking forward to hearing the details from his "private eye". The man's spot had been more than filled, however, by the reappearance of several reporters eager to record a sound bite from the prosecution's one-sided summary of the case.

"Ladies and gentlemen of the jury," Judge Patel announced when everyone was properly assembled and seated, "please give your attention to Ms. Nakamoto, who will deliver the opening statement on behalf of the state of Washington."

Nakamoto stood up and nodded to the bench. "Thank you, Your Honor. May it please the court, counsel, ladies and gentlemen of the jury." It was a formal introduction, archaic even. But jurors liked prosecutors who were formal. It meant they were taking their jobs seriously. If a criminal defense attorney was too formal, they would think him disingenuous, maybe even mocking. Raine couldn't pull off the "may it please the court" spiel, but that was okay. He never liked it anyway.

Nakamoto stepped out from behind the prosecutor's table and took up a position directly in front of the jury box. She straightened her suit coat. She took a breath. Then she began.

"Love. Betrayal. Anger. Greed. These are some of the strongest emotions we can feel as human beings. But extreme emotions can lead to extreme actions. Actions we never thought we were capable of, but actions we fully intended in the moment. Actions that are no less criminal for those emotions. Actions like murder."

She turned to point back at Abigail seated at the defense table next to Raine.

"Abigail Willoughby felt all of these emotions as she ended her decade-long marriage to her husband, Jeremy Willoughby. She loved him. Then she was betrayed by him. Then she was angry at him. And finally, all of those emotions merged with greed and entitlement and blind rage, and she murdered Jeremy in her own home. She literally smashed his skull in on her living room floor only hours after losing a hearing in divorce court and threatening him for all the world to hear. She loved him, but that love soured. She thought she was going to walk away a millionaire, but he betrayed her. She threatened him, and then she made good on that threat."

Nakamoto squared her shoulders to the jury box again. "And now we are all assembled here today because Abigail Willoughby carried out that threat. Abigail Willoughby murdered her husband, and during the course of this trial, we will prove that to you beyond any reasonable doubt."

Raine knew better than to make faces during an opposing counsel's opening statement. Any one of the jurors could be watching him for reactions. He kept his eyes lowered and took notes of what Nakamoto was saying. Not so much because he would ever refer back to them, but to give himself something to do and to look lawyerly for his audience in the jury box. But inside, he was frowning. Nakamoto's introduction was solid.

Nakamoto took a step to her right, indicative of a change in tone. Good trial attorneys didn't pace, and most prosecutors got enough practice to become good trial attorneys, especially by the time they had worked their way up to homicides.

"We are going to call a lot of witnesses in this case," she informed the jurors. "You're going to hear from police officers, including patrol officers and detectives. You're going to hear from forensic experts, like medical examiners and accountants. And you're going to hear from Jeremy's family, specifically his son and his ex-wife. And you will see documents, specifically a proposed divorce settlement and Jeremy Willoughby's last will and testament. Each of these pieces of evidence will tell you a different piece of the story, a different part of the tale of how and why Abigail Willoughby murdered her husband. But right here, right now, I can put all of those bits and pieces together and tell you the story from beginning to end. I can tell you what the evidence is going to show. And what it's going to show is that Abigail Willoughby is guilty of murder in the first degree."

Another step, back to her left, taking up that formal, in-command position directly in front of the jurors.

"Abigail Willoughby used to be Abigail Thompson. She met Jeremy Willoughby through mutual friends. They travelled in similar circles, or at least Abigail wanted to travel in Jeremy's circle. Jeremy Willoughby was a successful technology entrepreneur. He was also married. Not to Abigail. Not yet. He was married to a woman named Bethany, Bethany Carter-Willoughby. In fact, they had been married for almost fifteen years when Abigail met Jeremy, and they had a son who was just starting high school. Everything seemed to be going well for Jeremy and Bethany. It was everything Abigail wanted for herself. So she took it."

Raine stood up. "Objection, Your Honor," he interrupted, trying to sound annoyed rather than angry or, worse yet, afraid of what Nakamoto was saying. "Ms. Nakamoto is trying to smear my client's reputation with innuendo and conjecture about her romantic feelings a decade ago. This case isn't about how or when or why my client married her husband. It's about who murdered him, because it definitely wasn't her."

Patel pointed an angry finger at Raine. Raine was fine with that. He knew Patel was going to overrule any objection he made, but he didn't mind it if the jury started to get the feeling that the judge was being a little hard on him and maybe pulling a little too much for the prosecution.

"You will get your chance to make an opening statement, Mr. Raine," the judge barked. "Until then, you are to remain silent. Is that understood?"

Raine didn't answer. He couldn't promise not to object if the prosecutor said something objectionable. He had a job to do. Instead, he simply sat down again, signaling his acknowledgement that his objection had been, at least tacitly, overruled.

"Please continue, Ms. Nakamoto," Judge Patel instructed.

Nakamoto took a moment to nod to herself, then to the jury. "My opponent makes a fair point." She was good enough to not simply ignore Raine's objection, but to use it against him. "We aren't here for what Abigail Thompson-Willoughby did to start her marriage with Jeremy Willoughby. We're here for what she did to end it. I will let it suffice to say that Jeremy's marriage to Bethany had not ended prior to his relationship with Abigail beginning. Ms. Carter-Willoughby can tell you the rest when she testifies."

It didn't matter if Nakamoto said it out loud. The jurors knew what Bethany was going to say. Nakamoto moved on.

"Fast-forward ten years and what do we find?" Nakamoto asked rhetorically. "We find a marriage, once fresh and young and exciting, now on its last legs. Maybe it was Jeremy who didn't find Abigail fresh and young and exciting anymore. Or maybe that was how Abigail felt about Jeremy. The one thing we do know is that Abigail decided to divorce Jeremy. And she wanted half of his fortune. The fortune he had built before he married her."

Say my client is a gold digger without saying she's a gold digger, Raine thought.

"There was only one small problem," Nakamoto continued, "and that problem was the prenuptial agreement Abigail signed before marrying Jeremy. It's standard practice to execute a prenuptial agreement when a rich person marries someone who is maybe not so rich. That's even more true when the rich person is exceedingly rich and the not-so-rich person is, well, very not so rich. That was the case with Jeremy and Abigail. And after Jeremy finalized his divorce from Bethany—which she filed, by the way, for the reasons she'll tell you—Jeremy was not going to get married again without a prenup. Abigail gladly signed it. Then ten years later, she tried to get out of it. She failed. Then she..." Nakamoto held up a hand to the jurors. "But I'm getting ahead of myself."

Nakamoto was a good storyteller, Raine had to give her that. He knew he'd need to be at least as compelling. He also knew that would be a challenge without being able to name a specific person as the star of his "Who Murdered Jeremy Willoughby?" show.

"Let's take a moment to be very clear about the options the defendant was facing when she decided to file for divorce from her husband." Nakamoto took another practiced step, this time to her left. A change in tone again, but instead of more familiar like last time, it was more businesslike. Factual. Bullet points.

"First, she could have filed for divorce, accepted the financial settlement she agreed to in the prenuptial agreement, and moved on with her life. She rejected that result.

"Second, she could have filed for divorce, fought the financial settlement she agreed to in the prenuptial agreement, won that fight, and walked away with half of Jeremy's fortune. That was the result she wanted.

"Third, she could have filed for divorce, fought the financial settlement she agreed to in the prenuptial agreement, and lost that fight and get only what she agreed to minus tens of thousands of dollars in legal fees. That was the option she was staring at the morning of the murder, when she went to court, asked the judge to throw out the prenuptial agreement, and lost."

That wasn't entirely accurate, Raine knew, but it was close. And it wasn't like Patel was going to sustain his objection. Raine would just clarify in his own opening statement.

"Or fourth…" Nakamoto trailed off. She stepped back in front of the jury. "The only way Abigail Willoughby was going to get any substantial portion of Jeremy's fortune was if she was still married to him when he died. If she inherited it through Jeremy's will, which still listed Abigail as the only beneficiary for his entire estate. And she would need to hurry. If she went back to him, he was certainly going to make her sign an even more restrictive prenuptial agreement—technically called a postnuptial agreement since it's executed after the marriage rather than before it. And he was probably going to change his will too. Maybe leave it all to his son or, worse, his ex-wife, who he probably had feelings for. Feelings can linger even after a divorce."

Natalie's face flashed through Raine's mind. He forced it

away with a grimace. He shook his head slightly to stay focused on Nakamoto.

"So again, the defendant had four options, but two of them were gone after the very first hearing in her divorce case." Nakamoto held up four fingers, but lowered two of them as she spoke. "File for divorce and accept the prenuptial agreement: gone. File for divorce, fight the prenuptial agreement and win: gone. File for divorce, continue to fight the prenuptial agreement, lose, get nothing and owe a bunch of legal fees: still very much on the table. In fact, the most likely option. Or four: end the marriage a different way. End it while still married to Jeremy. Murder Jeremy. And that's the option she chose."

Raine understood the logic of Nakamoto's argument, as the jury did as well, he was sure, but it was missing something. People didn't usually do a cost-benefit analysis when deciding to murder someone. Unfortunately, Nakamoto knew that too.

"Now, I'm not suggesting the defendant went home and wrote all of this out on a whiteboard and then decided to murder the man she'd spent the last ten years of her life with. Rather, what I'm suggesting is that, at some level, she was aware of how things were going. Even if she didn't fully grasp it on a whiteboard level, she understood it at an emotional level. That's why, after she lost that hearing, she went out into the hallway and in front of everyone there, in this very courthouse, she shouted at Jeremy and threatened him. She told him, 'You're not going to get away with this', and 'I'm going to be the one who makes sure you don't get away with it'. And she told him it was 'a promise'. She may not have known what she was going to do, but she was starting to feel it.

"And then he came to her home that night."

Very ominous, Raine thought sarcastically, *but also accurate.*

Jeremy definitely went to Abigail's home that night. There was no denying that.

"And he came with that new financial agreement I was talking about," Nakamoto continued. "It wasn't a postnup. They weren't getting back together. It was a divorce settlement. One for less than what she was entitled to under the prenup. But if she signed it, he'd pay all of her legal bills. They'd be divorced, but she would get almost nothing. Just some stock options. He had won. She'd set the game in motion, but he'd won, just like he always did. Just like he did when they first met and he dropped Bethany for her, and just like he was about to do when he dropped her too. She probably wondered if there was a new woman already waiting in the wings. Maybe even waiting in the car. We don't know. We don't know exactly what she was thinking. But we know what she had been feeling that morning because she screamed it across the courthouse lobby. And we know what she was feeling that night because she picked up a heavy marble statuette and slammed it against the back of Jeremy's head."

Well, somebody did, Raine thought.

"Jeremy fell forward onto the floor," Nakamoto half-pantomimed what happened next, leaning forward like Jeremy, then straightening up again to act like Abigail standing over him. "We don't know if he was still conscious, but we do know he was in no condition to defend himself. You're going to see that marble statuette, the one that ended Jeremy Willoughby's life. It's heavy and it's sharp. And Abigail smashed it into Jeremy's skull again. And again. And again.

"The medical examiner is going to tell you that there were at least seven blows to the back of Mr. Willoughby's head," Nakamoto told the jurors. "And the forensic experts who examined the crime scene are going to tell you that the blood spatter on the walls indicated that Mr. Willoughby was already motionless on the floor when most of those blows were struck. The first, unexpected blow, with his back to the defendant, rendered him helpless. Then Abigail Willoughby made a decision. She chose option number four. She didn't take Jeremy's offer. She took his life. In those moments, she made a conscious premeditated decision to kill her husband. She chose violence. She chose murder."

Nakamoto centered herself in front of the jurors again. She straightened her suit again. And she brought her story to a close.

"So, ladies and gentlemen of the jury, at the end of this trial, after you've heard all of the evidence, I'm going to stand before you again and ask you to return a verdict of guilty to the crime of murder in the first degree. Thank you."

She turned and walked crisply back to her seat at the prosecution table.

She had done a very good job. Raine had to do better.

He ignored the fact that the reporters were already filing out of the courtroom before he'd said a single word. They only wanted the official story. That was fine with Raine. They weren't his audience anyway.

"Now, ladies and gentlemen of the jury," Judge Patel said almost begrudgingly, "please give your attention to Mr. Raine, who will deliver the opening statement on behalf of the defendant, Abigail Willoughby."

25

Ask a dozen trial lawyers what the most important stage of a trial was and you'd get a dozen different answers. There were those who swore you won or lost your case in closing argument. Others were convinced it was the first witness. Some even claimed the case would be won or lost in jury selection, a proposition Raine had felt was the most outlandish. In his opinion, every stage was important, and it was the sum of them that would determine the outcome. But if there was one stage that was more equal than the rest, it was the opening statement. You couldn't win a case in the opening statement, but you could definitely lose it.

As Nakamoto had told the jurors, the witnesses would be coming in piecemeal, to tell their little slice of the story. There was only one time when the entire story could be told from beginning to end, let alone by an experienced and passionate narrator with a professional interest in the outcome. That was the opening statement. Whoever told the better story had a significant leg up once those disjointed snippets of testimony started being extracted from a series of inarticulate or even hostile witnesses. Nakamoto had told a cohesive story, compelling and believable, featuring realistic characters with relatable motivations. It was too bad Raine couldn't do the same.

Raine's defense was the classic "SODDI defense"—some other dude did it. And he wasn't even allowed to say who that other dude was, largely because he didn't know himself. But he didn't have any other story to offer—what the career defense attorneys called a "counternarrative". There was no great tale to be spun about Abigail sitting in her car alone while some unknown assailant murdered her husband inside her home.

If one lawyer stood up and told a credible story and the other side stood up and said, "Oh yeah? Prove it", the jury knew immediately the story was true. Raine couldn't just hide behind the presumption of innocence and proof beyond reasonable doubt. There lay the refuge of the guilty. Raine couldn't leave it at that, but he didn't have a counternarrative. He needed to connect with them, and he knew how to do it.

Jurors on a weeks-long murder case were a relatively homogenous group. They needed to be able to take a lot of time off and not worry about losing their jobs or shuttling their kids to school and activities and doctor appointments. And they took the jury summons seriously enough to show up and agree to sit on a jury despite the interruption it would have to their daily lives. Maybe because of it. That meant, generally speaking, they were older. They were retired or had saved up a lot of leave time. Their kids were grown and could take care of themselves. The only thing a trip to the court-house would interrupt was the daily boredom of their other-wise quiet and empty lives.

They had been married, and over half of the marriages in the United States ended in divorce. Of those remaining, a healthy percentage probably suffered from the same maladies and deficiencies that led others to call it quits. Raine couldn't offer the jurors a counternarrative. But he could offer them the truth.

He stood up, thanked the judge without the "may it please the court" language, and took up the same spot Nakamoto had claimed for her opening statement.

"Divorce," he began, almost scoffing at the word. "The prosecutor just told you that the motive for this murder was divorce. She told you that this was a crime of passion, forged in the fire of love and anger and whatever else she said at the beginning of her comments. Passion. From a divorce. Ha."

Raine shook his head. "The only thing that tells me is the prosecutor has no idea what a divorce is really like." He sighed. "Unfortunately, I do."

Raine wasn't one to talk about his personal problems. But he was one to give his all for his client. Abigail Willoughby had told him she was innocent. The least he could do was tell the jury why.

"Divorce isn't about passion," Raine continued. "Divorce is about the loss of passion. It's about the death of passion. It's about whatever small ember of passion that might still remain being extinguished by the process and formality and bloodlessness of going to court and obtaining a piece of paper that finally and formally terminates the strongest feelings of joy you'd ever experienced.

"Divorce is about the torment of remembering the passion that no longer exists. The passion from that first meeting, the first eye contact, the first brush of a hand on an arm. The passion of the first kisses, the first nights together when time didn't matter and you tried everything you could think of, laughing when it didn't work and exploding when it did. The passion that made you never want to be apart from that other person. The passion that made you ask them to never leave you. The passion of saying yes when they ask you that. The passion of finding the perfect person for you, and of being that perfect person for them too."

Raine took a moment to swallow. His mouth was drier than he expected. He hadn't poured himself a cup of water before starting. He didn't pause to do it then.

"Divorce is about that passion slowly ebbing away, so slow sometimes, you don't even notice. So fast other times, you can't help but notice. It's about realizing that perfect person never helps you with the dishes. It's about them realizing you never finish projects you promise to finish. It's about sick kids and late bills and bodies that age and change and expand and sag. It's about passion being replaced by exhaustion, by resentment, and worst of all, by indifference. It's about how, even after all that, even when you both know it's over and you agree it's over and you hire lawyers to make it be over, how, even after all that, there's still a small, stubborn, ridiculous spark in your gut that fights to stay alive. It's about going back to your office and finding your wife, the woman you loved more than you thought you could ever love anyone, waiting for you, one of your kids sitting next to her and your other kid in the car, the final divorce papers in her hands. Divorce is about how your gut burns when you sign the order, and she leaves, and that last spark of passion dies. Divorce is about the dull, passionless hole that remains."

Raine took a moment to come to the surface of his remarks and assess how they were landing. To be sure, there were a few jurors looking at him like he had lost his mind. But there were far more who wore expressions of understanding, even fellowship. Sixteen middle-aged and older people in a box. That meant, statistically, eight of them were divorced. Three or five more wished they were. Raine had connected with them. He just needed to explain why it mattered.

"Divorce isn't about passion," he repeated. "It's the opposite of passion. It's pain and loss and grief and failure and loneliness. Do you want to know where Abigail Willoughby was after she lost in court that morning? First you need to understand what she lost. She didn't lose some motion about a prenuptial agreement. She didn't lose money. She lost her husband. She lost her last unspoken hope that he might beg her to stay, to try to work it out, to fix things."

He looked back at his client—compassionately, he hoped —then back to the jury.

"They say when a couple gets divorced, one of them has a psychological advantage because they've been thinking about it and preparing to ask for the divorce, while the other person never saw it coming. They didn't know the towels on the floor were that big a deal. They would have taken the kids to more doctor appointments. They didn't know it was over. They don't want it to be over. They promise to pick up the towels and finish the projects and see a doctor about the snoring. They beg the person—*their* person, they thought—to stay. Sometimes it even works out. But not always. Not even usually. But the person who files for divorce can expect that kind of reaction. In fact, they might even want it."

Another glance back at Abigail.

"So when Jeremy Willoughby not only agreed to the divorce Abigail initiated, but doubled down on it by wanting to enforce an agreement they had entered into before ten years of living, loving, and growing together, Abigail wasn't angry. She was hurt. She was sad.

"Did she lash out and yell at him immediately afterward? Yes. And I would submit to you that no one with an actual intent to harm someone else would broadcast that in a courthouse. But do you know what she did afterward? Do you know what she did when she realized the passion was gone, the fairy tale was over, her once mighty love would be reduced to nothing more than a dull ache when she heard his name or imagined his face? She cried."

That was believable, Raine knew. He really knew.

"She left her house and drove to where she used to go when she was sad when she was younger. When she was a teenager and feelings were always just too big. She drove to Gas Works Park, and she sat in her car, and she cried because her marriage was really over. The kind of crying where you let yourself feel all the things you didn't even realize you weren't letting yourself feel. The kind of crying you don't want anyone else to see. The first honest cry in a very, very long time. And when she was done, she went home again. She thought she was going home to straighten the kitchen and turn down the bed and get ready for the next day, not confident in what it might hold but resigned to face it anyway. But instead she came home to police cars and flashing lights, to a dead man in her home and hand-cuffs on her wrists. I wish I could tell you who murdered Jeremy Willoughby. I wish I could tell you why Jeremy was inside Abigail's home when she wasn't even there. I wish I could tell you what happened that night, but I can't. Because Abigail wasn't there. She doesn't know. So I don't know either."

Raine gestured at Nakamoto. "But the prosecutor also doesn't know. Not really. She told you a compelling story, but it was all made up. All she knows is someone murdered Jeremy Willoughby and it happened in my client's home. Everything else is a guess or, worse, fiction. Like the idea that divorce is about passion.

"Abigail Willoughby wasn't overcome by some murderous rage. She was overcome by the sadness that truly accompa-nies divorce. That's the truth. And she didn't murder her husband. That's the truth too. So, at the end of this trial, I'm going to ask you to return the only true verdict: not guilty. Thank you."

Raine turned and walked back to the defense table. He didn't make eye contact with anyone on his way and didn't look to see if anyone was in the gallery to witness his confessional. But when he sat down, Abigail squeezed his arm. "I'm sorry you felt like you had to tell everyone all that. But thank you for doing it."

Raine patted her hand. "Let's just hope it was worth it."

He felt confident he hadn't lost the case in his opening statement, but there was plenty of time for that.

"We will take our morning recess now," Judge Patel announced before departing the bench. "Please be ready to reconvene in fifteen minutes to begin the testimony of the State's first witness."

The bailiff called everyone to their feet, and the jurors filed into the jury room. Raine was debating whether to use his time to check in with Abigail further, organize his notes for the cross-examination of that first witness, or run to the restroom. Then he saw Sommers in the back of the courtroom.

"I'll be right back, Abigail," he said. "I want to check in with Rebecca."

"Maybe she found the real killer," Abigail quipped.

Raine almost wouldn't put it past Sommers, but he wasn't going to hold out any hope for such an expeditious ending to the trial.

"Wow," Sommers said when he reached her. "Overshare much?"

Raine shrugged off the criticism. "Do you believe she cried alone in her car?"

"I believe you sure did," Sommers answered.

Raine decided to change the subject. "Did you figure out who that guy in the back of the courtroom was?"

"Is," Sommers corrected. "He was here for your therapy session, too, but stepped out when the judge called the recess."

"So who is he?"

"Edwin Plunkett," Sommers answered. "Certified CPA and inactive member of the Washington State Bar Association."

"Wow, okay. Cool." Raine appreciated the information. "How did you figure that out? Did you trail him to his office? Run his name through some sort of sales database?"

"Nope. I asked him."

Rain cocked his head. "Seriously?"

"Yep," Sommers confirmed. "I just followed him to the coffee cart in the lobby and struck up a conversation. Everybody likes to talk about themselves. Ask a person about themselves and they'll tell you their life story if you let them. He didn't know I had anything to do with the case, so he had no reason to hide anything from me. Although I did have to look him up on the Bar Association website to confirm he was inactive. He hasn't practiced law for five years now."

Raine was impressed by Sommers's grasp of human nature. But there were questions remaining. "What's an accountant with a law degree doing sitting in on this trial? Who does he work for?"

"Himself, near as I can tell," Sommers answered. "Someone must have hired him to monitor the case."

"He didn't tell you that part of his life story?"

Sommers shook her head. "Nope. When I tried to probe into who had hired him, he clammed up. That's part of it, though. He was showing me what a reliable professional he is. And important, too. Like a secret agent."

"Or a private eye," Raine returned with a grin. "Thanks."

Sommers returned the smile. "So what now?"

"Now," Raine said, "I have to pee. Then the first witness. Let's see if I can top that opening statement."

Sommers shook her head. "Only way you top that is with a therapy couch and a valium."

26

Nakamoto stood after the recess to announce, "The State calls Jillian Crenshaw to the stand."

There were a few different ways for the prosecution to start a murder case. If it was a simple assault case, then it was easy: you start with the victim. The victim tells the jury what happened, and if they do it well enough, the rest of the testimony isn't really all that important. Kind of like painting the face first in a portrait. If you nail the likeness, it doesn't matter if the folds in the shirt don't look quite right. But in a murder case, the victim was in no condition to speak to the jury. That meant introducing the victim through a surrogate, and there were basically two choices of which victim to introduce first: the live one or the dead one. The prosecutor could start with a member of the victim's family to introduce a photograph of the victim at some happy time prior to their death. Or that first photograph of the victim could be what Nakamoto had opted for: the victim dead on the floor of the crime scene.

Detective Jillian Crenshaw entered through the doors at the back of the courtroom and made her way to the front to he sworn in by Judge Patel. She was forty-something, Raine guessed, with dark blonde hair and a strong build. She wore a blazer over a button-up shirt. Her badge was on her leather gun belt, which creaked as she sat down on the witness stand after swearing to tell the truth, the whole truth, and nothing but the truth.

"Please state your name for the record," Nakamoto began. There was a series of introductory questions the prosecutor always asked of each new witness. Name, rank, and badge number.

"Jillian Crenshaw," came the answer.

"And how are you employed?"

"I'm a detective with the Seattle Police Department," she answered.

"How long have you been a detective with the Seattle Police Department?"

And so it went. Nakamoto asking questions she already knew the answers to, and Crenshaw slowly reciting her résumé to the jury. When it was done, everyone knew Crenshaw had been a cop for sixteen years, a detective for nine of those, and assigned to the homicide and major crimes unit for the last three and half. She knew what she was doing.

Ordinarily, that might have bothered Raine. Usually the defense attorney attacked the lead detective. He hadn't encountered Crenshaw before, but she seemed pleasant enough. He wasn't particularly interested in attacking her, but he would if necessary. The thing was, Raine doubted it would be necessary. Crenshaw was going to describe the crime scene. Raine could hardly contest that Jeremy Willoughby had been violently murdered in Abigail's home. Attacking that would make him look like he would attack anything and therefore none of his attacks mattered. Instead, he expected to use Crenshaw to his advantage. Maybe they could even be friends afterward.

Nakamoto moved on to the actual case at hand. "Could you tell us how you came to be involved in the investigation regarding the death of Jeremy Willoughby?"

"Of course," Crenshaw replied. She turned to the jury to deliver her answer. Cops were taught to do that at the academy. It made the jurors feel more included, which made them like the witness, which made them want to convict. *Ah, due process*, Raine thought with a small shake of his head.

"The call came in shortly after eighteen hundred hours," Crenshaw began, then remembered to translate. "That's six p.m. Sorry."

Raine suspected the lapse into cop talk was intentional. She pulled it off in a very endearing way. They probably taught that at the academy too.

"It was an anonymous call," Crenshaw continued, "from a blocked number. They reported 'trouble unknown' at 4406 Larkspur Drive in Seattle, then hung up."

Raine was familiar with the call.

"That's the Madison Park neighborhood?" Nakamoto asked.

"It is," Crenshaw confirmed.

"And why were you, as a homicide detective, dispatched to a 'trouble unknown' call?" Sometimes the lawyers had to ask the questions they knew the jurors were wondering.

"Good question," Crenshaw replied. "The answer is, I wasn't. Patrol officers were dispatched, but when they arrived and saw what they were dealing with, they called the major crimes unit."

"And what were they dealing with?" Nakamoto prompted.

"A murder," Crenshaw answered. She looked again to the jurors. "Definitely a murder."

Then it was time for the crime scene photos. A picture was worth a thousand words, and crime scene photos were probably worth more than that. It was hard to fully describe a murder scene, especially one as violent and bloody as Jeremy Willoughby's murder. The best way to really burn the images into the deepest parts of the jurors' brains was to project the photo onto a three-foot-tall screen and have the detective describe what they were all looking at.

Raine had already seen the carnage up close and personal. The photos weren't particularly shocking to him. But he knew they would be to Abigail, and that was why he had never shown them to her. Not just because it would have been traumatizing to see your husband's beaten and bloody body for the first time, but because Raine wanted that reaction to happen in front of the jury. The jurors were going to look immediately from the first bloody crime scene photo to Abigail, if only because they assumed she was guilty and wanted to see the person who had committed such an atrocity. He wanted them to see her react with the same horror and disgust they felt. More in fact, because she had loved the man, even at the end, as Raine had tried to explain in his opening statement. If she didn't react strongly enough because she had already seen the photos with Raine, the jurors might reasonably conclude she wasn't reacting strongly enough because she had witnessed the scene with her own eyes, standing over Jeremy's dead body with a bloody statuette in her hand.

"Oh my God!" Abigail shrieked. She buried her face in her hands and began crying, her body racked by the sobs.

Perfect, Raine thought. He placed a comforting hand on her back, but only because the jurors were looking. The last thing he wanted was for her to stop.

Nakamoto seemed surprised by the outburst as well. Unprepared, anyway. She hesitated, unsure how to proceed with her questioning with the courtroom filled by the defendant's sobbing.

"Um…" she said after a few moments. "Perhaps we should take a recess?"

One thing Raine had noted about Nakamoto in their limited interactions was that she seemed to be a decent person. A worse person would have assumed Abigail's reaction was an act, rolled her eyes, and pressed ahead, raising her voice to shout at the detective to go ahead and describe the grisly murder scene. But Nakamoto's instinct was to give Abigail a moment. That signaled at least the possibility that Abigail's reaction was genuine.

"I think that's a good idea." Raine stood to agree with Nakamoto's suggestion. "Perhaps ten minutes for my client to compose herself, Your Honor?"

Judge Patel frowned. He would have been the prosecutor who shouted over the sobs. "Five minutes. No more. We have a lot of witnesses to get through in this trial. We aren't going to take a break in the middle of every one of them."

Raine didn't need any more breaks. He'd already won the first witness.

The jurors were excused to their jury room, the judge left the bench, and Crenshaw and Nakamoto stayed seated in their respective locations. Raine put his hand on Abigail's back again. "Are you going to be okay?"

Abigail had managed to reduce her sobbing to more of a whimper. She wiped her nose with the back of her hand. "I'm sorry. I just, I had no idea. I mean, I heard the descriptions, but to see Jeremy like that… I just… I'm sorry."

Raine smiled slightly. "Never be sorry for being authentic. I'm sorry I didn't prepare you better," he lied. "Take a minute, and then we'll get back to it. The judge is right. This is going to be a long trial."

Abigail sighed and sniffled loudly, sucking her sadness back up her nose. "I thought I knew what to expect. I was wrong."

218   STEPHEN PENNER

Raine nodded. That was trial work.

After the break, the rest of Crenshaw's direct examination was uneventful. She was able to walk the jury through the crime scene, with only minimal sniffling from Abigail. She explained what a lead detective does at a major crime scene, which consisted mostly of delegating important tasks to the experts who did those tasks. Then they came to what the law enforcement types called "suspect contact". Abigail had arrived home while the cops were still there, but as soon as she realized what was going on, she'd declined to answer any questions. Smart. And problematic for the prosecution. Nakamoto wasn't allowed to tell the jury that she had invoked her right to remain silent. That would be a comment on that right and an invitation to draw an adverse inference from it. Only guilty people refuse to talk to the police, right? Maybe, but the prosecutor couldn't argue that to the jury. That meant Nakamoto had to pretend any effort at questioning never took place.

"Did you have any contact with the defendant that evening?"

"Yes," Crenshaw answered.

"Where did that take place?"

"Outside the residence."

"And eventually, based on all of the evidence, did you place Ms. Willoughby under arrest for the murder of her husband?"

Crenshaw nodded and looked again to the jury. "I did."

"No further questions, Your Honor," Nakamoto announced.

It was finally Raine's turn.

Cross-examination was one of the harder aspects of trial work. There were entire seminars offered on the subject. The keys to effective cross-examination were focused inquiry, leading questions, and using the expected testimony to advance your theory of the case. Ineffective cross-examination would start at the top and challenge everything the witness said. Not only was that unlikely to succeed, especially with an experienced professional witness like a homicide detective, it also provided the jury with a rerun of the State's case. Raine didn't need them to hear Crenshaw repeat everything she had already said, just in case they missed something. He needed them to think there was potentially a problem with the State's case. He needed to strike fast and hard and sit down again. Nothing exuded confidence like a limited cross-examination on a specific subject. And it wasn't like Raine was challenging the fact that Jeremy Willoughby had been murdered inside Abigail's home. He just needed the jury to think maybe she wasn't the one who did it, despite appearances.

"Ms. Willoughby was not at the home when police arrived, correct?" He began his questioning even as he stepped out from behind his table and approached the witness.

"That's correct," Crenshaw confirmed.

"And it's common, is it not, that a murderer leaves the scene of the murder before police arrive?" Raine followed up.

"Very common," Crenshaw agreed.

"In fact, that's what usually happens, isn't it?" Raine asked.

"Yes," Crenshaw answered. "We don't usually have the murderer still standing over the victim when we arrive. My job would be a lot easier if that was what normally happened."

There were a couple of light chuckles from the jury box at that comment. Nothing too loud. It was a murder trial, after all, but they liked Crenshaw. That was okay. Raine liked her fine too.

"It is uncommon, though," he put to her, "that a murderer

would return to the scene of the crime while the police were still actively investigating it. Wouldn't you agree, Detective?"

Crenshaw took a moment. "Well, we've all heard of the suspect going back to the scene of the crime, but I would have to agree that it doesn't happen very often that they do so while we're still there. It's usually before the police detect the crime, maybe to clean up possible evidence, or after the police have left, to sort of gloat over it."

Raine nodded along. "In fact, you've never had another case where the prime suspect returned to the scene of a murder while the police were still actively investigating the crime scene, have you, Detective?"

Raine was taking a risk with that question, but it was a calculated risk. He thought the answer was going to be what he wanted, but even if it wasn't, he expected to be able to draw a distinction between whatever that case was and Abigail's case.

"I had one shooting," Crenshaw recalled after a moment, "where the shooter came back to the bar to surrender himself. He was a young kid. Barely eighteen. Got into an argument in the parking lot and shot the other party. He went home and told his mother what happened, and she made him come back and turn himself in."

Another few light chuckles from the jury box.

"But that's not what happened here, is it?" Raine asked. Then, before Crenshaw could draw any actual parallels between the two situations, he changed the question. "When Ms. Willoughby arrived at the residence, it was more like a homeowner returning to find her home burglarized, rather than the burglar turning himself in, wasn't it?"

Crenshaw frowned slightly. "I'm not sure, counsel. I wasn't the first person to speak with her. I just know that based on everything I saw, I placed her under arrest."

Raine thought that sounded like a pretty big jump to a pretty big conclusion. He hoped the jury agreed.

"Where did she go?" Raine asked. "And why did she come back?"

Raine knew Crenshaw didn't know the answers to those questions. He just wanted the jury to know it too.

"We believe she may have left the scene to dispose of evidence," Crenshaw answered, "then returned to perhaps clean up the scene before the police arrived, but it was too late."

"You believe?" Raine repeated. "So you're guessing."

"It's more of a deduction, counsel," Crenshaw insisted.

"A deduction?"

"Yes."

"Which is a fancy word for guess," Raine challenged. "What evidence would there be to get rid of? The murder weapon was left at the scene."

"Well, that's just it," Crenshaw answered. "We don't know what she got rid of because she got rid of it. Maybe it was just to change clothes."

"Change clothes, but then return to clean up the scene and get the new clothes bloody too?" Raine questioned.

Crenshaw shrugged. "These are just working theories, counsel."

"Guesses," Raine repeated. "Okay then, why would she stop and contact the police if she knew what was inside? Wouldn't you expect her to just keep driving? Maybe all the way to Canada, even?"

Crenshaw shrugged. "I try not to guess why a murderer would do what they do."

Raine crossed his arms and cocked his head slightly at Crenshaw. "Actually, Detective, that's all you do. No further questions."

Raine turned and walked back to sit down next to his

client, who offered a "good job" pat on his arm. Nakamoto had the option to conduct redirect examination, to follow up on and try to rebut anything Raine had asked about. But he'd kept his questioning short, and even after all of the Q&A by both attorneys, the moment that stood out the most from Crenshaw's time on the stand was when Abigail burst into tears. A few more questions wouldn't change that.

"No redirect, Your Honor," Nakamoto stood to inform the judge.

Patel seemed disappointed, likely in Nakamoto, and frowned. "All right then. May the witness be excused?"

Whenever a witness finished testifying, the judge could either excuse them from any further testimony—in which case a new subpoena would be needed to compel their return —or dismiss them "subject to recall", meaning the original subpoena was still in force and they were still considered a potential witness for later in the trial.

"We would ask the detective to remain subject to recall," Nakamoto answered. Prosecutors always had the lead detective be subject to recall, just in case.

"No objection to that, Your Honor," Raine concurred.

Crenshaw departed the courtroom, for the time being anyway, and Judge Patel looked down at Nakamoto. "Call your next witness."

"The State," Nakamoto announced, "calls Marshal Eric Bautista."

The guard who had been standing guard outside the divorce courtroom, Raine knew. It was going to be a long trial.

27

Raine recognized Bautista as soon as he walked into the courtroom, passing the exiting Detective Crenshaw in the doorway. Nakamoto had her witnesses lined up and waiting in the hallway. She was good at her job, Raine would give her that.

Bautista was wearing the same marshal's uniform he had been sporting the day he had to step between Abigail and Jeremy. Hell, he was probably doing the same thing that day and just testifying on his break before heading back downstairs. His calm demeanor from that morning was still there as well, as he strolled comfortably to the front of the courtroom to be sworn in. He took the witness stand, and Nakamoto began her questioning.

"Please state your name for the record."

It was the same name, rank and badge number routine. Except instead of Jillian Crenshaw, detective, it was Eric Bautista, courthouse marshal. He told the jurors the same story Raine had watched unfold in person. He had been working as security outside the main family law courtroom. A man later identified as Jeremy Willoughby departed the courtroom with his lawyers after his hearing. He appeared to be in good spirits. Shortly after that a woman later identified as Abigail Willoughby, the defendant, and her lawyer, the same guy in the courtroom with her today, came out of the courtroom. She did not appear to be in good spirits. Words were exchanged, and eventually Abigail shouted a series of threats at Jeremy.

"What did she say exactly?" Nakamoto asked. "If you recall."

Bautista frowned slightly. "To the best of my recollection, she yelled, 'You're not going to get away with this!' and 'I'm not going to let you get away with this!'"

Nakamoto's mouth tightened. "Anything else?" she prodded.

"Oh, and 'You're going to get what you deserve!' and either 'That's a promise' or 'I promise you that' or something about it being a promise."

Nakamoto's expression relaxed. She had extracted what she needed. "Thank you, Marshal. No further questions, Your Honor."

Raine stood up and approached Bautista even as Nakamoto returned to her seat.

"A promise?" he repeated.

"Right," Bautista confirmed.

"Like when someone says 'It's not a threat; it's a promise', right?" Raine said. "So it wasn't a threat."

"Well, I'm not sure about that," Bautista replied.

"As a marshal, you're a commissioned peace officer, correct?" Raine seemed to change tack.

"Um, yes," Bautista answered after a moment.

"That means you can arrest people, right?" Raine translated.

"Right," Bautista confirmed.

"I mean, what's the point of a guard outside divorce court

if you can't arrest someone who goes off after losing a hearing, right?" Raine pointed out.

"Exactly."

"If they commit a crime, I mean," Raine clarified.

"Of course," Bautista agreed.

"And threatening someone"—Raine adopted a thoughtful expression—"that's a crime, isn't it? Criminal Harassment, right?"

Bautista frowned at the lawyer.

"Do you need me to cite you the exact statute number?" Raine asked. "You and I both know I know it. You know it too, don't you?"

"Revised Code of Washington 9A.46.020," Bautista recited begrudgingly. He was losing his air of affability.

"Very good!" Raine congratulated him like a teacher praising a struggling student who finally got an answer right.

"But it's not a crime to threaten someone unless it's a credible threat, right?" Raine continued. "The victim has to believe the threat is going to be carried out, and it has to be objectively reasonable to think that. Isn't that correct?"

Bautista nodded. "That is correct."

"And"—Raine raised a professorial finger—"if the reasonably credible threat is a reasonably credible threat to kill, that even makes it a felony, doesn't it?"

Another reluctant nod. "Yes."

"Marshal Bautista, you wouldn't let someone commit a crime in front of you and not arrest them, would you?" Raine asked him. "Especially not a felony, right?"

Bautista didn't answer.

"You wouldn't let someone commit a felony right in front of you and not arrest them, now would you, Marshal?" Raine asked again. "Especially not if that was your entire job, correct?"

Bautista took a moment, then finally nodded slightly. "I would not," he admitted.

Raine smiled broadly. "And the reason you didn't arrest my client that morning for Felony Criminal Harassment was because she didn't make a specific threat, did she? And even if a threat was implied, there was no indication that she meant it, that Jeremy Willoughby was afraid she meant it, or that if he had been afraid, it would have been reasonable for him to be afraid. Isn't that all correct, sir?"

Bautista struggled to answer. So Raine kept talking.

"She was just blowing off steam," Raine simplified it, "and no one, not even you, thought she really meant it. Right?"

Bautista nodded. "Right."

"Because you would have arrested her, wouldn't you?"

"I would have."

"And you didn't."

"I did not," Bautista had to agree.

"No further questions," Raine declared triumphantly and marched back to his seat.

Nakamoto stood up for redirect examination. "Knowing what you know now, Marshal Bautista, do you wish you had arrested her for Criminal Harassment?"

Bautista frowned. He did seem like a decent enough guy. He couldn't arrest everyone who left divorce court angry. They didn't have a jail big enough for that. But he probably felt guilty about what had happened that night anyway.

"I do my job to the best of my ability, ma'am," he said. "That's the only way I can answer that."

Raine was fine with that answer.

28

A fter Bautista, it was a parade of cops and the like, none of whom had anything particularly interesting to say, but each of whom did something small on the case. The patrol officers who put up the crime scene tape and made sure no one entered. The forensics officers who photographed and collected the evidence. The technicians from the medical examiner's office who took the body to the morgue. Raine wasn't contesting that Jeremy had been murdered, so there wasn't much cross-examination to do. He had considered asking each and every one of them, "You don't know who murdered him, do you?" but he suspected the jury would tire of that kind of gamesmanship fairly quickly.

Eventually, there came a break in the State's case-in-chief. The cops were done, and it was time to turn to the victim's family. But it was late in the day on a Wednesday, and the next planned witness wasn't in the hallway. Nakamoto had told them to appear first thing Thursday morning. Raine was taking less time to cross-examine everyone than Nakamoto had anticipated. Had Raine asked to knock off early one afternoon, Judge Patel not only would have denied the request, but he likely would have excoriated Raine in front of the jurors for not managing his case better. But since it was the prosecution asking for the early recess, Judge Patel was only too happy to oblige.

"Court is adjourned until tomorrow morning at nine o'clock." He punctuated his announcement with a bang of his gavel, then retired to his chambers.

The jurors were led away, and the rest of the assembled also bled slowly toward the exits. Abigail, despite her fancy clothes, was still in custody and taken away by the guards before Raine could say much more than, "See you tomorrow."

Nakamoto left without any small talk, and the gallery was empty. Even the mysterious Mr. Plunkett, who had sat through every word of every witness, was the first one out the door when the judge's gavel hit.

Raine took out his cell phone in the empty courtroom and dialed Sommers's number. "Can you meet me at my office in, like, thirty minutes? I want to talk more about that guy in the back of the courtroom."

"Make it an hour," Sommers replied. "I'm about to close a deal, but the other side needs a little more handholding to get there. You don't want to be around me after a deal falls through."

Raine didn't doubt that. "I'll see you when you get there."

———

SOMMERS ENDED up needing less than an hour to close the deal—"I'm good"—and was at Raine's office about forty-five minutes after their phone call. It was approaching five, but not quite. Laura was finishing up her tasks and keeping an eye on the clock so she didn't miss her bus home. Raine welcomed Sommers in the lobby, and they adjourned to his office to talk strategy.

"I want to find out who this Plunkett guy is working for," Raine said. "Maybe you could tail him or something?"

"Tail him?" Sommers laughed. "Sure, boss. You want me to wear a wire too? Maybe make him some cement shoes or something? Should I pack some heat?"

Raine wasn't amused. "I just meant—"

"Don't worry, Dan." Sommers chuckled again. "I already dug up all his connections, and I can narrow it down to two likely employers."

"Did you follow him?"

"Did the tall, beautiful, platinum blonde woman who flirted with him at the coffee cart follow him without him noticing?" Sommers exposed the silliness of Raine's question. "Um, no. He noticed me just standing, goddess-like, in the courthouse. He definitely would have noticed me following him around town."

"You think a lot of yourself, huh?" Raine observed.

"Nothing unearned," Sommers responded. "Looks and confidence get you a long way in life, and especially in our fields."

"I think intellect helps too," Raine countered. "At least in my field."

Sommers smirked. "I'd bet you dinner that the handsome lawyers do better with juries than the smart ones."

"Are you saying I'm handsome?" Raine inquired.

"You haven't won your case yet, Romeo," Sommers pointed out.

Raine was enjoying himself, but he hadn't invited her over for banter. "What did you find out about Plunkett? Who's he working for?"

"So like I said"—Sommers was ready to pivot back to business as well—"I dug into his business dealings a little deeper to find any connections he might have. He does consulting work now under a privately owned LLC. Want to know who two of his biggest clients are?"

"Yes," Raine answered. "Obviously I do."

"Willoughby Enterprises," Sommers answered, "and Mayfield Anderson, Attorneys at Law."

"Jeremy's company?" Raine was surprised by that. But not as surprised as by the second business. "Smith's lawyers? The ones who served me with the cease-and-desist letter?"

"Correct," Sommers answered. "My guess is he's monitoring the trial for one of those."

"Or both," Raine considered.

"Smith probably wants to know the moment you try to utter his name in open court," Sommers surmised. "Who better to hire than some half-retired lawyer who would understand what's going on but not have his own cases to worry about."

That did make sense, Raine thought. "But what about Willoughby's company?"

"Maybe they want to know if Abigail is going to be the next CEO or not," Sommers suggested.

Raine leaned back in his chair and put his hands behind his head. "That's good intel. I'm not sure what to do with it. But thanks. I guess you could have just told me that over the phone. Sorry I asked you to come all the way over here."

Sommers shrugged off the apology. "No worries. I'm usually pretty worthless after closing a big deal. I wasn't going back to my office anyway. I just figured you were lonely."

Raine didn't want to think about whether that was true.

"I always celebrate a big deal by buying myself a drink," Sommers continued. "You want to join me? Strictly business."

"I've got a big day tomorrow," Raine demurred.

"Come on. One drink," Sommers encouraged. "On me. You can grab something to eat too, then get back to work."

Sommers had a point. He would need to eat. And it was early enough, he could get back to the office and work as late as he wanted to prepare for the next day's testimony.

"Okay, you talked me into it," Raine relented. "Where should we go?"

"Abscess," Sommers answered.

"Excuse me?" Raine asked, standing up. "Is that a real place? Is it 'Absinthe' maybe?"

Sommers stood up too. "Definitely a real place," she assured him as they headed toward the lobby. "And definitely 'Abscess'. It's a little speakeasy hidden in the basement of a pool hall down on Occidental Avenue. I'll drive."

As they rounded the corner into the lobby, Raine called out, "We're going to grab a drink, Laura." It wasn't until he and Sommers had completely entered the lobby and Laura nodded, wide-eyed, toward the front door that he saw Natalie standing just inside the entrance.

"Nat," he said, surprised, "what are you doing here? I mean, I didn't expect—"

"Obviously not," Natalie replied with a glance toward Sommers.

"Oh, right." Raine fumbled. "This is Rebecca Sommers. She's my, um—"

"Real estate agent," Sommers said at the exact time Raine said, "Investigator."

"It's complicated," Raine offered.

"I'm sure." Natalie offered a tight smile. "Well, I was going to invite you to a family dinner with the boys this weekend at the house. I was driving by and thought I might catch you before the end of the day. But I can see now that you're busy."

"Oh!" Raine exclaimed. "Yes. That sounds great. Of course. Oh, wait. I'm in trial."

"Of course you are," Natalie responded. She nodded vaguely toward Sommers. "No time for frivolities when you're in trial, right, Dan?"

"I think I'll wait in the car." Sommers spoke up. "Nice to meet you, Mrs. Raine."

"Ms. Raine," Natalie corrected as Sommers slipped past her. Once Sommers was outside, Natalie shook her head at him. "That didn't take long."

"It's not what it looks like," Raine insisted.

"Your going out to drinks with your beautiful, blonde investigator-slash-real-estate-agent-slash-who-knows-what isn't what it looks like?" Natalie replied. "Of course not. And never mind about dinner. The boys were asking about you, but I'll just tell them you're in trial. Again."

"Nat," Raine implored.

"No, Dan, it's fine. Really," Natalie said. "It's not like we aren't used to it."

"That's not fair, Nat," Raine said. "You were always busy with work too. We both were."

Natalie nodded her head slightly. "Fine. You're right. And I don't want to have this argument again. It doesn't matter anymore. It's over. But can I give you some advice, Dan?"

"Of course," Raine answered.

"Don't let the kids get used to you being gone all the time," Natalie told him. "That's what happened to us. They deserve better."

With that, Natalie left. Again. Raine stood there for a moment, acutely aware that Laura was staring awkwardly at his back. And Sommers was waiting in her luxury SUV, watching Natalie walk to her mid-level sedan. Raine didn't feel like dinner anymore. But he sure wanted that drink.

29

The drink was less festive than Sommers probably would have liked. But the meal was mercifully short. After a single Manhattan and a happy-hour burger and fries, Raine walked back to his office to allow Sommers to enjoy her deal closing without his oppressively depressed company. It was all for the better probably. He did have a big day the next day, and when he arrived in Judge Patel's courtroom the next morning, he was as prepared as he possibly could be.

It wouldn't matter.

Nakamoto's first witness of the day was Bethany Carter. She was dressed impeccably in a designer suit with matching gloves and shoes. Her purse probably cost more than Raine's car. She walked into the courtroom as if she owned the place but didn't care that she owned it. She stopped in front of the judge and raised her right hand to be sworn in. Once she'd made the requisite affirmation to tell the truth, the whole truth, and nothing but the truth, she sat down on the witness stand, more than ready to answer a few questions about her ex-husband and the woman who'd stolen him from her.

Instead of name, rank, and serial number, it was name, relationship to the victim, and number of years in that relationship.

"Bethany Carter."

"Jeremy Willoughby was my ex-husband and the father of my child."

"We were married for fourteen years. We divorced ten years ago."

Everyone in the courtroom could do that math. But Nakamoto hadn't called Bethany to make Abigail seem like a bad person. Not just for that reason, anyway. She had called her to establish motive. More specifically, to establish that Bethany didn't have a motive.

"Did you and Jeremy have a prenuptial agreement prior to your marriage?" Nakamoto asked.

Bethany shook her head. "No. Jeremy hadn't struck it rich yet. We were just two kids in love and ready to take on the world. There were no assets to worry about. I think our biggest asset was probably the car my grandmother gave me when she went into a retirement home. So no, I didn't make Jeremy sign a prenuptial agreement to protect him from getting half of that car."

More light laughter from the jury box. That was fine, Raine thought. Bethany was likable enough. The danger was if the jury decided they had to choose between Bethany and Abigail. Like Jeremy did.

"So is it safe to say that when you and Jeremy divorced," Nakamoto continued, "you received a sizable settlement?"

Bethany nodded. "That would be safe to say."

"Was it structured as monthly support or a lump sum?" Nakamoto asked.

"It was a lump sum," Bethany responded. "By then, Jeremy had made most of his fortune, but I had become a successful professional myself. I had no need for alimony, but

I was going to receive my fair share of what we had built together during our marriage."

"So, then, is it accurate to say"—Nakamoto finally got to the point—"that Jeremy's death did not result in the termination of support payments to you or anything like that?"

"That would be accurate," Bethany agreed. "It would be even more accurate to say that Jeremy's death had absolutely no financial impact on me whatsoever."

That was Nakamoto's real point, Raine knew. She walked to the counter in front of the bailiff and returned with a document from the row of exhibits.

"Ms. Carter, I'm handing you what's previously been marked as State's exhibit two," Nakamoto stated for the record as she did so. "Could you please identify this document?"

Bethany took a moment to peruse the exhibit, then looked up to answer. "It says 'Last Will and Testament of Jeremy Willoughby'."

"Does it appear to be his most recent will?" Nakamoto asked.

Bethany shrugged. "It's dated a little over a year ago. I can't say whether he changed it after that."

Nakamoto nodded. "Of course. But I'd like you to assume this is the most recent will and there is no evidence of any changes since the date of execution on that document."

"Okay," Bethany agreed.

"Could you please examine the exhibit and tell us whether you were a beneficiary in Jeremy's will?"

"I don't need to examine this to know that," Bethany answered. "I was not a beneficiary in his will. He wrote me out as soon as the divorce was final. He wrote Lucas out later, when he refused to follow in his father's corporate footsteps."

Nakamoto smiled at the answer. "We'll be talking to Lucas next. Let's restrict your answers to you personally. Could you please go ahead and read the document, Ms. Carter, and confirm you were not a beneficiary? Just to be sure."

Bethany sighed, but then returned her attention to Jeremy's will. After a few more moments, she looked up again. "As I said, I am not a beneficiary in this will."

"Who is the beneficiary?" Nakamoto asked.

Bethany looked past Nakamoto and pointed at Abigail. "She is. Abigail Willoughby. She gets everything."

Raine could only appreciate how well that came together for Nakamoto. He knew she was smart enough to take the win and announce: "No further questions, Your Honor."

It was Raine's turn. He didn't have much to cross-examine her on. He could try to draw out her bias against Abigail, engendered by finding her in bed with Jeremy while they were still married, but to what end? There was no place for bias in the mathematical fact that Jeremy had left nothing to Bethany and Lucas and everything to Abigail. Provided Abigail wasn't convicted of murdering him, that was. There was little to be gained by attacking a woman who had come across as likable and independent.

"No questions, Your Honor," Raine announced. "Thank you for coming to court, Ms. Carter."

He could at least try to score some points with the jurors for being polite.

The next witness could give Raine more of an opportunity to elucidate why Jeremy might have wanted to give everything to Abigail.

"The State calls Lucas Willoughby to the stand."

Lucas was considerably less put together than his mother, a fact of which he seemed to be both aware and proud. He wore torn jeans and a paint-stained T-shirt under an equally paint-stained unzipped hoodie. His face was clean, but his hair looked like it probably wasn't, sticking up randomly at the back corners. He marched into the courtroom immediately after his mother had left it, and had to be directed by Nakamoto to walk up to the judge, who was waiting, hand raised, to swear him in. He answered the judge's question about affirming to tell the truth with a less than convincing, "Sure," and flopped down on the witness stand.

At least he was going to be more entertaining than Bethany, Raine suspected.

He even made name, rank, and serial number more difficult than they needed to be.

"Could you please state your name for the record?" Nakamoto started.

"Lucas," came the answer.

"Lucas what?" Nakamoto prodded.

"Uh... Lucas, ma'am?" he ventured.

More laughs from the jurors, albeit quickly stifled.

"What's your full name, sir?" Nakamoto directed him.

"Oh, right. Right." Lucas nodded. "My full name is Lucas Jeremy Willoughby."

Name: check.

"Did you know a man named Jeremy Willoughby?"

Nakamoto wasn't allowed to ask leading questions of her own witnesses, so she couldn't just say, "Jeremy Willoughby was your father, right?" But most witnesses understood that and could answer an awkwardly phrased question appropriately. Lucas, not so much.

"I thought I did," was Lucas's reply, "but do any of us really know anyone else?"

Of course, the rules did allow for some leading questions when absolutely necessary, and you could ask any question so long as the other side didn't object. "Jeremy Willoughby was your father, correct?"

Raine refrained from objecting. Although he would have enjoyed prolonging Nakamoto's struggle, the jurors would not have appreciated it. And it was all about the jurors.

"He provided the DNA to my mom, who formed me in her womb," Lucas answered. "I don't know if I can say he was really a father to me."

Raine allowed himself a small grin. There was no way he was going to object to anything during the direct examination of Lucas Willoughby. It was going to be highly entertaining all on its own.

"Well, let's talk about that, then," Nakamoto assented. It was to her advantage anyway that Lucas was estranged from his father. "When was the last time you spoke with him before his death?"

"Well, I didn't speak to him after his death obviously," Lucas quipped. No chuckles from the jurors for that one. "So the last time we spoke? Probably five years ago. It was after I refused to take a job at his company. He just couldn't understand why I wanted to pursue my art instead of letting my soul wither and die in some corporate cubicle."

"So you're an artist, then?" Nakamoto followed up.

"I try," Lucas answered with a shy grin. "But yes, I'm an artist. I work primarily with paint but have been expanding into more multimedia pieces lately. I'm not sure I can say I'm expanding confidently, but I'm—"

"And your dad didn't approve, is that right?" Nakamoto cut him off. No one wanted to hear Lucas expound on his artistic influences and interests.

"He did not," Lucas confirmed.

"You said you didn't talk after that," Nakamoto recalled. "Did he also cut you off financially?"

"Yes, he did," Lucas answered. "He thought that would make me come crawling back. He didn't think I could make it on my own. He was wrong, though. And I think that made him even more angry."

Angry. Raine noted the use of that particular word.

"When was the last time you received any financial assistance from your father?" Nakamoto asked.

Lucas shrugged. "Just before we stopped talking. He sent me a check and dared me not to cash it. He said if I really wanted to be my own man, I would tear up the check. Or I could cash the check and show up at his office the next day at eight a.m. sharp, in a suit. I didn't even own a suit." He gestured at his paint-stained attire. "I still don't."

"What did you do with the check?" Nakamoto asked.

"I tore it up," Lucas said. "And then I recycled it. I'm not a sociopath. The earth is dying, man."

"What about his will?" Nakamoto finally got to it.

"What about it?" Lucas replied.

"Will you get anything from your father's will?"

Lucas shrugged. "I don't know. I don't think so. Mom said he left everything to her." He pointed at Abigail, and all eyes turned to the defendant. Raine put a comforting hand on his client's arm, if only because everyone was looking and he wanted them to think he supported her. "If he left me anything, I haven't seen it yet. But that's cool. I haven't needed anything from him for years. I don't need anything now."

"Thank you, Mr. Willoughby," Nakamoto concluded. "No further questions."

"Cross-examination, Mr. Raine?" Judge Patel invited.

Raine stood up and made his way toward the witness stand. Again, he wasn't likely to convince the jury that Lucas had committed the murder. He didn't believe it himself, for one thing. For another, Lucas's demeanor on the stand had been somewhat annoying but also earnest. He wasn't playing the part of starving artist. He was relishing it. But maybe Raine could take the edge off some of the prosecution's other evidence.

"That thing with the check," Raine began, "that was kind of messed up, wasn't it?"

Lucas nodded. "Yeah. Totally messed up."

"Like, either give you the money or don't, right?" Raine followed up.

"Exactly," Lucas answered. "But that was the point, right? It was never about the money. It was about control."

"He wanted to control you?"

"He wanted to control everybody," Lucas confirmed. "And he tried to use his money to do it. I mean, it usually worked, too, right? Most people, they like money, right? They need it. And hey, I understand. Food isn't free. Housing isn't free. It should be, but it's not, because of people like him. If we actually took care of each other and made sure everyone had a roof over their heads and a meal on the table, then those rich capitalists couldn't control all of us, you know?"

Raine appreciated Lucas's passion, but wasn't really interested in discussing economic philosophies just then.

"Did you ever see him use money to control your mom?" Raine asked.

"I saw him try"—Lucas lifted his chin slightly—"but she couldn't be bought. She left his ass and took her fair share. She didn't need him, so he couldn't control her anymore. I think that's why he tried so hard to control me, in part. To get to her."

Raine nodded along. "What about his new wife, Abigail?" He pointed at his client. "Did you ever see your dad try to control her with money?"

Lucas took a few moments before answering. He leaned forward and rubbed his unshaven chin. "Look, Abigail's my stepmom, right? I was a teenager when Dad divorced my mom and married her. She was always nice to me, so I don't want to say anything bad about her."

"But?" Raine prodded.

"But"—Lucas leaned back in his seat again—"their entire

relationship was about Dad controlling her with money. He had all the money, and she had none."

"Do you think he ever pulled a trick like he did with you and that check?" Raine pushed.

"I'm sure he did," Lucas answered. Raine liked that answer. But he didn't like what Lucas said next. "I mean, isn't that what happened when she murdered him? Like, he went there with some bullshit divorce papers for her to sign and give up everything, and she finally had enough and just lost it and smashed his self-righteous skull in? Look, man, I don't blame her. I thought about doing the same thing a dozen times myself. I got away from him by tearing up that check and choosing my own life, but I'm not going to judge her for finding a different way to get away from him. She probably didn't see any other way."

Raine stood there, stunned. He couldn't have Lucas unsay what he'd just said. And questioning him further about it would just be underlining it.

"No further questions," he practically admitted, and returned to his seat.

"Any redirect examination, Ms. Nakamoto?" the judge inquired.

"Oh, no, Your Honor," Nakamoto chirped.

"May this witness be excused?" Patel followed up.

"Yes, Your Honor," Nakamoto answered.

"Please, Your Honor," Raine agreed.

As Lucas made his way out of the courtroom, Abigail leaned over and whispered into Raine's ear, "That's not what happened. I never saw that settlement agreement."

"I know," Raine whispered back, "but it's what could have happened. That's enough."

Amazingly, it was about to get even worse.

30

The next witnesses, the last witnesses in fact for the State's case-in-chief, were the experts. The ones who could explain to the jury the sorts of things that most jurors wouldn't necessarily understand from common experience. Things like autopsies. And accounting. Two things that might not normally go together but which Nakamoto was going to use as a one-two punch to end her case.

She stood and announced the first punch. "The State calls Desmond Mitchell to the stand."

Raine turned and watched Mitchell enter the courtroom. He looked like the very tall cat accused of eating the canary even though he didn't even know there was a canary. His eyes darted around, landing on practically everyone in the courtroom. Nakamoto, Raine, Abigail, the judge and the jurors, even Plunkett, who was again seated in the back by the doors. Mitchell walked tentatively down the walkway to the front of the courtroom, clutching a leather satchel of papers to his chest.

Judge Patel raised his right hand and instructed Mitchell to do the same. "Do you swear or affirm you will tell the truth, the whole truth, and nothing but the truth?"

"Of course," Mitchell answered. "I mean yes. Yes, I swear or affirm all of that. Yes."

Raine was surprised by how nervous the accountant seemed, but then again, he supposed, he was an accountant. He had been comfortable enough in his office, but the last place any accountant wanted to be was in a courtroom, a judge and a pair of lawyers about to grill him about his book-keeping.

Mitchell walked around and sat down in the witness chair. Nakamoto gave him a moment to get comfortable, then began.

"Could you please state your name for the record?"

"Um, Desmond Mitchell." He leaned forward to deliver his answer directly to Nakamoto.

"How are you employed, sir?"

"I'm an accountant."

"Do you work for yourself, or do you have an employer?"

"I have an employer."

Raine could tell it was going to be like pulling teeth with Mitchell. He didn't suppose that mattered. It wasn't like Mitchell was going to say anything earth-shaking. Or so Raine hoped, after Lucas Willoughby's testimony.

"Who is your employer, Mr. Mitchell?" Nakamoto continued.

"Willoughby Enterprises," Mitchell answered. "I'm the senior executive accountant for Willoughby Enterprises."

Rebecca should add "senior" to her "executive Realtor" title, Raine thought absently.

"How long have you been with Willoughby Enterprises?"

Name, rank, and serial number for nervous accountants.

"Um, twelve years and five months on the first of next

month," Mitchell answered. "I've been the senior executive accountant for less than that."

Nakamoto smiled. "I supposed. It sounds like you've been with Willoughby Enterprises for a long time."

"Yes, ma'am."

"And you're familiar with its corporate structure and business accounts?"

"Very familiar, yes, ma'am," Mitchell agreed. "That's my job."

"Very good." Nakamoto gestured to the jury box. "Could you please explain to the jury the corporate structure of Willoughby Enterprises?"

Mitchell looked wide-eyed at the jurors. "Um, what exactly should I tell them?"

Nakamoto took a deep breath, but kept her pleasant, encouraging smile. "Well, let's start at the top. Is it a corporation or a sole proprietorship?"

"Oh, it's a corporation," Mitchell answered. "Of course."

"Of course," Nakamoto acknowledged. "Is it privately held or publicly traded?"

"Oh, I see." Mitchell nodded. "Yes, it's a privately held corporation. It is not publicly traded. You can't just go and buy stock on NASDAQ or anything."

"Is there a majority owner?" Nakamoto continued.

"Yes," Mitchell answered, then frowned. "I mean no. I mean, well, I'm not sure. It's complicated. Mr. Willoughby was the majority shareholder. But he's, well, he passed away. So I guess there isn't a majority shareholder right now. It's actually a very difficult position to be in."

"For the company or for you?" Nakamoto inquired.

"Both, actually," Mitchell admitted. "I'm not used to having to make so many decisions by myself. I worked very closely with Mr. Willoughby."

"Is there a board of directors or some other entity that is

currently handling the day-to-day operations?" Nakamoto continued.

"There is, but they are a bit hamstrung," Mitchell answered. "While Mr. Willoughby was still alive, they functioned mostly as an advisory body. They would make recommendations, but Mr. Willoughby had the final say."

"Because he was the majority shareholder?"

"Exactly."

"Can't the next largest shareholder make the decisions now?" Nakamoto inquired.

Mitchell shook his head. "It doesn't work like that. The next largest shareholder has barely five percent of the remaining stock. There's simply a very large body of voting stock and no one to cast that vote. We're all just waiting."

"Waiting for what?"

Mitchell shifted in his seat and threw an uncomfortable glance at the jurors. "Well, to see what happens in this case."

Nakamoto nodded. "Please explain."

"Um, well, okay." Mitchell nodded. But he didn't look at the jurors. He obviously didn't go to the law enforcement academy. "Mr. Willoughby's will bequeathed all of his shares in the company to his wife, Ms. Willoughby over there." He nodded at Abigail, who nodded slightly in return. Raine wished she hadn't. "But we received a court order blocking any such transfer and freezing all accounts related to her and the company until the resolution of the criminal case. Apparently, you can't inherit from someone if you're convicted of murdering them."

"So if Ms. Willoughby hadn't been charged with the murder," Nakamoto expounded, "she would be in charge of Willoughby Enterprises right now?"

"That's correct," Mitchell confirmed.

"That's a very valuable company, isn't it, Mr. Mitchell?"

But Mitchell shrugged. "It's less valuable without Mr. Willoughby."

Nakamoto frowned slightly. "How so?"

"Well, he was the driving force behind it, wasn't he?" Mitchell answered. "He was the one who had a vision and a plan. He was the one who was always looking for small start-ups with bright new ideas so he could buy them out and take those ideas for himself. Without him at the helm, the value of the company has dropped significantly."

"By how much?" Nakamoto asked.

"It's difficult to say as long as the court order prevents us from doing anything," Mitchell explained. "It's difficult to measure the liquidity of the company when we can't actually sell it, but I expect there will be offers to purchase the company now. Those offers are already lower than they were in the past."

Nakamoto paused and retrieved a document from the shelf in front of the court clerk. "Mr. Mitchell, I'm handing you what's been marked as State's exhibit eleven. Could you take a look at that and tell us what it is?"

Mitchell took the document gingerly and examined it as one might examine an electric eel. "It says 'Final Settlement Agreement' at the top."

"Does it say who the parties are?" Nakamoto continued. "It's a final settlement agreement for whom?"

"Yes," Mitchell answered. "It's the final settlement agreement between Jeremy Willoughby and Abigail Willoughby. Well, it would have been if they had signed it, but it doesn't look like that ever happened."

"Do you notice anything else about the document?"

"It has large dark spots all over most of the bottom of each page," Mitchell answered. "You can't really read what's written there."

"I'd like you to assume that exhibit eleven is a photocopy of the document found clutched in the hand of the victim," Nakamoto said. "And I'd like you to further assume that the dark spots are the result of the document being stained by the blood it was lying in."

"Um, okay." Mitchell held the document a bit further from him.

"Is there anything in that proposed settlement agreement regarding stock in Willoughby Enterprises?"

Mitchell hesitated. "May I look at the document?"

"I expect you would have to," Nakamoto replied. "Yes, please do."

Mitchell nodded, then perused the exhibit. He flipped through, reading what he could. Then looked up.

"What did you see regarding stock valuation?" Nakamoto asked.

"It appears to say the settlement will be mostly in stock options," Mitchell answered.

"And there's a reference to an attachment that includes tables regarding current and expected stock valuation, correct?"

"Um, correct," Mitchell confirmed.

"Are those tables attached?" Nakamoto asked.

Mitchell examined the document again. "No, it doesn't appear so."

"So whoever committed this crime left the scene with a portion of this settlement agreement," Nakamoto posited, "the one that would show how valuable Mr. Willoughby thought the stock would be."

Mitchell just stared at Nakamoto. "Is that a question?"

"I suppose it wasn't," Nakamoto admitted. "Would you agree, someone took those tables?"

"It does appear that way," Mitchell answered.

"That would be pretty valuable information for someone

who might end up selling the company later," Nakamoto suggested, "if they found themselves in control of the company, I mean. Wouldn't you agree?"

Mitchell shrugged. "I would agree with that, yes."

"Have there been past offers to purchase the company?" Nakamoto continued.

"Well, not the entire company, of course," Mitchell answered, "but a controlling share of the stock, yes. Mr. Willoughby always turned them down. I don't know if the new owners, whoever they end up being, will be as motivated to keep the company out of his hands."

"Whose hands?" Nakamoto asked reflexively, doing that thing where the lawyer asks the question the jurors would naturally have at that moment.

Raine tried not to show his excitement. He couldn't be the first one to mention the name, but if Nakamoto opened the door through her questioning of her own witness, there was a chance he could slip through that crack.

But Mitchell didn't seize the opportunity. "I, uh..." He looked up at the judge. "I'm not sure I'm allowed to say."

Raine stood up. "I would ask the court to instruct the witness to answer the question, Your Honor."

Judge Patel scowled at him. "You're out of order, Mr. Raine," he barked.

"I'll withdraw the question, Your Honor," Nakamoto said.

"Well, then I'll just ask it," Raine interjected.

Patel pointed down at him. "No, you will not."

Door not opened, Raine knew. He frowned and sat back down.

"The question is withdrawn, Mr. Mitchell," Judge Patel instructed the witness. "Do not attempt to answer it. Ms. Nakamoto will now pose a new question. Answer only that question and the questions that follow."

Mitchell nodded. "Okay. I mean yes, Your Honor."

Nakamoto took a moment to formulate the next question carefully. "So without naming any potential purchasers, is it safe to say that whoever ends up being the eventual controlling shareholder of Willoughby Enterprises could sell their share for a very substantial amount of money?"

Mitchell listened intently to the twists and turns in Nakamoto's question, then nodded. "That is correct."

"And if Ms. Willoughby is allowed to inherit from Mr. Willoughby's will," Nakamoto continued, "she would be that controlling shareholder, correct?"

"That's my understanding, yes," Mitchell confirmed.

"What if she is not permitted to inherit from Mr. Willoughby's will?" Nakamoto asked. "Who will control Willoughby Enterprises then?"

"It's my understanding from our lawyers," Mitchell answered, "that the secondary beneficiary in Mr. Willoughby's will was the company itself."

"So the company would control the company?" Nakamoto asked. "How does that work?"

"It means the board of directors would decide what to do," Mitchell answered. "And they would almost certainly sell to Mr.—I mean to a potential buyer."

Almost. Raine shook his head slightly.

"Either way, the company gets sold," Nakamoto opined.

But Mitchell frowned. "I don't think so. I think Ms. Willoughby would try to run the company, at least at first. I think the sale is most likely if she doesn't obtain control over it."

Finally, Raine thought, *some good testimony.*

Nakamoto frowned. "That's speculation, though, isn't it?"

"It is, ma'am," Mitchell confessed. "I'm sorry."

"Nothing to be sorry about," Nakamoto assured him unconvincingly. "But let's just take a moment to confirm the thrust of your testimony. If Ms. Willoughby gets away with the murder of her husband, then she will control his company and could use it to her own ends, including but not limited to selling it out from under everyone else. Is that correct?"

Mitchell frowned and looked over at Abigail again. "I'm not sure I would phrase it that way, but yes, I suppose that's accurate."

"Thank you, Mr. Mitchell," Nakamoto said. "No further questions."

It was Raine's turn. Judge Patel invited him to cross-examine the witness, but also warned him. "You may cross-examine, Mr. Raine, but be mindful of this court's previous rulings. I will not hesitate to impose appropriate sanctions for violation of my orders."

Raine had no doubt about that. "Understood, Your Honor." Mitchell wasn't going to be allowed to say the name "David E. Smith III", but Raine could get him to say everything except that.

"Willoughby Enterprises is a very valuable company, correct, Mr. Mitchell?" he began.

"Correct, Mr. Raine," Mitchell replied nervously.

"A multimillion-dollar company?" Raine ventured.

"To say the least," Mitchell agreed.

"And there have been a buyer or buyers who have previously expressed interest in buying the company, is that correct?"

"Mr. Raine..." Judge Patel growled a warning at him.

"I'm simply inquiring about valuation, Your Honor," Raine assured the court with raised palms. "I will not ask about any specific buyers. Valuation goes to motive, Your Honor. I think I'm entitled to test the State's theory as to motive."

Patel frowned. "Be careful, Mr. Raine."

Raine turned back to Mitchell. "There have been previous offers to buy Willoughby Enterprises, correct?"

"To purchase a controlling share in the company, yes," Mitchell clarified.

"Right, right." Raine accepted the clarification like a lawyer who wasn't an accountant. "And the moment Jeremy Willoughby died, the purchase price for that controlling share dropped. Isn't that also correct?"

Mitchell nodded. "Maybe not that exact moment, but as soon as that information became public, yes."

Raine considered asking the obvious next and last question: "So that unnamed person who previously tried to buy the company benefitted directly and substantially from Mr. Willoughby's death?" But he also suspected that doing so would lead to him being held in contempt and dragged away in handcuffs in front of the jurors. Not a good look. And he didn't need to ask the question anyway. Mitchell had given him the "two plus two". He could, and would, argue the "equals four" in his closing argument.

"No further questions," he conceded and returned to his seat.

He didn't expect Nakamoto to bother with any redirect examination based on his questions, but she apparently wanted to get the last word. A one-two punch loses its effectiveness if the first punch is too long before the second.

"To be perfectly clear, Mr. Mitchell," she stated more than asked, "the defendant, Abigail Willoughby, will gain control of her late husband's company unless she is found guilty of his murder, correct?"

Mitchell hesitated. He looked again at the jurors, then back to Nakamoto. "That is my understanding, yes."

"No further questions."

Raine didn't have any more questions either, but rather than allow Mitchell to be excused, Raine asked for him to remain on call, just in case. Mitchell looked dismayed at the prospect of returning, but Raine didn't have time to explain. Nakamoto announced her final witness. "The State calls Dr. Frederick Bannister to the stand."

Bannister was the medical examiner who had conducted the autopsy on Jeremy Willoughby. He was a middle-aged man with thick glasses and unruly black hair. He entered the courtroom as Mitchell hurried out of it. Plunkett also departed after Mitchell left. Raine supposed he was going to report to Smith's lawyers that the damned defense attorney was still pushing to name him as the real killer.

Bannister's demeanor was the opposite of Mitchell's. Mitchell had been nervous and obviously uncomfortable with everyone looking at him. Bannister couldn't have looked more at ease, and he flashed a broad smile to the jurors as he took his place on the witness stand.

Nakamoto took him through the name, rank, and serial number, then into the explanation of what an autopsy was. Raine found himself only half-listening. There was little of value for him in Bannister's testimony. Someone had definitely murdered Jeremy; Raine was just arguing it wasn't Abigail.

Bannister explained the different categories of injuries he might see when conducting an autopsy.

"There are several broad categories of injuries I look for. In addition to visible contusions and minor skin lacerations, which can be common on any person living or dead, I am looking for more substantial injuries that could have been the cause of death. Blunt force trauma. Sharp force trauma, which can be large lacerations, stab wounds, or puncture wounds. Gunshot wounds, of course. In this case, there were multiple impacts of blunt force to the posterior of the decedent's skull."

Then Bannister explained the four categories of manner of death that he could put on the death certificate.

"Natural causes is what it sounds like. A person dies from disease or from old age and the related failure of vital organs. Accident means that some sort of unexpected trauma was visited upon the decedent, but there was no intentional agency by anyone to inflict that trauma. Suicide means the fatal trauma was intentionally inflicted by the decedent themselves. And the last category, homicide, means an unexpected and fatal trauma was visited upon the decedent with the intent to cause the death."

Time for that second punch.

"There has been previous testimony regarding the legal and financial effects of a finding of murder in this case," she said. "Were you able to make a determination as to the manner of death in this case?"

"Yes, I was." Bannister turned to the jury to deliver his answer. "The death of Jeremy Willoughby was a homicide."

"Thank you, Doctor. No further questions." Nakamoto returned to her seat, ready to rest her case.

Raine stood up. He didn't really have any disagreement with Bannister's findings. But he couldn't let the prosecution's case end on Nakamoto's assertion.

"Homicide isn't the same as murder, is it, Doctor?" Raine challenged.

"No, it's not," Bannister admitted. "Homicide is a medical determination. Murder is a legal determination."

"Because murder is an illegal homicide, correct?" Raine knew.

"Correct," Bannister agreed. "All murders are homicides, but not all homicides are murders."

"So you can't actually say whether this was a murder, can you, Doctor?" Raine challenged.

He expected a quick no from the doctor because that was

the correct answer. But Bannister thought for several moments before answering. When he did, Raine wished he hadn't.

"As I said"—Bannister turned to the jurors—"all murders are homicides, but not all homicides are murders. For example, an execution would be a legal homicide, but that's a very specific and generally rare occurrence. The most common way that a homicide is not a murder is if the homicide was committed in self-defense. Sometimes, that can be difficult or even impossible to determine from an autopsy. I can't tell if a gunshot wound was fired without provocation or after the dead person fired several shots themselves first. But in this case, the injuries are completely inconsistent with self-defense. There was an initial blow to the head, which would have incapacitated the decedent. Then there were at least seven additional blows. It's difficult to count above that number because of the extensive damage caused to the soft tissue by the first several strikes, but I counted seven distinct cracks in the skull. At the time those injuries were inflicted, the decedent would not have been able to move, let alone act in a threatening way toward the killer sufficient to justify the killer acting in self-defense. Forensically, this was not self-defense. So, legally, it was almost certainly murder."

Raine was finished. In more ways than one.

"No further questions," he conceded.

Nakamoto had no need for further questions. Bannister was excused, and she rose to announce, "The State rests."

Judge Patel turned quickly to Raine. "Is the defense prepared to call its first witness, if any?"

"If any"; Raine stopped himself from shaking his head at the judge's subtle comment in front of the jurors.

"I would ask the court to start fresh in the morning," Raine requested. "I will need some time to line up our witnesses so they are waiting in the hallway. I also need to have a conversation with my client about how we will be proceeding."

That conversation, the lawyers all knew, was about whether Abigail would testify. She didn't have to, and if she didn't, Nakamoto wasn't allowed to argue that it meant she was guilty. It would gut the right to remain silent if the prosecution could argue adverse inferences from exercising it. In fact, judges weren't even allowed to ask defense attorneys in front of the jury whether the defendant would be testifying. Raine was hoping that by alluding to the general topic of whether his client would testify, and the legal landmines associated with any specific conversations about it, Judge Patel would have to grant his request to start fresh in the morning. Such a request would have been granted as a matter of course by any other judge. With Patel, Raine wasn't sure.

Raine didn't dare tell him the real reason he needed the extra time that afternoon: to try to serve a subpoena on a certain rival businessman who might have benefitted directly and substantially from the death of Jeremy Willoughby. A general accusation that "Madison Davey" was in town and had a motive wasn't going to work. Patel would require iron-clad specifics. Raine needed time to get them. Time Patel wouldn't give him if he knew.

The judge frowned and looked to Nakamoto. "Is the State ready to proceed now?"

Nakamoto threw Raine a bone, although for her own reasons, he knew. A conviction wasn't a conviction if it was overturned on appeal, and a defendant's right to decide whether or not to testify could be infringed by the judge not giving the defendant enough time to talk it over with their lawyer. Nakamoto didn't want to put all of that effort into the trial only to have to do it all over again after losing an appeal because her friendly judge was a little too prosecution-friendly.

"We have no objection to adjourning until tomorrow morning, Your Honor," Nakamoto said. "The jurors might appreciate the break as well."

It would also let her evidence sink in one more night before Raine started his case-in-chief.

Judge Patel frowned, but he'd painted himself into a corner with his question to Nakamoto. "All right then. Court is adjourned until nine a.m. tomorrow morning."

He banged his gavel, and people started to leave the courtroom. Raine needed to talk with Abigail, but the guards weren't going to allow that to happen right then. She was going back to her cell.

"I'll come by in a bit," Raine assured her. "We have a lot to talk about."

"How are we doing?" Abigail had to ask. "That didn't seem like very good testimony for me. Are we okay?"

"Right now?" Raine asked. "We're in trouble."

"Oh," Abigail replied.

"But I have a plan," he assured her. "Go back to the jail. I'll see you in an hour."

He needed that hour to come up with that plan. He also needed a partner to come up with a better one.

"That went well." Sommers emerged from the gallery and walked up to the defense table. "I'm joking, of course. That was not good."

"You came to watch me?" Raine smiled at his "partner".

"I came to watch Mitchell," Sommers corrected. "It sounds like prime office space might be changing hands soon."

Raine's smile faded.

"You really want to pin this on Smith, don't you?" Sommers asked.

"It's the only way to win," Raine said. "Nakamoto proved Abigail had the opportunity, means, and motive. If I can't show that somebody else had an even bigger motive, she's going to get convicted."

"How are you going to do that?"

Raine frowned. "I'm going to need help."

31

"We are in trouble," Raine repeated an hour later in the meeting room of the King County Jail. He and Sommers were squeezed in on one side; Abigail was on the other. "They've proven Jeremy was brutally murdered inside your home, and the only suspect the jury has heard about is you. Unless we change that, literally tomorrow, the jury will have no choice but to convict you."

"He's right, Abigail," Sommers put in. "I was watching the jury during their testimony today. They were staring at you when Mitchell explained that you'd inherit everything. They didn't look happy. They looked even less happy when that medical examiner explained how you smashed his head in after he was incapacitated."

"I didn't do it!" Abigail shouted.

"Right," Sommers quickly corrected. "I meant whenever whoever did it did it. But they think it was you. I watched them. They really think it was you."

"So what can we do?" Abigail moaned.

"We give them someone else," Raine explained. "We give them David."

"But David didn't do it either," Abigail insisted. "I just know he didn't."

"Because he was with you?" Raine tried one more time. "I've got a process server out right now tracking him down to serve him with a subpoena to appear at nine a.m. tomorrow morning. He's going to take the stand right after Mitchell, who was none too pleased to receive my phone call telling him to come back to court tomorrow, let me tell you. So, after Mitchell sets him up, I don't care if Smith says he committed the murder or says he couldn't have because he was with you. Either of those get you off the hook, but it might be nice to know in advance."

Abigail looked Raine dead in the eye. "I was not having an affair with David Smith, and we were not together when Jeremy was murdered."

Raine paused. He believed her. Despite what he wanted to be true, he believed her.

"Okay, fine. I believe you," he practically admitted. "But that's too bad. We need to give the jury another suspect. Someone. Anyone. And now we've lost Smith for that."

"Maybe not," Sommers suggested. "When one door closes, open the other one."

Raine cocked his head at her. "That's not exactly how that saying goes," he pointed out.

"I like my way better," Sommers responded. "It gives you agency. And responsibility. Look, what are the two main reasons anyone does anything?"

Raine supposed there was a right answer to that very interesting philosophical question, but they didn't really have time for the Socratic method. "I don't know. Just tell us."

"Love and money," Sommers answered. "So, if it wasn't love..."

"It was money," Raine finished her thought.

"Does any of this matter?" Abigail questioned. "Didn't the judge say you can't call David as a witness?"

"He said I can't unless I have something specific to link him to the murder," Raine answered.

"Money," Sommers reminded him, "not love."

Raine nodded. "Okay. Mitchell gave me half of what we need today. He said Smith has been trying to buy the company, but Jeremy wouldn't sell to him. Now that Jeremy's dead, he can buy it, either from you or from the board of directors, and at a discount even."

Raine nodded as he considered this new tack. "Yeah, this might work. I'll tell Patel I'm calling him to the stand to testify about his attempts to buy the company just to establish valuation. I'll tell him I intend to show that Abigail would have personally profited more from a divorce settlement with the company valued high than she would have from murdering Jeremy and the company's value plummeting. I need to know the exact terms of the offers Smith made in order to do that."

"What if he lies?" Abigail asked.

"Oh my God, I hope he lies." Raine laughed. "That would be the best possible result. Why would you lie unless you're guilty?"

"But how will you know if he's lying?" Sommers asked. "He could make up any numbers at all. Or just deny ever making any offers."

"He could," Raine admitted. "And that's why I need proof of the offers he made in the past. And the one he made after Jeremy's murder."

"After?" Abigail asked.

"You heard Mitchell," Raine explained. "He let slip that there's already been an offer since the murder, and it was lower. That had to be Smith. I just need to find the proof and shove it in his face when he denies it. Then I've got him lying about a material aspect of the case. Patel will have to let me accuse him at that point."

Sommers shook her head. "I don't know, Dan. There are a lot of ifs in that plan."

"I know," Raine agreed. "But without it, there are no ifs, ands, or buts. Abigail is going to be convicted."

Abigail's shoulders dropped. "What do you need from me?"

"And me?" Sommers offered. "We're partners, remember?"

Raine smiled. He pointed to Abigail. "From you, I need information."

Then he pointed to Sommers. "And from you, I need access."

32

A bigail could tell them where they needed to look, but she wasn't going to be able to get them inside Jeremy's offices. If they had frozen her accounts, they had definitely deactivated whatever access devices she might have had. Using her expired badge to try to open a locked door would not only be unsuccessful, it would create a digital record of the attempt. They needed to gain access without seeming like they were gaining access. They also weren't going anywhere Abigail had a key to anyway.

They needed records of the company's financials going back at least ten years. Longer, if need be. Raine wanted the details of every purchase offer since Jeremy married Abigail. He wanted to show the jury that murdering Jeremy wouldn't just have been evil, it would have been financially imprudent. If he could show that the company and its stock were worth more to her with Jeremy alive, then Nakamoto's theory of the case would fall apart. But records that old weren't kept on-site. They were "in archives". Every business sent records to "archives", but no one really knew where that was. Jeremy was a tech guy, but Abigail said he was also a paper guy. He knew the limitations and vulnerabilities of tech. Online records could be hacked and changed. But paper stored in boxes in some warehouse in the light industrial district south of downtown? What idiot would ever try to break in there?

Or pair of idiots.

"For the record, I'm not super comfortable committing a burglary as part of my defense strategy in a criminal trial," Raine commented as he rolled his car to a stop up the street from their target, an unmarked one-story warehouse at the edge of Seattle's SoDo District. "SoDo" was the name of that light industrial neighborhood south of downtown. It was short for SOuth of the DOme, a reference to the Kingdome, former home of Seattle's professional football and baseball teams. The Kingdome had been demolished more than a generation earlier, but people still called the area "SoDo". It just had a nice ring to it. It also had a lot of razor wire and a dearth of streetlights.

"Then keep up and shut up," Sommers answered as they exited the vehicle. "It's not a burglary if they invite us in."

"Kind of like vampires, huh?" Raine observed.

"A lawyer who believes in vampires." Sommers grinned. "Hard to believe."

Raine missed the reference, but he appreciated Sommers's confidence.

Abigail had given them the address to the archives building, and it was a good thing because there were absolutely no signs or other indications of what the building was. No large gold W like on the forty-fourth floor of the Columbia Center. It was just a one-story cement building, its outline diffused by the rain that had settled in after the sun went down. Its few windows were painted over with black, and the only visible entrance faced the street. A faint light flickered through the small, thick windowpane in the center of the metal door.

"Lovely place," Raine commented. "Very inviting."

"Discourages the vampires," Sommers quipped.

Raine shook his head slightly. He wondered when the silly jokes would stop and the dizzying charm would start. Just inside the front door, it turned out.

"I'm here!" Sommers called out as she flung open the heavy door and exploded into the tiny lobby jammed inside. She didn't even seem to take the time to notice whether anyone was present to appreciate her dramatic entrance. "Tell him I'm here and ready for the tour."

There was in fact someone there. A young man who couldn't have been more than twenty sat behind the gray counter on the other side of the cramped entryway. He had what was trying very hard to be a mustache on his upper lip and long black hair pulled back over his ears. He looked up from his phone with a mixture of surprise and boredom. "Who are you?"

"Who am I?" Sommers called out. "Young man, I am Rebecca Sommers, the number one commercial real estate agent in Seattle, downtown core and, um, SoDo District."

"Three quarters running," Raine put in.

"Yes, three quarters running," Sommers agreed with an exaggerated gesture toward her companion. "And after we close this deal tonight, it will be four quarters running. I'll show that Jenkins bitch who's the boss."

"We're kind of closed, lady," the attendant said. "It's, like, late."

"Of course it's late, young man," Sommers replied. "If you want to get ahead in this world, you don't stop working at five. Quitting time is for quitters, I always say. Isn't that what I always say, Jack?"

Raine grimaced at the name, but appreciated the anonymity she was offering him. "That's what you always say, Ms. Sommers."

She sidled up to the counter and leaned into the young

man's personal space. "What did you say your name was?" she purred.

"Um, Jared?" He didn't seem sure himself.

"Jared. I like that." Sommers twisted a strand of her platinum hair. "I'm here to meet with someone, and I need you to get them for me. Can you do that for me?"

"Uh, um, okay, sure," Jared stammered. "Who is it?"

Sommers thought for a moment, then looked back at Raine. "What was his name again, Jack?"

Raine had no idea whom her imaginary meeting was with. He could only shrug.

Sommers turned back to Jared. "I think it was something like Taylor? Tyler? Baxter?"

"Barry?" Jared suggested.

"Yes! Barry!" Sommers placed a finger on his chest. "Where is Barry right now?"

"Um, he's down on three, doing document destruction," Jared answered. "I can go get him."

But Sommers would have none of that. "Absolutely not. You have a job to do, Jared, and that job is to be here, watching that door, making sure no unsavory characters cross that threshold."

Jared squinted at the door. Raine wondered if he knew what the word "threshold" even meant.

"Don't bring Barry to us," Sommers continued. "We will go to Barry. Where are the elevators, my dear Jared?"

Jared turned and pointed down a narrow hallway. "Down there, but you need a security badge." He held up the one hanging around his neck.

Sommers reached out and took ahold of the badge, and his hand. "May I borrow yours, Jared? I promise I'll bring it back to you when I'm done."

Jared probably would have cut off his own foot for Sommers at that point. His acned face was flushing at the jawline, and his breathing was rapid. "Um, sure. Yes. Of course. Whatever you need, Ms., um..." He'd forgotten her name. He'd probably forgotten his own name.

"Call me Rebecca," Sommers breathed as she pulled the lanyard over his head. "Now watch that door for us. We don't want any vampires sneaking in, now do we?"

"Vampires?" Jared asked.

Raine nodded. "They can't come in if you don't invite them in."

Jared looked again at the entrance, and Sommers and Raine headed for the elevators.

"That was impressive," Raine admired when they were out of earshot.

Sommers chuckled. "Not really. Men are idiots. If they think they have any shot to fuck you—I mean any shot, like one in a million—they'll do whatever it takes to keep that option open."

Raine frowned. "All men?"

"Almost all men," Sommers clarified. She flashed Jared's security badge over the card reader and pressed the elevator call button.

"Have you tried that on me?" Raine wondered aloud.

Sommers smiled at him. "It doesn't work on certain men if they're at a certain place emotionally."

"Where's that?" Raine asked.

"The rare times when they actually aren't trying to fuck another woman," Sommers answered. "At the beginning of a new relationship, or at the end of one they don't want to end."

Raine knew which category she thought he was in. "I'm not—"

"Yes, you are," Sommers told him. "You'll get over her, Dan, but you're not there yet. Until you are, you wouldn't notice if I threw myself at you."

The elevator doors opened with a ding.

"Have you done that?" Raine asked as they stepped inside.

"Definitely not," Sommers assured him. "I already told you, you're not my type. And I'm not Natalie."

Raine's heart jumped at the sound of her name. Maybe Sommers was right. He decided he didn't want to talk about it anymore. "So, anyway, what floor are we going to?"

Sommers grinned as the elevator doors closed. "Any floor but three."

There were five floors, descending from street level. Sommers pressed the bottom button. "Let's try five. The best stuff is always buried the deepest."

And in the dark, Raine considered as the elevator doors opened. They were confronted with a dim maze of makeshift cubicle walls and stacked boxes. When they stepped off the elevator, the overhead lights nearest them brightened with an audible click and buzz. Raine supposed it made sense to save energy by keeping the lights down if no one was there. He also appreciated that it indicated no one else was on the floor with them.

"Okay, I got us in," Sommers said as she ventured forward a few steps, triggering another light to brighten. "Now, what are we looking for?"

"Mitchell said the appendix to the agreement Jeremy wanted Abigail to sign was probably a way to value the stock options he was offering her," Raine answered, "and he said the best way to do that was to look at actual sales of stock. I think it was a trick to get her to give up actual money for the promise of increased stock value, but you can't buy groceries with increased stock value."

"Well, actually, you can," Sommers replied. "You use the stock as collateral and borrow against it. A company like Willoughby Enterprises is only going to increase in value."

"Until the owner dies," Raine pointed out.

"Fair point," Sommers conceded. "So, just a record of

every single stock transfer in the history of the company. That should be easy to find. Meet back here in five minutes?"

They both knew it was going to take considerably longer than that to locate anything to support Raine's gambit for the next morning. Not only did they need information about the inside stock value, they also needed evidence that David Smith had been the one who tried to purchase a controlling share of those stocks in the past. Abigail wouldn't benefit from a drop in share value, but Smith would.

An hour later, they hadn't found anything. An hour after that, they were still empty-handed.

Raine made his way over to where Sommers was sitting on the dusty ground, going through yet another box of records. "Maybe this isn't going to work after all," he admitted. "I can always just accuse Smith without proof and hope he confesses out of sheer guilt."

Sommers frowned up at him. "I thought you said the judge wouldn't even let you put him on the stand without the documents we're looking for."

Raine nodded. "Yeah, that's true. I've got it all lined up too. I called Mitchell and that lead detective, neither of whom were excused, and told them to be there at nine. My process server is good. He'll find Smith, and Smith will be there too, although probably with a team of lawyers ready to try to quash the subpoena. I put Mitchell on first to authenticate these documents—if we can find them—and tell the jury they show Smith tried to buy the company at price X, and now that Jeremy is dead, he can buy it at price Y, especially if Abigail is behind bars for murder and the board of directors gets to make the decision to sell. Then I put Smith on the stand and confront him with all of that. He can deny it, but it won't matter because the jury will have already heard it from Mitchell and seen the receipts." He gestured at the labyrinth of records surrounding them. "If we can find the receipts."

"What about the detective?" Sommers asked. "Why are you recalling the detective to the stand?"

"Oh, I'm not," Raine answered. "But I want her there in case Smith actually confesses so she can arrest him. Nakamoto will have to dismiss the case if they arrest someone else for the murder."

"Well, I would hope so." Sommers laughed.

"She will." Raine nodded. "She's just doing her job. She told me to get her proof it was someone else. This is my last chance."

Sommers glanced around the subterranean room. "Well, then we'd better keep working. Barry and Jared have probably gone home for the night. We've got the place to ourselves and a few more hours before dawn. Let's find the proof."

THEY EXHAUSTED the records on five and moved up to four, then three. They were about halfway through the records on the third floor when Sommers called out, "I think I found something!"

By then, Raine would have been willing to take anything that simply suggested David Smith was aware of Willoughby Enterprises. It was nearly 6:00 a.m. He needed to be in court in just a few hours, and he was definitely going to need a shave and shower before appearing in front of the jury again.

"What is it?" he asked in a lower voice as he approached her position in one of the corners of the room. Just because Barry and Jared had left didn't mean Betty and Jennifer wouldn't be coming onto shift soon.

Sommers squinted at the binder in her hands. "It's an old ledger. I think the entries are for stock transfers."

"So exactly what we're looking for," Raine hoped aloud.

"Maybe," Sommers cautioned. "It's from, like, seven years ago, and the details are minimal. I can't tell if these are internal or external to the company."

"What's that?" Raine pointed to a corner of a page sticking up at the back of the ledger.

Sommers grasped the paper and pulled. "Not sure. It's stuck between some pages. Hold on."

She turned to some empty pages at the back of the ledger to find an unevenly folded up piece of paper. She unfolded it.

"What is it?" Raine asked.

Sommers smiled. "It's a handwritten table of some additional stock transfers."

"To who?"

"It looks like just initials," Sommers answered, "but they're the exact right initials. DES."

"David E. Smith," Raine was excited to say.

"He didn't just try to buy shares of Jeremy's company, he actually did it," Sommers said. "And it looks like someone was trying to keep it off the books."

"That's exactly what I need to show Patel," Raine said. "We need to take pictures of each page of the ledger with entries and also that extra piece of paper."

"Why don't you just take the entire ledger?" Sommers questioned.

"That would be stealing," Raine answered. "I don't want to explain to the Bar Association why I committed a crime against the victim in a murder case."

"We're already trespassing," Sommers pointed out.

"Are we though?" Raine challenged. "Jared gave you his security badge."

Sommers seemed to appreciate the point, but before she could agree, a deep male voice shouted out from across the floor, "Hello? Who's in here?"

"Oh shit," Sommers whispered. "We're busted."

She pulled out Jared's security badge and shoved it into Raine's hand. "Quick, circle around back to the elevator." Then she pulled out her phone. "I'll take the pictures and text them to you."

"I'm not going to just leave you here," Raine protested.

"You have to," Sommers replied. "You have to get out of here. You have to get to court."

Raine knew that was true.

"Damn it!" Sommers hissed, holding up her phone after the first photo. "There's no reception down here."

"Don't move!" the voice shouted. It was getting closer. "Stay right where you are!"

"You need to go," Sommers implored. "I'll handle things here. You handle things in court."

Raine was about to protest further, when Sommers cupped a hand next to her mouth and called out, "Barry? Is that you? I've been waiting forever!" She scowled at Raine and waved him away. "Go!" she hissed.

"Stay where you are, ma'am," the voice commanded. "Don't touch anything. The police are on their way."

Raine knew he couldn't be detained by the police. He would have to trust Sommers. After everything they'd been through, he did.

Sommers hurried to take the rest of the photos while Raine circled around behind the boxes until the way to the elevators was clear. He flashed Jared's badge, and the elevator doors opened immediately, the car still waiting there from its descent carrying whoever was about to detain Sommers until the police arrived. She was good at talking her way out of things. Jared would have to admit he'd given her his badge. Hell, if Sommers was right about almost all men, he'd be glad to help her if it meant increasing his odds to two in a million.

The elevator opened on the first floor, and Raine turned away from the main entrance, hoping to find a back door he could slip out of. He was successful and found himself in the parking lot behind the building. The rain had stopped, but puddles filled the uneven pavement. He ran toward the street and to his car. He had less than three hours to get to Judge Patel's courtroom and nothing concrete to show for his night at the archives. He was going to have to rely on that last resort of the trial lawyer.

He was going to have to bluff.

33

Raine kept his phone on him constantly as he drove home, jumped in the shower, got dressed, and drove to the courthouse. He even took it off silent mode so he would hear the notification if she managed to text the photos to him, or even just text that she was okay. But there was no word from Sommers. She had probably been arrested on suspicion of burglary, and her phone confiscated. Raine could go to the jail and try to arrange for her release, but not until after he was done with court. Although that might take less time than he had originally wanted.

When he arrived outside Judge Patel's courtroom, he was greeted by a nervous Desmond Mitchell, a nonplussed Jillian Crenshaw, and an incensed David Smith and his lawyers. And another gaggle of reporters who must have gotten wind of the appearance of one of Seattle's richest citizens at the trial about the murder of another of Seattle's richest citizens. Raine was intent on ignoring the reporters, which was facilitated by being immediately confronted by Smith himself.

"Do you have any idea who I am?" Smith stormed up to

him, drawing up just shy of actually bumping Raine's chest. "This will not stand."

"David Smith, I presume?" Raine replied without stepping back. Smith was almost the same height as him and obviously took care of his physical fitness, with a strong frame under an expensive suit. "Nice to meet you."

"We will be moving the court to quash your subpoena," one of the lawyers called out over his client's shoulder. It was Mayfield from the confrontation in Raine's parking lot.

"Nice to see you again, Mr. Mayfield." Raine nodded toward him. "I expected no less. Not with your little toady sitting in on the trial and giving you daily reports of whether I was really going to go after your client."

Mayfield frowned. "I'm sure I have no idea what you're referring to."

"Sure, whatever." Raine wasn't surprised by the denial. "But before you and I can lock horns, I have another witness to get through before we get to the question of your client's testimony. But I will ask the judge to hear from you before your client is sworn in to testify."

It was a reasonable response, and the only real way forward. Mayfield knew that, to his chagrin. "Yes, well, you'd better, Mr. Raine."

Raine pointed at Crenshaw. "You're last, Detective. I need you to just wait here in the hallway until called inside. Understood?"

"Roger that," Crenshaw answered. "I'm on duty, so I'm getting paid either way."

Protect and serve, Raine thought sardonically.

He pointed next to Mitchell. "You. Come inside now. You're first."

Mitchell stood up. "Okay." He wasn't the type to disagree.

Raine could hear the reporters following as well, but they weren't his concern just then.

There were several people already inside the courtroom by the time Raine walked in. Abigail was at the defense table, waiting for him and flanked by two jail guards. Nakamoto was also at her table. The bailiff and the court reporter were at their stations. And Mr. Plunkett was seated in the back row again.

Before Raine could wonder about that, Judge Patel stormed into the courtroom to the surprise of even his bailiff.

"All rise!" the bailiff called out belatedly. "The King County—"

"Never mind that!" Patel shouted. "I want to know why there are a half dozen lawyers in the hallway outside my courtroom with a particular well-known business leader I specifically told you, Mr. Raine, that you were not going to be allowed to smear with accusations of murder."

Raine quietly instructed Mitchell to sit down in the front of the gallery, then stepped forward to address the judge.

"Good morning, Your Honor. May it please the court—"

"It most definitely does not please the court," Patel boomed. "Give me one good reason I shouldn't hold you in contempt right now, Mr. Raine."

Raine considered for a moment. He looked to Nakamoto, but she was very much looking away from him.

"Well, Your Honor, I suppose the best reason you shouldn't hold me in contempt right now is that I haven't done anything contemptuous yet," Raine answered. "I understand that it looks like I'm preparing to, and maybe I will, but I don't want to, and I will try my best not to. I'm just making sure I have all of my potential witnesses ready in the unlikely event Your Honor allows me to go down a road that I would like to go down."

"You want to accuse David Smith of murdering Jeremy Willoughby," Patel said. "And I've told you that you can't do that."

"And I haven't," Raine pointed out. "Not yet anyway. Your Honor's ruling was that I couldn't introduce other suspect evidence without some concrete evidence linking the other suspect to the crime. I couldn't just say that 'Madison Jimmy' was in town, so to speak. It is my hope and intent to produce that evidence with my first witness this morning, Desmond Mitchell. If, after his testimony, I believe I have failed to do so, then I will go out in the hallway, thank and excuse Mr. Smith for honoring my subpoena, and then call my client to the stand to tell the jury she did not commit the murder."

Patel frowned at Raine's explanation, but didn't interrupt.

"On the other hand," Raine continued, "if I believe I have succeeded in presenting the specific evidence necessary to permit the introduction of evidence that Mr. Smith had not only the means and opportunity to commit the murder but also a motive far stronger than any my client might have had, then I will first ask the jury to be excused and then request, outside the presence of those jurors, the court's permission to call Mr. Smith to the stand. If the court agrees with me that sufficient foundation has been laid, then the court can allow Mr. Smith to testify. And if the court does not believe the foundation has been laid for Mr. Smith's appearance at this trial, then I will humbly and very much non-contemptuously accept that decision."

Judge Patel stared at Raine through narrowed, angry eyes. "There is nothing humble about what you're trying to do, Mr. Raine."

Raine supposed that might be true. But humble wasn't going to win the trial.

"What do you think of all of this, Ms. Nakamoto?" Judge Patel demanded.

Nakamoto turned back to face the proceedings. She took a moment, then stood up. "I think the court should avoid holding Mr. Raine in contempt until he does something worthy of being held in contempt. And then I think the court should do it immediately and punish Mr. Raine accordingly."

Gee, thanks, Raine thought with a frown.

"I very much doubt," Nakamoto continued, "that Mr. Raine will be able to lay sufficient foundation to call Mr. Smith to the stand, and I'm not in any way afraid of whatever testimony he plans to elicit from Mr. Mitchell. I think the court should bring in the jury, let Mr. Raine call Mr. Mitchell to the stand, and let the case proceed. I am more than prepared to cross-examine Ms. Willoughby today, and I think we are all eager to bring this case to a final and just conclusion."

Patel's frown lessened slightly. He clearly liked the prosecutor's idea of a "final and just conclusion", to wit: a conviction. "All right then. Mr. Raine, you will be on a very short leash with Mr. Mitchell. If I sense anything improper, I will terminate your questioning and you will find yourself in a jail cell. Is that understood?"

"Understood," Raine said. He could hardly say anything different.

With that parameter in place, Judge Patel instructed the bailiff to bring in the jurors. Abigail stood up next to Raine. "Did you find what you needed last night?" she whispered.

Raine frowned. "Rebecca did, but I don't have it."

"That's bad news, isn't it?" Abigail knew.

"Yes," Raine admitted, "but we're out of time. I'll do the best with what I have."

"I hope that's enough," Abigail tried.

Raine nodded to her. "Me too."

The jury was in the jury box, and the judge fairly glared down at the defense table. "Does the defense wish to call any witnesses?" he had to ask, since a criminal defendant was under no obligation to call witnesses.

"Yes, Your Honor," Raine answered, since a jury always

still wanted the defense to call witnesses regardless of the niceties of the Constitution. "The defense recalls Desmond Mitchell to the stand."

Mitchell stood and approached the judge again.

"I remind you, Mr. Mitchell," Patel said, "you are still under oath."

Mitchell nodded and returned to the witness stand. He didn't have his leather satchel, but he did have a small stack of papers.

Raine needed to accomplish three things with Mitchell. First, have him reaffirm that there had been previous offers to purchase a controlling share in the company. Second, explain that the cost of such a controlling share had gone down since Jeremy's death. And third, that a lower company value from Jeremy's death would benefit a certain "DES" far more than Abigail.

He just hoped the records Mitchell had brought with him could support that. He pulled out his phone one more time before starting his questioning to see if there was any word from Sommers. There was not.

"Mr. Raine?" Patel interjected. "Are you going to ask questions or play with your phone?"

Raine shoved the phone back in his pocket. "Of course, Your Honor. Thank you, Your Honor. I was just checking something. But here we go."

He turned his attention to his witness. "Mr. Mitchell, are internal records kept of actual or potential sales of Willoughby stock, even though the company is privately held?"

"Of course," Mitchell answered.

"Why is that?" Raine asked.

"Well, we need to know who owns how many shares so we know things like how many votes a person might have."

"Even though Mr. Willoughby maintained the majority of voting stock?" Raine challenged.

"The only way we know that is if we keep track," Mitchell explained.

"That makes sense." Raine pointed to the papers under Mitchell's hand. "Did you bring some records with you today regarding such sales or proposed sales?"

"Well, yes," Mitchell answered. "You told me to."

Raine smiled. "I did, didn't I? And do they show what I asked for? That is, is it a complete list of stock transfers for the last ten years, with attendant values?"

Mitchell picked up the document in his hands. "It is."

Raine took the papers from him and handed them to the bailiff. "Your Honor, the defense offers this as defense exhibit one."

There had been over a hundred State's exhibits during Nakamoto's case-in-chief. It was nice to have at least one for his side.

Patel looked to Nakamoto. "Any objection from the State?"

Raine handed the charts to Nakamoto for her review. It wasn't anything she didn't already know from Mitchell's previous testimony. And it did not include the name or initials of David E. Smith anywhere.

"No objection," Nakamoto answered.

"Defense exhibit one is admitted," Judge Patel ruled.

"Thank you, Your Honor." Raine handed the papers back to the witness. "Now, Mr. Mitchell, is this the sort of document that would have been attached to the proposed final settlement agreement you examined when you testified previously? The one with the bloodstains on it?"

Mitchell grimaced slightly at the memory. "Yes. It was probably something similar to this."

"Why?"

"Well, this shows the value of the stock in real and incontrovertible terms," Mitchell explained. "Analysts can guess at how much a stock is worth, but when it's actually traded, that creates a price data point. A chart like this would be as close as you could come to giving a concrete number on how much a package of stock would be."

"But this document you prepared for court today"—he pointed at the exhibit—"that doesn't include the names of who obtained the stock, does it?"

Mitchell took a moment, then shook his head. "No, it doesn't."

"Why not?" Raine asked.

"Because you didn't ask me to include that," Mitchell answered. "And it's irrelevant anyway."

"You mean irrelevant for the purpose of determining the stock value?" Raine asked.

"Yes," Mitchell confirmed.

"But it might be relevant for other inquiries, correct?" Raine suggested.

Judge Patel leaned forward. "Be careful, Mr. Raine," he warned.

Raine didn't have a lot of options left, and being careful wasn't one of them.

"As the senior executive accountant for Willoughby Enterprises," Raine began what he hoped would be a long and complicated enough question to get it all out before Nakamoto objected and Patel ordered the guards to arrest him, "you must keep all sorts of records, records that include all sorts of additional information, information that maybe even just you alone need or want to know, information such as—"

Ba-bing!

An electronic chime filled the courtroom.

Ba-bing! Ba-bing!

Raine stopped. It was his phone. He'd forgotten to put it back on silent mode. It had been a hell of a night.

Ba-bing! Ba-bing! Ba-bing! Ba-bing! Ba-bing! Ba-bing! Ba-bing! Ba-bing! Ba-bing! Ba-bing! Ba-bing! Ba-bing! Ba-bing!

"Mr. Raine," Judge Patel growled at him.

Raine fumbled to fish his phone out of his pocket. "I apologize, Your Honor. I'm very sorry. Let me just—"

It was the texts from Sommers, with the photos attached. She must have gotten her phone back somehow.

"Mr. Raine?" Judge Patel prodded.

"Um, yes. Sorry, Your Honor." Raine pulled up the first few pics. They looked exactly like the chart Mitchell had brought. Except for the "DES" entries. He flipped to the last text with the last image. The handwritten entries for transfers to "DES". "I just need a moment, Your Honor."

Raine approached Mitchell and took the exhibit from him. He turned to the second-to-last page of the ledger, with the entries from about a year earlier, and compared it to the handwritten chart.

The handwritten entries had been left off the document Mitchell had prepared for his testimony that morning.

There was no legitimate business purpose to leave off purchases by David Smith.

But Raine knew Mitchell wouldn't have left them off without a reason. A very good reason.

Raine looked up to the judge. "I'm going to forward some documents to your bailiff's email, Your Honor. I would ask that they be printed out and marked as an exhibit."

"My bailiff is not your secretary, Mr. Raine," Patel replied impatiently.

"I'm trying to avoid asking for a recess, Your Honor." Raine knew how to use the judge's impatience against him. "I'm sure it will only take a moment."

It took several moments, actually, but after some awkward

silence and the sound of the bailiff's in-court printer, Raine had defense exhibit two in his hand.

He returned his attention to Mitchell. "How long did you work for Mr. Willoughby?"

"Uh, as I mentioned earlier," Mitchell said, "I started with Willoughby Enterprises over twelve years ago."

"And how long did it take you to become the senior executive accountant?"

"I was promoted to that position approximately five years ago."

"Does it pay well?" Raine asked.

"Well enough," Mitchell answered.

"What you're worth?" Raine pressed.

Mitchell shifted in his seat. "What Mr. Willoughby thought I was worth."

"Of course," Raine replied. "So, as senior executive accountant, you must have worked very closely with Mr. Willoughby?"

"Yes, I suppose so."

"I mean, if nothing else, you had to make sure he kept the majority of voting stock, right?"

"Yes," Mitchell answered, "although he did that himself as well, of course."

"Of course." Raine nodded. "He would want to know who controlled what shares of his company, wouldn't he?"

"I imagine he would," Mitchell agreed.

"And Mr. Willoughby was probably a pretty hands-on manager, wasn't he?"

"I think that would be fair to say."

"Because, I mean, you don't get that rich and successful by letting everyone else do your work for you, do you?" Raine asked.

"He was very involved in the day-to-day operations, yes," Mitchell confirmed.

"Did he ever give you last-minute tasks?" Raine asked. "Even last-second tasks? Like, drop everything and do this right now?"

Mitchell shrugged. "I suppose so. I think most bosses do that sometimes, probably."

"Sure, sure," Raine agreed. "Kind of like I did when I called you yesterday and said bring a chart with every stock transfer for the last ten years."

Mitchell laughed lightly. "Yes, kind of like that."

Raine tapped on the exhibit still clutched in Mitchell's hands. "But you were able to do that. Pretty amazing, actually."

"Um, thank you?" Mitchell ventured.

"You already had that ready, didn't you, Mr. Mitchell?"

Mitchell frowned. "I'm not sure what you mean."

"You had already prepared that document long before I asked for it, hadn't you?" Raine continued. "This is the document that was supposed to be attached to that final settlement agreement my client was supposed to sign the night Mr. Willoughby was murdered, isn't it?"

"Um, well, no," Mitchell answered. "No, I just, I mean, this is the sort of information I'm supposed to keep handy."

"Full and accurate records of all the stock transfers?"

"Yes."

"And you would need to know the exact and true numbers," Raine put to him, "even if Mr. Willoughby didn't. Or couldn't."

"Couldn't?" Mitchell questioned. "Why would you—?"

"If you own stock, you can borrow against that, can't you?"

"Um, yes. I mean, generally. It depends on the lender."

"And the stock, right?"

"Sure."

"Willoughby Enterprises stock," Raine said. "You could probably borrow against that, right?"

Mitchell nodded tentatively. "I suppose you could."

"And then later, after you paid the loan back, maybe you could put the stock back again, right?"

Mitchell hesitated. "Back again?"

"Before someone, say Mr. Willoughby, knew it was gone," Raine suggested.

Mitchell didn't say anything.

Raine finally handed defense exhibit two to Mitchell. "I'd like you to compare these two exhibits, Mr. Mitchell. I think you'll find they are identical with the exception of a handful of entries on exhibit two that are not on exhibit one."

Mitchell slowly raised his hand to accept the document from Raine. He pretended to look through the two exhibits, but Raine could see his eyes were unfocused. Mitchell knew what was in the documents without looking at them.

"There are several transfers of Willoughby Enterprises stock on exhibit two that are not recorded on exhibit one," Raine asserted. "Isn't that correct, Mr. Mitchell?"

Mitchell just nodded. It wasn't great for the record, but Raine wasn't playing to win the appeal anymore.

"And those entries are all marked with the initials DES, aren't they?" Raine continued.

Mitchell nodded again. "Yes," he agreed, barely audibly.

"DES," Raine repeated. "Those are the initials of David E. Smith III, one of Willoughby's chief business rivals, aren't they?"

A gasp flowed through the courtroom. The reporters thought they had their moment on camera.

Mitchell seemed to think so too. "Why, yes!" he was happy to agree.

"Or those three letters could be a name." Raine extinguished Mitchell's flicker of hope.

He snatched both exhibits out of Mitchell's hands and held them aloft in front of his target.

"You printed out the wrong chart"—Raine looked him dead in the eye—"didn't you, *Des?*"

Mitchell's eyes widened, then darted around the room, landing on the door in the back of the courtroom.

"You went with Jeremy Willoughby to Abigail's home that day. You were there to convince her the numbers were accurate and she should sign the settlement agreement. But you printed out the wrong chart because Jeremy surprised you and demanded it with no warning. You printed out the one you needed to keep so you knew how many shares you had to put back before Willoughby noticed. He just pulled it off the printer, slapped it onto the back of the agreement, and dragged you to Abigail's house. But she wasn't there. She was down at Gas Works Park, crying her eyes out. So he let himself in. That's trespassing, by the way, but hey, who hasn't done a little trespassing recently?"

Raine glanced performatively around the courtroom and spied Sommers sneaking in to sit in the back near Plunkett, who was quickly making his exit. He hadn't been there to keep Smith informed; he had been there to keep Mitchell informed. And he knew when to leave.

"But I digress." Raine turned back to Mitchell. "The two of you were sitting there, in Abigail's home, waiting for her to return from wherever she was. That must have been awkward. You got up and started pacing around. Willoughby started thumbing through the settlement agreement. Then he looked at the chart you had printed out. He thought he knew every share transaction, but he saw a bunch he didn't recognize."

Raine took out his phone again and held up the image from the ledger. "The ones that included off-the-books transfers to 'DES'. To you, Desmond Mitchell."

There were gasps from the jury box.

"And Jeremy Willoughby probably said something like,

'What the hell is this?' And you panicked. That statuette must have been right where you were standing, pacing behind him, when he discovered your embezzlement. You panicked, and you hit him over the head with that statuette."

Mitchell was just staring at Raine. But he wasn't denying it.

"But that wasn't going to be enough, was it?" Raine went on. "Because when he came to, he was going to remember what he saw. So, just like the medical examiner said, you walked over, and with a very clear intent, you murdered Jeremy Willoughby as he lay helpless on my client's floor."

Raine took a step back. "The only thing I don't know is whether you pulled the chart with your name on it out of his hand after you killed him, or if he had already separated it from the rest of the document when he discovered what you had done." He paused. "Do you want to answer that question, Mr. Mitchell? Des?"

Mitchell took a moment, then sat up very straight in the witness chair and folded his hands on his lap. "I decline to answer any further questions pursuant to my rights under the Fifth Amendment to the Constitution."

Raine spun around to face Nakamoto. "There! Is that enough?"

It was.

Nakamoto stood to announce it. "The State moves to dismiss the charge of murder against Abigail Willoughby."

EPILOGUE

The next day they were assembled once again in the office conference room: Raine, Sommers, and Abigail Willoughby. Abigail looked almost like the same woman who had burst through Raine's door all that time ago. The clothes were similar, but the expression she wore was different. Wiser. A bit sadder.

Sommers, on the other hand, was positively giddy.

"Explain to me again how you managed to get away from my husband's—I mean *my* employees—at the archives?" Abigail asked.

"The worst part was how long everything took," Sommers answered. "They took me to their break room to wait for the police to arrive. It was a very nice room, but it was still underground, on the second floor, so no windows."

"And your texts still couldn't get through," Raine observed.

"Right," Sommers confirmed. "We made small talk while we waited. There was a very large man named Earl and a rather small woman named Ava. They were polite, but Ava was trying to act tough, and Earl just stood blocking the doorway the entire time. I stuck with my 'executive Realtor' story and insisted that I had been invited into the archives by Jared in order to talk with Barry. When it was pointed out to me that Barry was hardly someone who could possibly close any sort of real estate deal, I simply asked how I was supposed to know that."

"Did you try your method on Earl?" Raine wondered.

Sommers frowned. "I didn't think that would work. I think he was sweet on Ava, and Ava was present, so that's another category that it doesn't work on."

"That's true," Abigail put in knowingly, a bit to Raine's surprise.

"By the time the police arrived, I think I had almost convinced them my story was true," Sommers continued. "When the first officer questioned me, he had already been briefed by them and seemed open to my explanation. But it took them forever to decide what to do. Ultimately, they held me there until they could get a hold of Jared. He's a heavy sleeper apparently. But eventually he answered his phone and confirmed, a bit reluctantly I imagine, that he had in fact given me his security badge."

"I'm just glad he answered his phone before Mitchell was off the stand," Raine remarked.

"I'm sure you would have figured something else out," Abigail said. "That was excellent work. Will Ms. Nakamoto be prosecuting Desmond now?"

"I'm sure she will," Raine answered. "Now that they have the actual killer, they'll be able to go back and track his movements, look for his DNA on anything collected from the scene, and tear apart his fake bookkeeping. I don't envy his attorney."

"Well, he can't have mine," Abigail said with a smile. She reached into her purse. "Which reminds me, I believe I owe you some money for the work you did on my behalf."

Raine hadn't had the chance to do a final tally of his hours. "I can send you a bill, Abigail. There's no need—"

"I believe this will cover it." Abigail handed him a check that more than covered it, twice over.

"Uh, I can't accept this..." he started.

"Of course you can," Abigail insisted. "I'm the new owner of Willoughby Enterprises. I have the means. And who knows, maybe I or my company will need your services in the future. I need to keep my people happy. I don't want them to start embezzling from me."

Raine and Sommers raised their eyebrows at each other.

"Too soon?" Abigail asked with a grin.

"Um, speaking of future services"—Sommers saw the opening—"in addition to my, shall we say, part-time work with Mr. Raine, I also dabble a little in commercial real estate."

"The Rebecca Sommers?" Abigail raised her own eyebrow. "Yes, I had my new team do a little digging on you as well, Ms. Sommers. I wouldn't be surprised if I start making some changes at WE. That may well include new space. Do you have a card?"

The business card was already out and on its way to Abigail's gloved hand. Abigail thanked her old lawyer and her new real estate agent and made her exit. Raine leaned back in his chair, bumping it against the wall, but he didn't mind. It had been a good win.

"Dan?" Laura interrupted them. "Natalie just called to say she might be running a few minutes late, but she'll be here by five fifteen at the latest."

Raine thanked Laura for the information, and Sommers smiled at him.

"A date with the ex?" Sommers ventured.

But Raine shook his head. "No, she's dropping off the boys. We're going camping this weekend."

"Oh, that'll be nice," Sommers said.

Raine frowned. "I hate camping. But Jason loves it."

"So no going back to Natalie, huh?" Sommers went ahead and asked.

"I don't think so," Raine admitted to himself. "But don't think that's going to make me susceptible to your mind games."

Sommers winked at him. "Like I said, Dan, you're not my type."

"Good," he replied. "We can't have that if we're going to keep working together."

Sommers leaned forward. "We are definitely going to keep working together."

Raine grinned. "You enjoyed it?"

"Murder? Mayhem? Getting arrested and getting away again?" Sommers laughed. "*Winning*? Oh hell yes, I enjoyed it."

"We won't always win," Raine cautioned.

"Maybe we will now that I'm on board," Sommers countered. She extended a hand. "Partners?"

Raine gladly shook it. "Partners."

WE HOPE YOU ENJOYED THIS BOOK

If you could spend a moment to write an honest review on Amazon, no matter how short, we would be extremely grateful. They really do help readers discover new authors.

ALSO BY STEPHEN PENNER

Rain City Legal Thriller Series

Burden of Proof

Trial By Jury